Lady 355

Mother of Freedom

R.A. Johnson

The Enclave Series
Book Two

CROW Books

To Emily, the bravest person I have ever met.

And

To Carol, my biggest fan.

PREFACE

This edition of *Lady 355: Mother of Freedom*, which was published previously under the author name Rob Johnson, is a significant revision of that story. Elements have been added and refined so it fits better in the overall arc of The Enclave Series.

As with the previous book in the series, *The Templar Lance*, I've included several historical figures in the narrative. I've done my best to represent these characters as historically accurately as possible. Of course, any specific thoughts, statements, conversations, and writings by those figures are completely made up by me. I have strived, though, to represent them through those fictional elements as accurately as possible.

The core mystery at the heart of the story, namely who was Agent 355, is, in fact, very real. And hers and the rest of the Culper Ring's influence on the course of the American Revolutionary War cannot be overstated. My fictionalization of their exploits is presented in the spirit of celebrating them.

As always, thank you, Faithful Readers, for spending your precious time with my characters and their compelling story.

Faithfully,

R.A. (Rob) Johnson
Pennsylvania, U.S.A.
January 2024

THE ENCLAVE TIMELINE

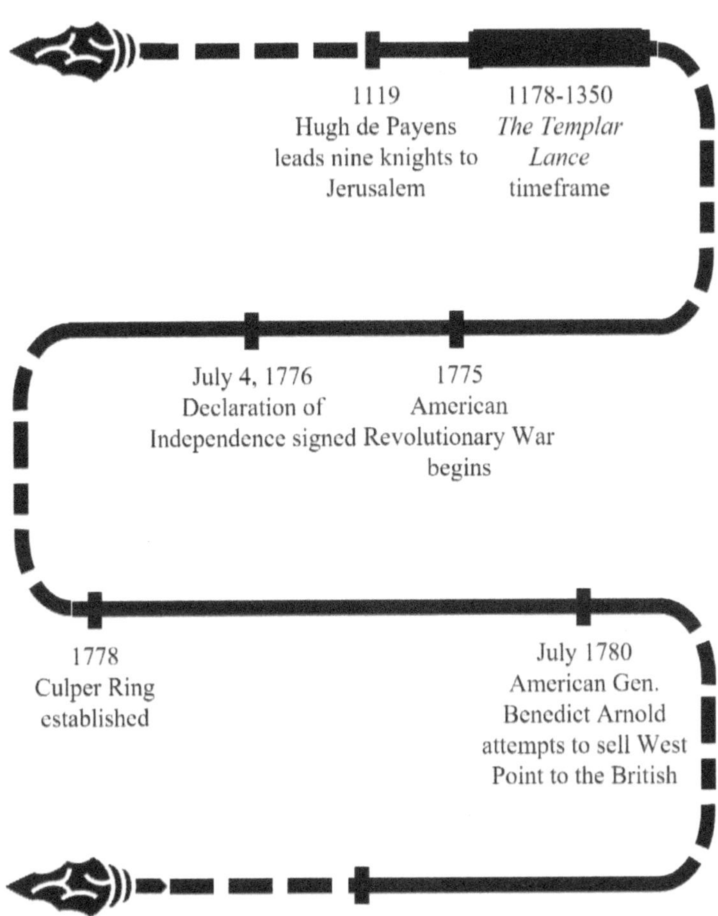

PROLOGUE

In 1118 AD, nine French knights set off for the Holy Land, ostensibly to protect Christian pilgrims visiting the holy sites there. Curiously, the King of Jerusalem, Baldwin II, gave them lodgings in the legendary underground stables of King Solomon on the Temple Mount. This led to them taking the name The Poor Knights of Jerusalem and the Temple of Solomon—soon to be known throughout the world as the Knights Templar.

Little is known of their activities during the first nine years of their residency, and there is no evidence that they ever sortied out to protect any of the many pilgrims coming and going. Yet, after these years of anonymity, their leaders suddenly rushed back to Rome and were granted an audience with Pope Honorius II, who immediately consecrated their group as the Catholic Church's first order of warrior monks. Subsequent popes granted more and more power to this secretive order until they became more powerful than any king in Europe.

Studying their history, several interesting questions arise. For example, what were those knights doing in Jerusalem for nine years? What event caused them to report back to the Pope, precipitating the birth of the most powerful international organization other than the church itself? And why did subsequent popes let them anoint their own priests, cross borders of kingdoms without interference, and amass lands and wealth beyond measure?

Clearly, those nine knights came into possession of some knowledge or relic that the Church was determined to either protect or hide. Given the absolute secrecy of the Templars and their rituals—which eventually led to their downfall—it is apparent that they discovered something that the Church would do almost anything to keep secret.

What that most valuable secret in Christendom was—or is—has been the subject of much speculation over the intervening centuries, but the truth ultimately became known only to one man, himself not much more than a boy, to whom it was entrusted in extremis as Jerusalem fell to Saladin's army.

Through the mysterious power of that secret, that man remained forever young and, in turn, founded his own clandestine group known simply as "The Enclave". That new order had a very different purpose from its progenitor. Tasked with learning and keeping the world's secrets, The Enclave has survived and thrived to the present day.

In an isolated area of rural Pennsylvania lies the village at the heart of The Enclave, where its founder and Grand Master still keeps those secrets, including the one that started it all. Father Dan, a brilliant, but naïve priest, was thrust into that Enclave to minister to its residents, continue his linguistic research, and discover those long-held secrets for himself. When he unraveled them and plumbed their meaning, his faith was shaken to its core.
As he will also come to discover, The Enclave and its archives contain many, many more mysteries to be solved. What follows is the story behind one of those mysteries.

PART I

Sarah Harkin
Autumn 1772

Nestled in the wilds of Colonial Pennsylvania, about twenty miles northwest of Philadelphia, lay the settlement known as The Enclave. Established before Pennsylvania Colony itself, its isolation afforded it an autonomy and independence unknown to the British subjects who were beginning to encroach on its boundaries.

Maintaining that autonomy was critical to The Enclave's underlying purpose—learning and keeping the world's secrets, a mission shared by many outposts of The Enclave Order spread across the Western world, of which the small village in Penn's Woods was the hub.

Born into that secretive group was a girl whose adventures and accomplishments would forever change the history of the world. This is her story.

Chapter 1

Fidget

S arah Harkin stood in the back corner of the classroom facing the row of pegs that, come winter, would be full of the children's heavy coats. That early in the school year, though, only the girls' mobcaps and the boys' felt hats hung there.

Standing still was not in Sarah's nature. She would rather have been outside running through the cornfields and climbing the trees in the apple orchard, but Mrs. Withers knew that. So instead, there she stood, staring at the teacher's cap and shawl hanging in front of her nose. Seething and imagining the pranks she could play on the Widow Withers, she shifted from foot to foot.

"Stop fidgeting, Child!" Mrs. Withers snapped the willow switch against the top of her desk.

Sarah froze while some of the other children snickered under their breath. She didn't want to feel that across her backside again. One thrashing didn't deserve a note home to her parents, but two certainly would. And her father's response to yet another report about her behavior would be far worse than three whacks with the willow branch from that old bat.

She told herself to hold still. Hold still!

Concentrating on keeping her feet flat on the floor, the tension built inside her like a devil on her shoulder, commanding her to move. Her hands, taking over for her feet, curled into fists until her knuckles were white.

Tonight, though. Tonight will be a good time to tell everyone about the Widow Withers's secret. She won't be so high and mighty when everyone knows what Sarah knows about her.

Everyone seemed to have secrets in the small village known simply as The Enclave, and Sarah knew most of them. Creeping about at night, listening at windows to whispered prayers and murmured confessions, Sarah risked more than the Widow Withers's willow switch. Getting caught would mean anything from a day in the stocks to banishment from The Enclave. That would be after a thorough beating by her Da.

Still, it would be worth the risk to know the gossips will be wagging their tongues over afternoon tea.

Chapter 2

Punishments

S arah's stomach growled as she lay in bed recounting the evening's events. The damnable old witch Withers had sent a note home, anyway, despite Sarah willing herself to be still and avoid causing any more disturbances in class.

That wasn't fair. Jimmy got the switch yesterday without getting a note.

But, deep down, Sarah knew two things. Mrs. Withers hated her, though she didn't know why, and Jimmy was a nice quiet boy, though slow to learn his lessons.

She couldn't be mad at Jimmy, not really. He was two years older, but still asked her to help him with his recitations. Though her one-room school spanned several grades, Sarah's love of reading and numbers had her way ahead of even the oldest children in the class.

Why couldn't they just let her read what she wanted? The primers her peers struggled with were childishly easy for her. Witch Withers couldn't read French or Latin herself, so she didn't want Sarah to show her up. When Sarah quoted Shakespeare from the folio in the village library, the teacher *tsked* and stood her in the corner again. Who knew the 'epee' in the play didn't refer to a sword?

Having a library in such a small village was quite unusual, but Abraham, The Enclave's Elder—who barely looked older than Sarah, and way younger than her father—insisted on keeping it up to date with the latest books published in Paris, London, and New York. It's shelves were open to all, and Sarah spent many hours lost in the stories it contained. If she was also hiding from her father's wrath, so be it.

She came straight home after classes, since there was no sense in putting off the inevitable. She had to present the note to her father, David, for him to sign, then she would return it to Mrs. Withers tomorrow. Sarah took the time until he returned from the fields to elicit some sympathy from her mother. They both knew what her father's reaction would be, as did Mrs. Withers.

Once, Sarah forged his mark on a note, but Mrs. Withers had seen it enough times by then to know it was fake. The punishment for that was double. She wouldn't make that mistake again. So, when he strode in the kitchen door, she handed the note to him with her head hanging.

He didn't bother reading it before said, "Another one?"

Although Sarah couldn't bring herself to meet his gaze, she heard the rage behind just those two words. The next ones she expected, though they were menacingly quiet.

"Go to the shed."

Turning quickly for the door, she strode across the small yard to the toolshed at the back of the Harkin property.

The shed, which had once been her hiding place and fantasy palace when she was a small child, was now, in her mind, a dungeon.

Opening the door to the low-roofed building, Sarah stepped into the space dimly lit by a single dirt-caked window. She left the door open so she could hear her father's approach—and prepared herself mentally for the ordeal to come.

She looked at the two loops of hemp rope hanging from a rafter just above eye level. With mounting terror, she reached up above her head and put a hand through each of the loops. A mantra started in her head.

I will not break. I will not cry out. I will become a stone statue that can't feel pain. I will not break. I will not cry out. I will become…

Her father's heavy tread on the step froze her defiant thoughts and melted her strengthening resolve.

Taking down the leather strap that had once been the reins of a horse's bridle, he said, "When are you going to learn discipline, child?"

Folding the strap in half and holding the two ends with his right hand, he continued, "Why can't you be like the other children, eh?"

The question distracted her enough that the strike of the strap on her backside came as a surprise.

She let out a faint grunt as her father continued, "Learn your household lessens from your mother."

Another strike landed, but she was prepared for it that time.

I will not break. I will not cry out. I will become a statue that can't feel pain.

"Find a young man who will put up with your nonsense." *Whack.* "Or one who has a strong right arm." *Whack*. "And become a good wife," **Whack**, "like your mother." ***Whack***.

I will not break. I will not cry out—

Realizing that Sarah had not made a sound after her initial grunt, David snarled and raised his aim. *Crack.* This blow landed across the small of Sarah's back.

She gasped, but clenched her teeth tighter. *Crack*. The well-aimed blow landed in the same strip of flesh. A whimper escaped Sarah's lips.

"What's that you say?" **Crack**.

Her mantra failed her, and Sarah cried out with wordless anguish. "It's about time," David said with a satisfied note in his voice. "And one for good measure." ***CRACK***.

Her spirit momentarily broken, Sarah broke down into uncontrollable sobs.

"No dinner for you. Get to your bed."

David hung the strap back on its hook and left Sarah hanging limply as the rough hemp bit into her wrists.

Chapter 3

Late Night Escapade

The European-Americans would not learn of the Native-Americans who lived a thousand miles or more to the west for several decades. Among those aboriginal tribes of the great open plains, prestige was earned by counting coup—sneaking close enough to one's rival, enemy or friend, to strike him with a coup stick adorned with beads and feathers. Doing so transferred the victim's honor to the victor.

Putting one over on a rival is a universal theme, though. Among The Enclave's children, they recognized Sarah as the best of her age at the Stealth Game, their equivalent of counting coup.

She started by drawing mustaches in charcoal on the faces of her friends while they slept. Charcoal progressed to painting her rivals, which resulted in much scrubbing and painfully scoured cheeks. But, it was because of the night after her the latest beating at the hands of her father that The Enclave's elders finally put a stop to her childish pranks.

That night, Sarah lay awake in the bedroom she shared with her younger sister, Jen. When she heard the rhythmic breathing of Jen and the whiskey-fueled, wall-rattling snores of her father, she slipped out of bed and tucked her nightgown into a pair of her brother's work pants. From under her bed, where it was firmly tied to the bedframe, she dropped the free end of a knotted rope out the bedside open window.

Relying on many nights' experience, she quietly descended the rope, crept through the village, and slipped past the night watch into the surrounding farmland. Out of sight of the village's houses, she ran with abandon from field to field, reveling in the freedom of being alone and unobserved.

Her frolicking had a more sinister purpose than just a ramble in the dark, however. As she passed from field to field, she uprooted one scarecrow after another from their watchful positions. When she had five of the constructs of straw, burlap, and ribbons, she tied them together beneath their arms with a length of twine and slid her head and shoulder through the loop. With the scarecrows, which were taller than she was, thus strapped to her back, she returned to the village. Slipping through the shadow of one house into that of its neighbor, she reached The Enclave's headquarters building.

The headquarters housed meeting rooms, offices, various storage rooms, and The Enclave library on the first floor. The second floor was occupied by Elder Abraham's office and apartment.

Abraham was the leader of The Enclave, whose settlement predated even the Pennsylvania colony which surrounded it. Sarah knew from previous midnight excursions that the ground floor doors and windows were kept soundly locked at night. But she also knew that Abraham opened the upstairs windows on warm nights to let the breezes in.

As she quietly hid in the bushes that bordered the yard behind the building, she knew her timing had been perfect. A three-quarters gibbous moon was just rising above the ridgeline to the east. Its pre-rising glow on the horizon had afforded her acute eyesight all the light she needed while stealing the scarecrows and slinking through the village.

Now, though, she needed extra illumination to navigate her way through the interior of the building. The quickly rising bright moon on the cloudless night would provide more than enough light.

In the few minutes it took for the moon to expose itself fully, Sarah surveyed the open space that lay between her hiding place and the back of the headquarters building. The yard was often used for holiday and birthday celebrations, or just as an outdoor gathering place for the community to enjoy a musical concert or theatrical. In the dim light, she saw the dozen or so long tables with matching benches stored close to the headquarters' low back porch.

One table in particular drew her attention. It still sat where she had staged it while a member of the cleaning crew after the previous festivities. The table sat just to the side of the porch roof's gable end. As was customary, the table's benches sat stacked on top of the table, making a perfect platform from which she could pull herself up onto the roof.

Slipping out of her hiding place, Sarah first made her way to the gate in the back fence and made sure her escape route was unlocked. The gate let out onto a path that wound its way behind the buildings on this side of the street, allowing her a hidden path back to her house, where the knotted rope she had used to descend from her bedroom was waiting for her return—an easy climb back to her bedroom window.

With a last check to make sure she wasn't observed, Sarah crossed to the strategically placed table. Once there, she unslung the bundle of scarecrows from her back, leaving them tied together, and lifted them onto the topmost bench. Opening the loop which had served as a sling, she tied the free end to her belt.

Having thus prepared her cargo to be hoisted up, she climbed onto the table, then onto the benches stacked atop one another. Her outstretched fingers were still about six inches below the framing of the roof's open end, but from a squatting position, she easily jumped high enough for her hands to grip the end truss's bottom chord.

In one continuing motion, she lightly hauled herself to the next handhold, the truss's web member, and brought her feet up to her first handhold. She had deliberately started her climb close to the roof's peak, so the gap between the horizontal bottom chord and the slanted roof was large enough to hold her crouching form.

There she rested a moment and listened for any reaction to the whisper-soft rustle of her climb. Hearing nothing but her light breathing, Sarah leaned out to grip the wood-shingled roof just above her head. This was the trickiest part of her climb, but she swung her legs out and up onto the roof with ease. The bundle of scarecrows she quickly hauled up beside her.

Five windows overlooked the porch roof. Sarah could see the reflection of the now fully risen moon in the glass of the window closest to where she crouched. By reconnoitering while volunteering for the headquarters cleaning crew, she had learned that the window before her opened into a guest bedroom that was currently unoccupied.

From that ingress point, she only had to sneak two doors down the hallway to reach Abraham's apartment. Although she had never been in the apartment proper, by pacing along the exterior wall while ostensibly cleaning up, she was confident she knew its size, if not exactly its layout.

No one had noticed that she had unlatched this window during her cleaning of the bedroom earlier in the day, nor that she had oiled the sash to ensure its smooth travel within the frame.

Silently sliding the window open, she slipped in and pulled the bundle of scarecrows in after her. Careful to avoid any contact with walls or doors that would make any noise to betray her passage, Sarah slipped through the bedroom doorway and made her way down the hall with the scarecrows under her arm.

Being over a century old, the building's hardwood plank flooring could emit various squeaks and pops, announcing the presence of a casual visitor. Sarah was a very careful visitor, however, and she had scouted the many spots that could emit telltale squeaks during her cleaning sessions. Using that mental map, she traversed the hall without a single sound.

A silent sigh of relief escaped her lips when she discovered that Abraham's apartment door was latched, but not locked. Her lock picking skills were still amateurish at best, learned by taking apart a door lock liberated from a maintenance storage room. By figuring out its mechanism, she had worked out how to defeat it, but her opportunities for practicing those skills had been scant.

While kneeling outside the apartment door, Sarah pulled a piece of river reed and a small phial of oil—another item she had lifted from the maintenance shed—from a pocket of the work pants she wore. Using the reed as a straw, she drew up a small amount of the oil, then blew it into the gap below the door latch's thumb lever. She drew up another squirt of oil from the phial and slowly depressed the thumb lever just enough to where she could feel the resistance of the latch. Holding the lever in that position, she blew the second bit of oil into the gap above the lever.

While giving the oil a few seconds to infiltrate the latch mechanism, Sarah noted the door did not hang flush against the stop. Visualizing the latch's hidden side inside the apartment, she knew the latch bar rested against the lip of its mating cusp, which was screwed to the interior doorframe.

Applying the slightest possible pressure, Sarah moved the door the fraction of an inch needed to center the latch bar, so it touched neither side. Then, with a well-oiled snick she could barely hear herself, she depressed the thumb lever and eased the door open just a few inches.

With the door in this position, Sarah repeated her lubricating trick on the three hinges that were now exposed between the door and the jam. Lifting the handle to take some of the weight off the hinges, she swung the door just enough to allow her to slip through with the scarecrows.

The light of the moon streaming through two windows illuminated a room which was a combination office and parlor. Across an expanse of about four yards was another door which stood fully open, no doubt to allow the free flow of the cool night breezes that passed between the open windows. Again, the friendly moon showed Sarah what she needed to see.

Although a few area rugs lay on the floor, she could see by the pattern of nail heads where the underlying floor beams ran. Her eyes picked out a path from beam to beam that should avoid any creaks and squeaks, a single one of which could awaken the bedroom's sleeping occupants.

After memorizing her chosen path, Sarah lifted her eyes to the open doorway. She could see a bed, occupied by two sleeping forms under the bedclothes, as she had hoped and planned for. Even her twelve-year-old mind knew that Abraham, a bachelor, should not have a nighttime companion. And she knew from her habitual eavesdropping who that companion was.

Having grown up in a farming community with bedrooms separated by thin plaster walls, the ways of mating, whether by cattle or people, held no mystery for the children of The Enclave. Sarah, therefore, understood completely why someone was sharing Abraham's bed.

She let satisfaction shine on her face. Two sleepers meant her coup would be complete, and the reaction of his bed companion would probably be a lot more dramatic than that of the notably stoic Abraham.

Creeping silently from beam to beam across the office, Sarah paused in the open doorway to the bedchamber.

A thick, intricately woven carpet of a type Sarah had never seen before covered almost all of the bedroom floor. Dropping to her hands and knees, she took a moment to dig her fingers into the deeply woven wool. The craftsmanship and style of the carpet, with its geometric shapes and abstract floral pattern, spoke of a sophisticated world beyond her experience.

For the first time in her life, Sarah realized there must be a world outside The Enclave. A world of which she knew nothing. That realization, and her natural curiosity, awakened in her a desire that she had never felt before. A desire to explore and understand that world.

Gathering herself from her momentary reverie, and refocusing on the task at hand, she crept around the perimeter of the room, first to the left of the doorway, then back around to the right. In each corner of the room, she raised up a scarecrow and leaned it against the wall facing the bed. With one scarecrow remaining, she looked around for a place to display it for the greatest effect.

Looking again at the bed, the optimal placement was obvious. As silently as the breezes wafting through the windows, she leaned the last scarecrow against the footboard of the bed, where it leered menacingly at the sleepers.

With a final survey of her handiwork, and a silently suppressed chuckle, Sarah reversed her path out of the apartment, through the guest bedroom window, and down onto the benches, table, then the ground. For her final trick, she retrieved a long iron pole from the porch. Using the pole as a lever, she moved her climbing table a good five or six feet away from the porch.

Let them figure that out, she thought as she replaced the lever in its well-known storage location.

Returning home and ascending the rope was routine. As she lay in bed, safely back home, Sarah reviewed the night's escapade in her mind. She thought back to each step of her adventure, trying to think of any way she had betrayed herself. Coming up empty, and with post-adrenaline exhaustion washing over her, she drifted off to sleep.

Chapter 4

Reckoning

S arah awoke, as did most of the other residents of the village, to blood-curdling screams. Rushing downstairs, and barely able to keep the grin from her face, she was stopped by her father before she could rush out the door.

He was pulling on his trousers as he called to her, "Sarah! Wait right here until I figure out what's going on."

Knowing that her father was not a man to cross, as the welts on her back testified, Sarah froze in her tracks.

It wasn't until he had yanked on his boots and taken his flintlock down from its place over the fireplace that David saw the look on Sarah's face. He didn't like that expectant, fearless expression.

"If you had anything to do with this, Young Lady—"

The unspoken, and unnecessary, threat hung in the air as he threw open the door and ran into the street.

Sarah's secret joke lasted until mid-morning. Her class's recitation of their vocabulary lesson was interrupted by Johnny Sutherland's father. Burly Jack Sutherland was The Enclave's blacksmith, guard, watchman, and Abraham's all-around enforcer.

He simply opened the classroom door, nodded to the teacher, Miss Jackson, who was filling in for Mrs. Withers that morning, and scanned the room for Sarah's head of unruly auburn hair. When he found her trying to hide behind Danny Roberts's wide shoulders, he simply looked her in the eye and jerked his head toward the hallway.

Sarah felt the whole classroom's eyes, including Miss Jackson's, on her as she stood.

"Miss Jackson, may I be excused?"

There was no sense piling an infraction for leaving the class without permission on top of whatever punishment she was now facing.

"I do not think you, nor I, have much choice in the matter," was the teacher's frosty response.

Sarah grimaced and marched out the door, then followed Mr. Sutherland into the hall. Behind her, she heard the class break into loud chatter while Miss Jackson rapped on her desk and called for quiet.

Sarah looked sideways up at her escort. "How bad is it going to be?"

Jack just shook his head slowly and shrugged. The lack of any other response told her she was really in for it this time.

Silently, the two walked down the main street from the schoolhouse to the site of the previous night's escapade. When Jack started up the stairs to Abraham's office, Sarah's knees felt so weak she could hardly climb the steps.

At the door to the office, Jack rapped his knuckles twice and, without waiting for a response, pushed open the now well-oiled door and preceded Sarah into the room.

The scene they walked into was tense. Abraham stood behind his desk, poised as if ready for a fight. Sarah's mom sat sobbing in the corner, with her face buried in her hands. This part of the tableau Sarah took in during a single heartbeat as she stepped across the threshold.

Before she could process the scene, though, her father sprang from where he stood to the left of the door, fist raised, fully intending to give Sarah the thrashing she was expecting—and used to.

Before David Harkin could take his second step, however, Big Jack met his charge with a straightened arm to the chest. Knocked off stride, David's eyes went wide and his unthinking anger climbed to an even higher level. He was not the only one caught by surprise, however.

Sarah, who flinched like a beaten dog when she saw her father's attack coming, stood equally stunned. Surprise registered first on her face, followed immediately by the astounding recognition that Jack Sutherland was there to protect her.

In a blinding rage, Sarah's father gathered himself for another rush, this time at Jack, but Abraham's voice whipped across the room.

"Stand down!"

His tone of absolute command froze David involuntarily in his tracks. Able to move only his head, he turned his attention in astonishment to Abraham.

When he saw he had David's undivided attention, Abraham said in a soothing, but nonetheless imperative tone, "We'll have no violence here."

Unbelievingly, Sarah saw her father's shoulders fall and his whole demeanor change. He looked again at Jack Sutherland, this time appraisingly. With his rational mind once more engaged, he nodded in recognition that he hadn't stood a chance against the man.

"Sarah, come here, please."

Abraham didn't commanded her as he had her father, but she hurried to his side anyway, putting his heavy oak desk between herself and her father. Understanding her haste, Abraham lightly touched her shoulder. Without words, that simple, gentle touch told her she had nothing to fear.

"You've caused quite a stir this morning, Young Lady."

Sarah's innate integrity would not let her even try to deny what she had done. But she also wasn't prepared to confess just yet. Seeing he would get neither a lying nor a remorseful response, Abraham nodded.

"You've caused a bit of damage to a young widow's reputation, you know." He paused, and a slight smile crossed his face. "Of course, we knew the risks we were taking."

The shocked gasp which escaped from her mother at Abraham's matter-of-fact discussion of his indiscretion drew a sharp response.

"Really, Woman? This is shocking to you? Didn't I hear you just last week gossiping with my housekeeper about this very thing?" Getting nothing other than a wide-eyed, but silent response, Abraham settled the matter. "Let us keep our hypocrisy to a minimum, please."

He pulled out his desk chair and indicated to Sarah that she should sit. When she had, he spun the chair to face himself. Standing over her with arms crossed, he assessed Sarah's attitude, which had progressed from fear, through astonishment, to defiance. Then, he turned to a shadowed corner of the room.

"Well, what do you think?"

Spinning in her seat to see to whom Abraham was speaking, Sarah was surprised to see a man she didn't recognize standing there. Up to that point, she had not known there was anyone else in the room. Stranger still, she never imagined there was anyone living in the village that she didn't know. With his eyes locked on hers, he stepped out of the shadows.

"Well, let's see. She collected up those silly scarecrows, but that was a simple matter of waiting for the night watch to pass. Nobody watches the cornfields at night." He paused a moment to organize his thoughts, then continued. "After that, though, she accomplished a lot. We still haven't figured out how she got up here."

Sarah couldn't keep a little smirk off her face, which this mysterious man plainly saw. He grinned a little in return.

"Regardless of how she did that, working in pitch blackness, she clearly unlatched and opened your office door, which I note doesn't squeak anymore."

Abraham raised his eyebrows as if he hadn't noticed that in the morning's hubbub.

The other man continued, "She then hauled those scarecrows across your notoriously squeaky floor." He put his weight heavily on his right foot and the plank he stood on dutifully let out a loud screech. "And for the *coup de grace*," he couldn't keep the smile from his face, "she surrounded you and your, ah, companion with those stupid scarecrows! All while you both snored away." He shook his head and chuckled appreciatively. "I have to say she's ready."

Ready? For what? Sarah was totally confused, but something compelled her to speak.

"It wasn't pitch black."

It was Abraham and his advisor's turn to be confused. After a second, though, understanding dawned on the mystery man's face.

"Ah, you waited for the moon to rise. I bet it shone right through those windows." His appreciation was clear in his tone.

Feeling more comfortable than she could have conceived of a few minutes before, Sarah asked the question that had been on her mind since Mr. Sutherland came to collect her.

"What gave me away?"

Abraham and his friend met each other's gaze and Abraham nodded. He looked down at Sarah.

"You left four footprints leading back to your house."

Sarah shook her head violently. "I couldn't have! I stayed off the bare parts of the path the whole way."

"True, you didn't leave any prints in the mud. But you did on the flat stones you stepped on to avoid that mud." Seeing Sarah's confusion, he continued, "The heavy dew on the grass alongside the beaten path…"

Sarah felt crushed. She had never considered the dew or what marks the soft leather boots she was wearing would leave behind, even though they were clearly wet when she took them off.

Abraham continued, "Don't be upset. In another hour, we never would have seen any evidence." Abraham looked down benevolently on Sarah with a big smile. "Although you would have been our prime suspect, anyway."

Leaving her to think that over, he then turned to Sarah's parents with a stern look. "We've decided. Say your farewells."

The flush of anger rose again in David Harkin's cheeks, and his wife broke into another round of sobbing. This was too much for Abraham.

"Stop your blubbering, Woman! It's not like you'll never see her again." When the sobbing continued, his voice cracked through the air like a bullwhip. "Look at me!"

Without conscious thought, Mary Harkin dropped her hands from her face and met Abraham's eyes. Her face, flushed from crying, was just starting to show the bruise below her left eye.

"Just as I suspected." Abraham turned to her husband, and though his voice was low, the threat was clear. "I've known for some time that you beat your wife. The entire village knows this. You've proven today that you beat young Sarah here as well. And if you haven't started in on her younger siblings yet, I'm betting you soon will."

Harkin started to protest, but Abraham cut him off. "Don't even try to deny it. Your wife's face and your daughter's reactions condemn you."

Turning to Jack Sutherland, he continued. "Jack, I give you the mission to watch over this family. I want to know if there is even the slightest hint that this coward abuses anyone else in his household."

Again, Harkin tried to protest, but this time, Jack grabbed his arm.

"If there are any more reports, you will be banished from The Enclave, and shunned by all of its members. Do you understand me?" Harkin just stared in disbelief. "Answer me!"

The words seemed to physically strike Harkin, and he staggered backwards. Abashed, he dropped his eyes to the floor and nodded.

"Say the words, Harkin."

"I understand you." His voice was so faint Sarah had to strain to hear it. She had never seen her father so cowed.

"Good. Now be gone, both of you. Mr. Sutherland will bring Sarah around later to collect her things."

Without another word, David Harkin slunk out of the office. Mary stood and looked her daughter in the eye, then ran from the room, wailing once again.

When they had gone, with a nod from Abraham, Jack followed them and closed the door behind him.

"Stand up, please." Abraham's voice didn't carry the tone of command it had earlier, but Sarah leaped to her feet, anyway. Pointing to the man from the shadows, Abraham continued.

"Sarah, this is Mr. Garrison. He is Headmaster of our *special* school."

Mr. Garrison held out his hand, and with mind racing, Sarah shook it.

Reading the unvoiced question in her eyes, Mr. Garrison said, "You've probably never heard of my school, although I'm sure you've noticed that some of your friends' older siblings have left the regular school here in the village."

Sarah nodded. "Ginny Winston's brother Josh stopped coming last fall. Ginny was sad for a week, but she wouldn't say where he went. I knew he hadn't died, 'cause there wasn't a funeral."

"That's right. Josh is very skilled at mathematics, and clever with puzzles. We have need of his talents, just like we have a need for the skills you demonstrated last night."

"So, this *special school* is my punishment?"

Both Abraham and Garrison laughed at that.

"Quite the contrary. You are being rewarded. Rewarded with an education you can't get anywhere else in the world. And, if you make it through your lessons successfully—which is a mighty big 'if', I assure you, you'll have adventures you've never even dreamed of."

Adventures? The twists and turns of the morning left Sarah dizzy.

Abraham stepped in to soothe her nerves. "You see, Sarah, the village has a very special purpose, and is a very important part of an ancient *order* called The Enclave. The Enclave has served for centuries as the Holy Father's eyes and ears. And sometimes as his mouth and fingers."

PART II

Father Dan and Elizabeth
Present Day

Lying forty miles northwest of Center City Philadelphia is the Enclave Borough. Adjacent to the small town of Kimberton, The Enclave's village nestles in an oxbow of the French Creek. Founded in secret on a land grant from King Charles I of England, years before William Penn settled in the wilderness that became Pennsylvania, the tiny municipality enjoys a status akin to that of Native American tribal lands—semi-sovereign, self-governing, and isolated politically, if not physically.

Crossing the well-protected border onto its ten-thousand acres means stepping into a world steeped in history, yet embracing technologies that allow its tentacles to reach out through a network of information sources to all corners of the worlds of government, politics, business, and finance.

Thrust into this secretive world was a naïve young Jesuit named Daniel Koprowicz. Assigned to the Enclave parish because of his linguistic talents, Father Dan passed a year-long test of his abilities, becoming not only a beloved pastor but also a trusted member of The Order of the Enclave. That was but the first of his many trials, though, including linguistic challenges, but also tests of his faith.

Joining him was the enigmatic Elizabeth. Though a native of The Enclave, she was more of an outsider than Father Dan.

Chapter 5

Elizabeth

The baggage carousel in Philadelphia's airport creaked and groaned as it crawled along its endless circuit. Elizabeth stood alone, watching the empty metal belt pass. The stale smell of burnt rubber and machine oil lingered in the air. She knew getting angrier than she already was wouldn't make her bag appear out of the black mouth that had disgorged everyone else's luggage. But each panel, as it jerked and screeched along its curving path, seemed to mock her. Finally, with a blast of an obnoxious buzzer, the belt slowed to a halt. Its groaning pause was like a switch being thrown, launching Elizabeth into motion.

"Where the hell is my suitcase?" she demanded even before she reached the Customer Service counter.

With her auburn hair pulled back into a low ponytail and her smooth, flawless skin, Elizabeth looked to be no more than twenty-five years old. But the way her deep blue eyes flashed stiffened the clerk behind the high counter when he looked up from his computer screen.

"I don't know, Miss, but I'm sure we can find out for you. May I see your boarding pass, please?"

His obsequious tone did nothing to mollify

Elizabeth's anger, but she held up the QR code on her cell phone. After scanning it, the clerk typed, and the keys clicked for a few seconds.

"Um, you had a connection in London on your way here from Brussels, correct?" Elizabeth just nodded. Beads of sweat appeared on his forehead. "Well, I'm sorry to say that your bag is on its way to Pittsburgh, which is the plane's next stop."

Elizabeth took a calming breath. "Why is it going to Pittsburgh? And when will I get it back?"

"Ah, I guess they missed it when the baggage crew unloaded here in Philly. I'm terribly sorry, Miss Deeloo?" He pronounced her name like an English bathroom.

"It's 'deLeau.' Pronounced 'de-low.'"

This just got a blank stare from the young man with dreadlocks whose nametag read 'An'dray.'

"Anyway, *Andy*, when will I get my bag?"

Confusion flickered across An'dray's features, but he quickly started typing again.

After a few moments, he raised his head and forced a tight smile. "I've notified our Lost Luggage office and scheduled it on a return flight which will arrive here in Philly, ah, about eleven o'clock tonight." His smile widened into his best I'm-helping-you-out-here grin. "And I've authorized the round-trip miles to and from Pittsburgh to be added to your account."

Scowling, Elizabeth said, "That's what, about five hundred miles? Don't bother."

"Ah, four hundred eighty-three…Oh."

He stopped mid-sentence as he noticed her seven-figure mileage balance and a notification flashed on his screen.

"I'm also authorized to offer you a hotel voucher for the Hilton here at the airport." The airline app on Elizabeth's phone dinged. "We'll be happy to deliver your bag to your room once you check in. Just enter your room number into our app." An'dray's smile seemed to stretch his entire face. "On behalf of New World airline, I apologize for the inconvenience. Is there anything else I can help you with?"

Without responding, Elizabeth turned on her heel and strode away toward the Global Entry kiosk.

She knew it was going to take some explaining at Customs, and that she had better play nice with them. She didn't want to spend the evening in a holding cell until her bag got there. At least by then there wasn't a line.

Striding up to the bored-looking Customs agent, Elizabeth's face lit up with the innocent smile that had gotten her out of many sticky situations—and had saved her life many times.

Chapter 6

Homecoming

Elizabeth drove her rental slowly through the parking lot of The Enclave Farm Market. As she waited for a mom and her two kids to cross to their SUV, she thought, *the "front" business looks like it's doing well. If these soccer moms only knew what's behind it.*

What lay immediately behind it was a stand of evergreens whose lowest branches swept the ground in the breeze. As she drove around the corner of the building and crawled along the access lane, she scanned the tree line for a gap. Between the eleventh and twelfth hemlocks, she saw what looked like a path for farm equipment and turned onto it.

She drove along the rutted dirt track through thick forest for a hundred yards, then over a small hill. Completely out of sight and earshot of anyone outside the farm market, the lane ended at a heavy security gate, which Elizabeth nosed her SUV up to. The double fence that ran away from the gate in both directions disappeared into the woods.

As she lowered her driver-side window, a voice came from a blank access panel set atop a thick steel post.

"This is a private entrance. Please use the turnaround

to your right and return to the Farm Market."

Looking into the eye of the camera on the access panel, Elizabeth kept her face neutral. She knew she had been under surveillance from the moment she rounded the market. Since her rental car didn't have the appropriate security IFF chips installed, the greeting was official-sounding and brusque.

"This is Elizabeth deLeau, returning home."

There was a momentary pause, then the front of the access panel folded down, revealing a camera, microphone, and keypad. Without prompting, Elizabeth stared at the camera while she entered a long string of digits on the keypad, then she repeated her name. After a moment while The Enclave's security system analyzed her face and voice, the panel beeped, closed up again, and the gate slid open.

"Welcome home, Operative deLeau. We have accommodations for you in Tallmadge House."

Well, that's appropriate. Perhaps one of John's little jokes.

With a practiced eye, Elizabeth spotted each of the surveillance cameras along the quarter-mile entrance road. When she pulled into a parking space in front of the Tallmadge House dormitory *cum* apartment building, she saw Karl Coolbaugh, the head of Enclave Security, waiting for her. She stepped out of the SUV as its back hatch rose. Karl reached in to grab her bag, but Elizabeth was quicker and lifted it out herself.

"Still completely self-reliant, I see." Karl had not

offered a greeting, and neither had Elizabeth. "You're back home much sooner than we expected."

Elizabeth shot him a scowl. It had been almost six months, after all.

"I got bored. Europe isn't what it used to be. Too…familiar. You go from one country to the next now, and the only thing that changes are the road signs. Even in France, almost everyone speaks English, though they may not admit it."

"Perhaps a change of scenery—somewhere like South America or Australia?"

Karl's tone was light, but his eyes were completely serious.

"You can't get rid of me that easily, Karl. Besides, there isn't a major city on any continent that I haven't visited. I still have apartments in several of them."

Karl said nothing as they walked toward the building's front door.

Elizabeth continued, "Tell John I need to see him right away, please."

Her tone made it an order, not a request. Karl's voice hinted at guilty pleasure as he opened the door for her.

"John is out of the country for at least a couple of days. I'll let him know you're here when he gets back."

"Message him tonight, please." Again, it wasn't a request.

"Of course. Do you still have the phone I issued you?" Elizabeth already had it in hand and raised it with another scowl. "Good. It will open apartment 355 for you."

As they walked into the building's lobby, Elizabeth

fished the pendant on the chain around her neck from inside her silk blouse. Wrought in heavy yellow gold were the numbers *355*. As she placed the pendant back between her breasts, her fingers also brushed the simple wooden cross tipped with silver that shared the chain.

"Well, make yourself comfortable." Karl pushed the elevator UP button. "Dinner is at six, as always."

Without waiting for a response, he turned and walked through the front door.

Chapter 7

Reacquaintance

F ather Dan Koprowicz walked with several of his parishioners from the small church to The Enclave's Commons building. The Commons housed, among its many functions, the main kitchen and dining room. As they walked, he chatted with Jenny Stafford on his left. She had recently switched from attending Sunday morning Mass with her parents to the Saturday evening service favored by those younger members who still bothered to come at all. Dan suspected she was more interested in him than she was in his homilies. Purely out of habit and without a conscious thought, he suppressed the pleasant thought this knowledge spawned.

"Did you enjoy the homily today?"

Jenny's sheepish look told him she hadn't been listening to what he thought had been a good one, but despite her embarrassment, her eyes never left his.

Feeling a bit creeped-out, Dan turned to his right where George Allworth, the twenty-year old son of The Enclave's Farm Manager, walked. George worked on his father's crew.

"Did you get much downtime during the winter?"

George's crew had just started the spring fertilization, so the "country air" smell of fresh manure pervaded the village.

George, who had eyes only for Jenny, yanked his gaze from her.

"Yeah, Father, we pretty much finished the maintenance on all of the field equipment a month or so ago."

As they approached the outer door of the Commons, Dan deftly sidestepped behind George and reached for the door handle and held it open.

"Well, I hope you used your free time to practice that guitar of yours. Do you have any gigs scheduled?"

George waited for Jenny to precede him through the door. As she did, she turned back to him.

"Thanks. I didn't know you play!" she said. "Where?"

Before he could answer, Dan chimed in. "He sings, too. You should hear him."

Now it was George's turn to hold open the inner door of the vestibule. Jenny's smile and shy "Thank-you" brought color to George's cheeks. Smiling at his own cleverness, Dan took the door handle from George so he could follow Jenny inside.

George mouthed his own "Thank-you" to Dan, who just winked in reply. He watched as the two of them, now clearly *together* sought out their friends' table.

Hearty greetings followed Dan from all sides as he entered the dining hall. He waved off several offered seats at various tables because he spotted a woman sitting alone against the wall opposite the darkening windows.

There were crowded tables all around her, but the way those closest turned their backs to her made it clear to Dan that something was amiss. The normally gregarious nature of The Enclave residents seemed absent in the space surrounding the young woman.

To Dan, it seemed there was a force field of unspoken agreement among all of those present that this woman wanted to be, and should be, left alone. Dan, of course, couldn't resist the challenge.

As he got closer, though, he realized he recognized her. Although their previous encounter had been very brief, she had left an indelible impression.

Her light hair cascaded around her bright blue eyes, high distinct cheekbones and small straight nose. Her elegant, yet subdued, blouse and trousers also made her stand out among the other, more casually dressed diners.

Looking up, she saw him approach, and her face opened into a smile as she, too, recognized him.

"May I join you, Elizabeth?"

"Of course, Father, it's good to see you again." He took a seat opposite her. "And please call me Liz." She held out her hand.

Dan shook it lightly. "It's good to see you, also, Liz. It's been quite a while since you were here to collect your aunt's things." She just nodded, so he continued, "I still pray for her soul."

Liz gave him an odd look that was almost a smirk.

"Oh, I don't think there is any need for that, Father. I'm sure she's firmly ensconced wherever it is she deserved to go."

The joking lilt in her voice kept Dan from taking offense.

"Well, I'm sure it can't hurt, anyway."

His chuckle told her they should agreed to disagree, and that perhaps their respective faith, or lack of it, wasn't the best topic of conversation.

Dan fixed his plate from the nearly full platters arrayed on the table. The food wasn't exactly hot anymore, but the beef stew and garlic mashed potatoes smelled delicious.

"What brings you back to our little village?" he asked around a mouthful.

"Well, it is like coming home to me." Dan's surprised look prompted her to continued. "I was born and raised here, you know."

"I didn't know that. Why did you leave?" Dan asked, but he thought he already knew the answer.

"Really, Father. Look at me." She looked all around the hall. "Most of these folks don't know me, or don't remember me, but they all know I don't belong here…" Liz's voice fell almost to a whisper, "anymore."

Surprised at the depth of resentment he heard in her voice, Dan's natural tendency to soothe another's hurts came forward.

"The Enclave is a bit closed-minded, I admit. But I came here as a stranger and now I feel at home. It took a while, but I feel I've been accepted here."

Liz tilted her head and leaned forward. "But you never *left*, Father." Dan was taken aback at the venom in her tone. "They don't give me the cold shoulder because I'm new here. They do it because they think I abandoned them."

Seeing his confused expression, she continued, "Even though they don't know who I am, the fact that I'm here inside tells them I was once one of them, and now I'm…not."

"But we often get visitors from other Enclave communities. You could easily be another of those visitors."

But even as he said the words, Dan knew the reactions of those in the hall belied his words. Looking around, he realized that the feeling he had ascribed to everyone was, in fact, only evident in a few of the older residents. They radiated that attitude, though, and the simpatico he had often observed in this tight-knit community spread their distrust throughout.

With this insight, he leaned back and studied Liz in a new light. Her hair looked to be its natural color and not a single grey strand or root was visible. Likewise, her face, which Dan had acknowledged the first time they met as stunningly beautiful, showed not a single line at either her eyes or mouth. The skin of Liz's long neck was similarly without flaw.

By all physical appearances, Liz could be no older than her early twenties. The poise she exhibited though, and her essential presence, even under Dan's obvious and somewhat rude assessing eye, contradicted her apparent youth.

One thing Dan's previous experiences of delving into the secrets of the shadowy organization known as The Enclave had taught him was to be very aware of contradictions. This led Dan to a suspicion that he couldn't discuss in such an open setting, but it was one he could verify later.

Rather than being uncomfortable under his scrutiny, Liz simply returned his stare until she saw this recognition dawn.

"You see, don't you, that some remember while others suspect? Such memories and suspicions poison the well of friendship."

Dan chose to interpret her cryptic remark, not as a rebuke, but rather as a plea.

"Suspicions can cut both ways, though. Suspicion of a pleasant outcome, of the beginning of a friendship, can also be called 'hope.'"

Liz's mouth turned up at the corners. "Indeed. I could use some hope right about now."

Seeing the opening, but not wanting to press the issue too hard, Dan simply nodded and matched her hint of a smile with one of his own.

Changing the subject completely, he nodded towards her neck, where the chain, pendant, and cross were visible.

"I see you're still wearing your Aunt Margaret's necklace."

Startled by the change of direction in the conversation, Liz reflexively touched her right hand to the pendant, running her fingers over its outlines, which formed the digits 3-5-5.

Dan continued, "Tell me again what '355' stands for?"

Regaining her poise, Liz dropped her hand and lifted

an eyebrow. "Come now, Father, someone with your background should know what a .355 caliber is."

It was Dan's turn to be startled that she would know he was the son of a world-renowned gunsmith.

"Of course, .355 caliber is the same as a 9-millimeter. I've made a lot of those."

That's not what she told me it meant last time. Is she that bad of a liar, or is she testing me? Another possibility presented itself. *Or, is she sending me a message?*

After a few seconds' lull in the conversation while Dan shoveled the rapidly cooling stew and potatoes into his mouth and thought this latest exchange through, he realized Liz had not answered his earlier question.

"So, again, what brings you home?"

Liz's mouth drew into a tight line. "I need to meet with our fearless leader, Mr., ah, Haviland, on a matter of some importance." She frowned. "But when I arrived, I found out he is out of the country for at least a few more days."

She paused, and when she resumed, her voice took on a sullen quality. "And they won't tell me where he is."

Her momentary pause at remembering John's last name was more revealing to Dan than she realized and added another weight to the scales of his own suspicions.

Feigning innocence, Dan asked, "What, would you have tracked him down? Surely your conversation can wait a couple of days."

Anger flashed in Liz's eyes, and Dan realized his earlier assessment of her apparent, but misleading, youth was spot on.

"Not everyone limps along at the leisurely pace that this place does. I assure you that if I knew where he was, I'd be on the next plane."

Dan knew exactly where John was, and why, but he just nodded and lifted a forkful of his now cold stew into his mouth. As he did, a young girl of perhaps ten years tapped Liz on the arm. Neither Dan nor Liz had seen her approach.

"You're new here. I've never seen you before."

Liz turned to the youngster without the slightest hint of annoyance.

"I've been away a long time. Probably since before you were born. What's your name?"

"Aimley! Get over here. Leave the *lady* alone." A matronly woman strode up and grabbed the girl by the arm, yanking her away from Liz.

"Hey. Be careful. She's not bothering me."

By way of reply, the woman simply scowled at Liz and turned a disapproving eye on Fr. Dan while she marched Aimley from the hall. Dan excused himself and followed the pair out the door.

Give her hell, Father, Liz thought.

Chapter 8

Aimley

E lizabeth flipped the pages of the fashion magazine without reading a single word.

Three days. Three eff-ing days with no word from John.

Looking up from the page, the reading circle at the other end of the library drew her attention.

Father Dan sat with about a dozen teenagers. They took turns reading from a modern translation of Homer's Odyssey. After each turn, Dan asked a question or two about the meaning and imagery of each passage.

The teens answered a smattering of the questions, but most were met with silence. After each of the awkward silences, Dan glanced to his left, and Aimley's much younger voice piped up with a well thought out explanation of the meaning of the Sirens' song, or Odysseus's crew's addiction to the Lotus.

Each time, Liz was impressed by the young girl's insight and her ability to connect Homer's epic tale to today's societal ills.

After Dan closed out the evening's readings and sent the kids home, he strolled over to where Elizabeth was now non-reading a travel magazine.

"I love to read about all those exotic travel spots."

Liz looked up and smiled. "Most aren't nearly as glamorous as they make them out to be."

"Yeah, but in general most things aren't." They both chuckled. "Have you visited many of them?"

Liz nodded and shrugged. "Most, actually. I like to travel, and thanks to my work for The Enclave, I can afford to."

Dan looked puzzled as he sat down. "I thought you said you had left The Enclave."

"I left this village, this place. The Enclave, Father, extends well beyond this backwater." Liz looked for either puzzlement or recognition from Dan, but he kept his face neutral and didn't react, so she continued. "There are other parts of The Enclave out there in the world, you know."

Dan nodded. "I haven't had the chance to visit any of them, though. At least not yet."

"Well, you seem to be doing a great job shepherding this flock." Dan smiled at the compliment as she continued, "Take that Aimley girl, for example. She seems like quite a precocious kid."

Dan nodded and sighed heavily. "Yeah, Amy's very smart. So much so that she's bored to tears in school, which is why I invited her to join the teens' reading circle."

"And she seemed to be the one with all the answers, even more than the older kids."

Dan nodded again. "We had a chat after the first time she joined the group. Amy kept jumping in to answer every question, and even cutting off the others when they did have something to say." Liz chuckled, but Dan got serious. "I've tried again and again to get her into classes with the older kids, but her foster parents keep refusing."

Liz's smile disappeared and was replaced by a look of puzzlement.

"Foster parents? What happened to her birth parents? And I thought her name is 'Aimley', but you keep calling her Amy."

Dan's face darkened. "'Aimley' is a derogatory nickname. It's short for 'Aimless Amy.' I hate that nickname."

The venom in Dan's voice shocked Liz. After a deep breath, he continued, "Amy's parents, ah, *left* The Enclave, also." Liz's eyes opened in understanding. "They were killed when their house was burglarized, so Amy came here, although she had never seen the place and had no surviving family. So, even though she's completely innocent, Amy's been ostracized and treated like a traitorous outsider by just about every adult—including the couple fostering her."

Liz felt an immediate affinity for the poor girl. "But, why? It's not her fault that her parents opted out."

"Unfortunately, this Enclave is so closed off from the world, it fosters closed minds as well."

Liz snorted in disgust. "Don't I know it! That's why I can't wait to talk to John so I can get the hell out of here."

Dan ignored the profanity. "I want to talk to John, too. I think it would be best for Amy to attend a boarding school somewhere. Unfortunately, she's too young for most of them in this area. I want to ask John if maybe he can pull some strings somewhere."

That's not what she needs, Liz thought.

Before Liz could voice the thought, though, both of their phones buzzed for attention. Pulling them out simultaneously, they read the same message on their respective screens.

Please come to my office at your earliest convenience.

John.

As one, they rose and headed for the spiral stairs leading to John's outer office.

"The Master summons, and the peons jump," Liz muttered.

Dan snorted and responded, "The *Grand* Master, you mean."

Chapter 9

Operative Elizabeth

N o, I don't have any assignments for you. And even if I did, I wouldn't give you one."

John Haviland, The Enclave's Grand Master, sat behind the desk in his spacious office. Before Elizabeth could object, he held up his hand and continued, "You, of all people, should know that the standard rule is at least a full year of downtime between operations. Especially ones that end as your last one did."

Heat rose in Elizabeth's face, but she kept her voice calm, knowing full well this was a test of her mental state as much as anything. She glanced at Fr. Dan, who sat in the other guest chair angled to face both Elizabeth and John's.

"I'm perfectly healthy—both in mind and in body. I don't want, or need, another six months of downtime."

"Six and a half months, actually." Dan spoke up for the first time. "You came in as 'Margaret' seven months ago. Dead, I might add, or so I thought."

Elizabeth looked in shock from Dan to John and back.

"Fr. Dan has full access to all our archives," John said quietly by way of explanation.

"I also gave you Last Rites." He raised an eyebrow, and she shrugged. "You were discharged several weeks later as 'Elizabeth.'

That was five months and two weeks ago." He sipped the brandy from the glass in his hand before continued. "Your records are quite extensive. Twenty-two operations, some of them quite long—multiple years, in fact. Dating all the way back to Sarah, born, as you told me earlier, right here at The Enclave…way back in 1760."

"You may know my history, but you don't know me."

"That's very true. Your after-action reports are spotty, at best. Twenty-two operations, all quite successful, but all of which ended in death and resurrection. Each with less and less downtime over the years."

Coldly, Elizabeth tried unsuccessfully to stare him down. "What is your point?"

John replied quietly, "I think you're addicted to these serial lives. Putting on a persona and fooling everyone around you for years. Gathering invaluable intelligence, I admit, but all while balanced on a knife's edge. You've gotten bolder and bolder, knowing full well that suspicion grows around you, but you've been unable to stop because of the lifeline you wear around your neck."

Elizabeth's hand flew to her chain, but she grasped the wooden cross, not the gold pendant.

John continued, "Perhaps you think the use of your cross to bring you back to life again and again will have a cumulative effect. That you will somehow become immortal through repetition?" He paused, but got nothing in response except Elizabeth's icy stare, so he shrugged. "You may be right. We don't know enough about the piece of the Lance you carry with you to know the full extent of its powers. But if you are right, if there's even a chance that you're right, I can't let that happen." He held out his hand, open palm up, and waited.

Realization of what he was demanding flooded her, and she wrapped the cross in her fist. "NO!" she cried out. "I won't give it to you. I've earned the right to wear it. For all the things I've done for this stupid Enclave for over two centuries."

John dropped his hand back into his lap.

"You're right. You have earned it, and I won't take that away from you. But I won't send you back into harm's way until Fr. Dan here tells me he believes you can handle it."

It was Dan's turn to look shocked. John had not discussed this aspect of his plan with him beforehand.

He remained silent though, as John continued, "Furthermore, if you use that cross to heal, or resurrect, yourself before that time, we'll tend to you and care for you and nurse you back to health as we always have. But you won't be wearing it when you wake up."

Elizabeth turned to Dan. "Are you qualified to make such an evaluation?"

Dan shrugged. "Seminary teaches us more than Catholic doctrine. I listen to many people talk about their troubles. Sometimes I can help them. Most of the time I just try to help them help themselves."

Her penetrating stare seemed to be trying to probe Dan's soul, but he didn't even flinch. Finally, she nodded.

"I agree. I'll stay here until the good Father pronounces me sane."

Dan and John exchanged a look that seemed to said, *That was too easy.*

John continued, "Just remember that I know more about you, or your history at least, than anyone you've fooled with your acting in the past."

It's far more than 'acting' but you'll never know that this cooperative *persona is just another one I can wear like a cloak,* she thought, but kept her silence.

Dan reached out to her, and she reluctantly took his hand. "I listen, Liz. And hearing what you've said so far, I suspect you've spent so much time undercover that you've lost the ability to form genuine relationships with others. Relationships with other people you aren't lying to all the time."

Liz snorted angrily and shook her hand loose. "They're all long dead and long gone."

Undeterred, Dan continued, "That's my point. I bet you spend the little downtime you take between operations alone." He raised his hands supplicatingly. "Of course, I don't want to jump to conclusions. As I said, I listen, which means you're going to have to talk. To tell me about your long life from the beginning."

Again, Liz held his gaze for a beat. *This one's deeper than I thought. Let's see if he can be trusted.*

She nodded. "We're going to need a lot of coffee—and bourbon."

Chapter 10

Amy

Liz and Father Dan sat in the spacious lounge area of the two-story library. At the far end from the library's double doors, the quiet space contained a cluster of club chairs, end tables, a low coffee table, and a few floor lamps that bathed the area in soft yellow light. This was Dan's favorite spot to chat privately with folks.

The low lighting and muffling acoustics offered a great deal of privacy, even in such a public space. Dan intended that night's conversation with Liz to be more convivial than their following discussions. Those would take place in John's office.

"Are you settled in?" Dan asked without looking up from the book he was reading.

"Unfortunately, yes." This made Dan looked up expectantly until Liz continued, "I didn't expect to be staying this long."

Dan smiled and put the book down. "Well, I, for one, am glad you're here. I have a lot of questions that I think our talks will answer."

"I don't know. I have even more questions than answers sometimes."

"Such as?"

Instead of answering, Liz looked around as if she sensed someone lurking in the shadows. Then she just shook her head.

Dan got the message and changed the subject. "Where are you staying?"

Liz grunted. "Tallmadge House, of course." Dan's quizzical look spurred her to explained. "It's one of John's inside jokes, I'm sure."

Dan shook his head. "I, ah…"

"Don't worry Father." She reached out and laid her hand on his arm. "We'll get there."

Just then, a whisper of fabrics rubbing together caught both of their attention.

Liz leaped to her feet into the defensive pose that Dan was just beginning to learn in his martial arts class.

"Hey! Show yourself."

Dan started toward the origin of the sound behind one of the leather sofas, but Liz grabbed his arm to stop him. Her grip was surprisingly tight and her arm strong. Dan stopped in his tracks.

In an imperious voice, Liz called out, "You have until I count to three, then I'm coming back there to kick your ass."

Liz's ultimatum was met by a small high-pitched whimper.

A pig-tailed head slowly emerged around the corner of the furniture. Dan relaxed, but Liz slowly drew herself up to her full height.

"Amy? What are you doing back there, Young Lady?" His voice was firm but gentle and non-threatening.

"I'm sorry." Amy's lip quivered, and the tears started. "I didn't mean anything."

Seeing the girl's tears and Liz's tense posture, Dan crossed to the sofa, knelt down, and gathered Amy into his arms. She buried her face in his shoulder.

Scowling over her head at Liz, he asked, "How come you're here? It's late and you should be in bed."

Her muffled voice answered, "Mrs. Warner went out with her friends and Mr. Warner fell asleep in his chair. I wanted to read more of that Oddity book."

Dan pushed her back and looked her in the eye. "Did you tell Mr. Warner you were coming here?"

Amy sniffed and rubbed her nose on Dan's outstretched arm, which made Liz grin and relax.

"I told him, but he didn't wake up."

"Probably passed out from what I've heard," Liz muttered.

Dan shot her a sharp look before standing and taking Amy by the hand. "Come on, we'll read more of the *Odyssey* tomorrow. Let's get you home now." He looked back at Liz. "If John calls, tell him I'll be back shortly."

Liz nodded and settled back down into her club chair.

As they left, Liz heard Dan said, "No more late-night escapades, Amy. If Mr. Warner wakes up, he'll be worried that you're not there."

As they faded out of earshot, Liz heard Amy's reply, "Oh, he won't wake up until morning."

"More trouble with that Aimley girl?" John asked as Dan entered his office. John and Liz sat in the more informal lounge area of the office. Both held a snifter in their hands, and seeing this, Dan raised a questioning eyebrow. John waved his hand toward the dry bar in the corner of the room and Dan made his way there.

"Her name is *Amy*, not 'Aimley.'" Liz was indignant. "You've got to get her out of that house, John. It sounds like a terrible situation."

Setting the decanter down, Dan carried his own snifter over to the others and took a seat in one of the overstuffed chairs.

He nodded in agreement with Liz and said, "The old man is drunk most of the time and his wife resents Amy as much as she does her own kids who left The Enclave and never looked back. Frankly, I can see why they did."

The last comment was quite out of character for Dan, and John's surprise showed on his face. He replied, "Bob didn't start drinking heavily until the kids left. Actually, not until Dolores started carrying that chip around all the time." He paused a moment before continued, "I thought Amy would be good for them. Snap them out of their funk."

Liz spoke up. "It seems it has had the opposite effect."

John gave her a thanks-for-stating-the-obvious look. "OK, see if you can find another couple who will take her."

Dan shook his head. "It won't be easy. She has a reputation now that Mrs. Warner has been bad-mouthing her all over town."

John just shrugged. Interpersonal matters were not his *forte*. Instead of offering further support, he just said, "OK, let's get to why we're all here. Dan needs to hear your story, Elizabeth. From the beginning, or at least from your nighttime raid on my bedroom."

Dan looked shocked, but also intrigued.

Liz waved her hand. "I was twelve, Father. And John—he was Abraham then, and I was Sarah—already had company in his bed."

PART III

Sarah
Summer 1776 – Autumn 1777

The unanimous Declaration of the thirteen united States of America

When in the Course of human events, it becomes necessary for one people to dissolve the political bands which have connected them with another, and to assume among the powers of the earth, the separate and equal station to which the Laws of Nature and of Nature's God entitle them, a decent respect to the opinions of mankind requires that they should declare the causes which impel them to the separation.

We hold these truths to be self-evident, that all men are created equal, that they are endowed by their Creator with certain unalienable Rights, that among these are Life, Liberty and the pursuit of Happiness.

Chapter 11

Training

In the four years Sarah spent at The Enclave's Operative School hidden in the woods, she learned the ways of the outside world. The Enclave enclosed an area of ten-thousand acres, most of which was covered by virgin Pennsylvania forest—oaks, maples, beech and stately elms. That expanse of land hid many secrets. The Operative School was just one of them.

The school challenged its students in many ways—physically, mentally, emotionally, and morally. Over the four years since she gladly left her family, Sarah learned to converse in French, Italian and German, using dialects as diverse as those that could be heard in the slums of Paris or among the elite upper class in the manor houses of England.

She learned equally well the manners of a lady and the art of spying. Those lessons shared much more in common than she ever would have guessed.

Tested at every turn, Sarah quickly became first in her classes and rose through the courses faster than any of the other students. At first resentful, the other students soon recognized that their instructors treated Sarah differently. They were more demanding in their assignments and harsher in their criticisms. Sarah understood this, as well, but accepted their challenges and rebukes as the lessons they were meant to be. She kept a positive attitude, seeing every correction not as a setback, but rather as a lesson learned.

On his infrequent visits, Abraham discussed in detail Sarah's progress with Mr. Garrison, the school's Headmaster. Each time, the focus of her training shifted, sometimes slightly, as when Abraham heard her beautiful singing voice for the first time and directed that her obvious musical talents should be expanded and refined. Sometimes, though, the shift in focus could be dramatic, as it was when Sarah turned sixteen.

"You need to accelerate her lessons in espionage," Abraham paused, "and the seductive arts."

He and Garrison stood in a concealed gallery overlooking the training floor, where Sarah sparred with three male students. While the instructor barked orders, Sarah disarmed and disabled all three opponents in short order, leaving them groaning on the floor.

Garrison raised an eyebrow at the last, but didn't address it. Instead, he said, "But she is only at the First Master level in three of the Seven Disciplines."

Abraham cut him off with a chopping motion. "And Second or Third Master in the others. I've seen the reports."

His tone softened as he turned his head back to the training below, where the teacher was leading Sarah through a succession of exercises, connecting the individual forms she knew so well into a series of devastating attacks. Nodding at his instructions, she launched into a whirling dance of kicks and punches delivered to a phantom opponent. Tumbling, leaping, and spinning the length of the practice floor and back again, Sarah ended her flurry in the very spot she had started from.

Sweat glistened on her brow from the heat of the July afternoon, but otherwise there were no signs of her exertions. The instructor broke into a smile—the most praise he ever expressed—as a gasp escaped from Garrison. Abraham just nodded. He had the confirmation he had come to see for himself.

"See?" He looked to Garrison, who nodded. "Maintenance only on her physical training from now on. We don't want her looking like a stevedore. If she wants to extend herself during her recreation time, fine. But I doubt she will have occasion to use those particular talents during the operation I have in mind for her."

Garrison turned a questioning look toward Abraham, who continued with a rueful smile, "These 'Americans' have named themselves independent of the British throne."

"Publicly?"

Garrison was not at all surprised by this turn of events. He and Abraham had discussed the possibility many times. Abraham nodded, but kept the excitement he felt out of his voice.

"Broadsides are being printed as we speak. Within a week or two, their 'Declaration of Independence' will be read in every town and village in the colonies." Garrison nodded his understanding as Abraham continued, "We have reached the fulcrum point in our plan, and that lovely young *woman* down there is our lever."

"She is very young."

It was a flat statement of fact, without any of Garrison's previous reservations. All of his objections had faded away with Abraham's news. His voice, if not his words, expressed his dedication to the path forward that Abraham had charted.

"Aye, she is young, my friend. But no younger than my first love was when she died, though that was a long time ago. Times have changed, but the desires of young men have not."

They watched as Sarah flew through another series of punches, feints, and whirling kicks. When she finally stopped, her tight-fitting exercise clothing clung, sweat-soaked, to her lean but feminine body.

"Indeed," was Garrison's only response.

Chapter 12

Rescue

The young, fresh-faced, maiden-who-wasn't walked toward Philadelphia with her baskets full of eggs. Sarah's proctor, Charles, had brought her on horseback to Germantown on the outskirts of Philadelphia town, which is where she was headed on the cold fall day.

Her mission, which Charles would observe and report on, was twofold. She would, of course, sell the dozens of eggs packed so carefully in the two wicker baskets she carried. Those business transactions, conducted routinely as they had been every week for the last two months, were secondary to her primary mission, however.

The trek on that cold, cloudless day was yet another exercise, a test on the road to proving to Charles, and more importantly to Abraham, that she, Sarah Louise Harkin, deserved to be an Enclave Operator. An Operator—a spy—for the oldest intelligence gathering organization in the world.

By sixteen years old, Sarah had showed her expertise in many forms of hand-to-hand combat, weapons of various sorts, and the art of extreme stealth. The past year's training, however, was decidedly different. Hours on the fighting floor had given way to hours on the dance floor. Sarah learned the value of silks and brocades, and other expensive fabrics used to make her fine dresses and gowns.

She also learned the value of *décolletage*, and how varying in the depth of her neckline appealed to men of different ages and social stations. A hint of cleavage to excite a young scion of a prominent family. A deeper plunge for his father.

Today, though, she presented the appearance of a rustic colonial girl straight from the family farm. Her gate and the general attitude she expressed had an air of responsibility mixed with excitement. Having established a routine of making this trip several times over the past few months, Sarah felt confident in her transactions as she met with the innkeepers and shop owners who were her regular customers.

To the proprietors and their wives, her wide smile and bright eyes evoked protective feelings of parentage for the poor girl, forced to brave the chilly wind to help feed her family. As a result, she usually returned from her excursion with a basketful of bread, besides the proceeds from her slightly overpriced eggs.

Not surprisingly, the shopkeepers' older sons made sure they were sweeping the floor or, better yet, working behind the counter when she came by selling her eggs. For those quick to blush, she peeked out from under her delicate eyelashes with a shy smile.

For those who seemed to inflate at her approach, throwing back shoulders, puffing out their chests, and finding as many ways as possible to flex the muscles of their arms, her manner was much different. A direct tilted-head gaze and banter that flirted with the edges of propriety usually let her manipulate those targets even more easily than she did the blushing stammerers.

Her flirtations served a deadly serious purpose, however. Philadelphia, previously the seat of the colonies' Congress, was now an occupied city. The British had captured the town without much of a fight the previous fall, and now they had troops quartered in every inn and most private houses within the confines of the city.

Sarah's customers, forced to interact with British troops and officers every day, were a deep pool of possible intelligence. Through subtle verbal probing, she had gauged the presence and depth of any patriotic fervor among those who had to feed and house those soldiers, sailors, and officers, most of whom treated their hosts like second-class bumpkins, rather than the loyal subjects of the Crown they were, or at least pretended to be.

Those who had already come to think of themselves in their heart-of-hearts as citizens of an independent nation especially interested Sarah. But Whichever direction their loyalty leaned, she could manipulate them with a subtle, seemingly innocent turn of phrase, to gossip about whom and how many officers were housed where, and what they overheard during their *guests* boisterous, often drunken gatherings.

The real wealth of information came, though, not from the adults, who knew the risks of even the hint of disloyalty; nor from their over-confident sons, whose bravado and too obvious patriotism easily marked them as dangerous to the occupiers. Many of those types disappeared to the ranks of the rebels, or worse, to the holds of the British prison ships, where they languished and died of thirst or malnutrition, or simply froze to death.

Among the more discreet residents, all patriotic conversations stopped, or veered to some mundane topic, when the British occupiers entered a room, or passed on the street. Sarah's best sources of information were those seemingly cowed innocents who moved freely and almost invisibly among the occupiers. Their hatred, felt as strongly as any rebel soldier on the field of battle, festered all the more for being suppressed.

Those blushing sons she flirted with often whispered to her the gossip they had picked up, or passed her notes from their parents in the guise of produce orders for market day—so many live chickens (new ships in the river), shanks of venison (recently arrived companies of soldiers), pork (Lieutenants and Captains), and beef (Majors and Colonels).

Fear, planted and cultivated by the occupiers, often yielded the best intelligence. And there were none more fearful in the occupied city of Philadelphia than the daughters and young wives who felt the threat of ruination from every pack of idling soldiers they passed. Reports of rape were commonplace and, if the uncaring officers meted out any punishment at all, it was accompanied by a wink and a nod.

As Sarah entered Philadelphia town, Eliza Adams was walking along Chestnut Street when a muscular arm grabbed her and a hand shoved a filthy rag into her mouth. Lifted off her feet and dragged into a coach alley between two houses, her attacker threw her face down on the ground with her arms pinned beneath her. The massive weight of her attacker pouncing on her back forced the breath from her lungs and prevented her from shouting out.

Unable to raise up the soldier's heavy body, she instead pressed knees even harder to the packed dirt of the alley, pinning her petticoats to the ground, and momentarily preventing her attacker's fumbling hands from yanking up her skirts.

This stalemate gained Eliza a few precious seconds, but when the drunken soldier recognized her ploy, she felt him raise up onto an arm centered on her back, pressing her even harder into the dirt. Gasping for air, she turned her head and saw his other hand ball into a massive fist. As he raised it to deliver a blow to the back of her head, Eliza knew her maidenhood, and maybe her very life was about to be taken from her.

As the edges of her vision blackened from lack of air, Eliza heard the distinct thud of a blow landing, though she felt nothing. A distinctive snapping crunch like a giant chicken being killed for the stewpot immediately followed the blow. As the oppressive weight rolled off her, and with adrenaline pumping, Eliza pushed to her feet to flee. Blocking the alley, though, the heavyset British mercenary lay motionless in the dirt, his head twisted at an impossible angle.

Movement at the opening of the alley caught her attention, and she looked up just in time to see the hem of a homespun blue dress disappear around the corner of the building to her left. By the time Eliza stepped over the dead soldier and ran from the alleyway, though, the blue dress was nowhere to be seen amongst the bustle of Chestnut Street.

Without looking back at the dead form lying in the dirt and hoping to avoid any official questioning and the investigation sure to follow its discovery, Eliza smoothed the wrinkles from her dress and walked briskly, without running, toward home.

Chapter 13

Recognition and Recruitment

Eliza's mother spread salve on the scrapes the girl suffered during the attack while Eliza gazed intently out her bedroom window onto the street below. She watched, fearful that at any moment a squad of British troops would crash into the shop below, bent on bringing retribution for the death of her intended rapist.

She was afraid, but for her family, not for herself. The attack in the alley had changed her, and the shaking she couldn't still was not that of a fearful victim. It was the physical manifestation of a newly seeded, but deep hatred—a steely resolve to fight, in any way she could, the monsters who oppressed her people, and those who condoned that oppression.

Waiting and watching for deadly British retribution, she was astounded to see the egg girl, Sarah, walking cheerfully along the street. Each moment of the day's terror was etched into Eliza's memory, as was the fleeting glimpse she had caught of her savior's dress. That very same blue dress that was turning into her father's shop below. Without hesitation, Eliza bolted from the room, interrupting her mother's ministrations.

Flying headlong down the stairway and bursting through the private door at the back of the shop, Eliza saw Sarah and her father quietly conducting their weekly business. When she started to speak, however, Sarah caught her eye and, with the tiniest shake of her head, silenced her.

Her father was still reeling from the story Eliza had recounted of her attack and miraculous escape, seemingly at the hands of a *woman*. Jonathan Adams's hands still shook as he counted out the coins for Sarah, but he saw the silent exchange between Sarah and his daughter. He, too, focused on her dress and understanding dawned like a hot summer day.

Fighting back tears, he grabbed Sarah's hand as she reached for the coins on the counter. With conditioned reflexes, Sarah twisted her hand out of his grip, grabbed Jonathan's thumb, and pinned his much larger hand to the wood. Her reflexive response would have broken his wrist had she not regained control of her muscles and stopped herself short of doing any permanent damage.

In a flash, Sarah realized that her reaction, and Eliza's obvious recognition of her role in girl's ordeal had exposed some of her abilities.

Were they patriots? Or Tories? She knew her life depended on quickly assessing this family's loyalties.

"Sorry, Mr. Adams. You startled me," Sarah said as she released his thumb from her twisting iron grip.

Before she could continue, though, he spoke with a voice choked by emotion.

"I saw a man from the country do that in a tavern once when a local tough tried to rob him." He rubbed his now sore and swelling hand. "That time, though, I heard the bones in the thief's wrist snap." Sarah merely raised an eyebrow. "I also saw that country man drop the other three hooligans who set upon him. He moved so fast that in a few moments, four men lay on the tavern floor. That country man then strode out the door as pretty as you please."

"I assure you that if I didn't like you, Mr. Adams, you would need a surgeon to set that wrist of yours."

Adams nodded. "And it probably never would have worked right again, eh?" Having recovered his composure, he even smiled a little. "I'm grateful you didn't like the beast who tried to have his way with my Eliza."

Sarah answered his smile in kind. "I've seen the drunken lout before, but we won't be seeing him again. And I assure you, sir, if it had been my own father that I caught in an act like that, the outcome would have been the same."

Although her words came out in a steady, calm voice, Sarah's heart thumped in her chest. She *killed someone!* Yes, he surely deserved it, but his family back home would never see him again...and that didn't bother her one bit. Her training had not yet included this lesson, but a teacher's words, delivered when she felt guilty about breaking her classmate's arm, came back to her.

"He placed himself in the position to suffer such an injury. You were simply the agent of the Fate that he created for himself."

Now she was Death's agent, as well.

As Adams continued to rub his wrist, the shop's door flew open and a British officer in full uniform, his saber sidearm rattling against the doorframe, strode into the shop, followed by two soldiers carrying muskets.

Sarah's world froze in time. The soldiers blocked any escape through the front while Eliza and her mother stood in the doorway to the back hallway and would certainly slow her down if she tried to run for it out through the back. Instead of bolting, though, she stepped back and lowered her head, keeping her eyes on the officer. Her body tensed beneath her gingham dress, ready for hand-to-hand combat.

The officer stepped to the counter, completely ignoring the three women. Mr. Adams smiled widely at him.

"God, Save the King!" he nearly bellowed.

Sarah cringed internally, but kept a blank expression. Wondering where Adams's loyalties lay, she scanned back through her memory. She left nothing of herself behind, so if he accused a simple farm girl selling eggs, he would look the fool.

"Yes, yes, God save the King," the officer responded impatiently. "Where have you been this morning?"

His tone and posture reeked of superiority and authority.

Sarah mentally prepared an attack plan. She was confident she could disable the officer quickly, but the two soldiers would be more of a problem.

To her relief, though, Adams replied, "Why, right here minding my store. Why, has something happened?"

Seeing the round belly barely covered by the shopkeeper's apron, the officer's tone turned from accusing to perfunctory.

"Have you seen a man running along the street this morning?"

"Well, no. Nothing out of the ordinary. Are you looking for someone in particular?"

Sarah knew he shouldn't asked so many questions, just answer theirs as simply as possible.

But Adams had never had her training. "Perhaps he is hiding in my shed out back?"

The officer looked askance at Adams. "We have already searched your property. Perhaps we should search your rooms upstairs as well."

He looked at Mrs. Adams and Eliza standing in the back doorway for the first time.

"Ah, certainly, Sir." Adams gestured to the door and his wife and daughter stepped out of the way, leaving the doorway open.

He was giving Sarah an escape route. Not out through the back, though. When the soldiers went upstairs, she could simply walk out the front door.

But the officer had no interest in rummaging through the rustic, homespun effects of these bumpkins.

"That will not be necessary." His tone was even haughtier, if that was possible. "If you see anything suspicious, report it to the garrison Commander immediately."

Without waiting for a reply, he spun on his heel and headed for the door.

"Of course, Sir!" Adams replied as the officer and his soldiers jerked open the door and clomped out.

Mrs. Adams let out a sigh of relief and Mr. Adams turned a now genuine smile to Sarah. But, seeing the serious cast of Sarah's face and her tensed posture, his smile faded, and he realized the debt he owed this wisp of a girl who had spoken so calmly of killing a man at least twice her size.

Placing his hand on his cashbox, he said, "How can I repay you, Miss?"

Relaxing her posture, Sarah raised her head and returned the shopkeeper's smile. Knowing she needed confidants, not debtors, she shook her head slowly from side to side and recited the beginning of a common aphorism she had learned. The litany was becoming a recognition sign among the local patriots, those who called themselves the *Cousins* of Liberty, in deference to their like-minded fellows in Boston, the Sons of Liberty. In order to gauge the leanings of new acquaintances, they asked the innocuous question which Sarah now echoed.

"What is a helping hand worth among those united in a common cause?"

Adams knew the response, as Sarah was confident he would.

"A helping hand in return."

"And when that cause is Freedom?"

Adams stood ramrod straight, but before he could respond, Mrs. Adams and Eliza stepped forward, holding hands. Mrs. Adams gently took her husband's injured hand with her own, and Eliza held hers out to Sarah. Sarah nodded and joined hands with Eliza and her father. The circle complete, the Adams all completed the litany in unison.

"Then we pledge to each other our Lives, our Fortunes, and our sacred Honor."

Sarah nodded, and her smile broadened.

Adams met Sarah's steady gaze. "I've heard rumors since my youth of a shadow colony out in the wilderness west of Philadelphia. A group with special abilities like those you surely possessed, My Dear. A people who serve no masters except themselves. I've always believed that the scene I witnessed in the tavern was evidence of such a group. And here before us now stands living proof in the guise of a farm lass." Sarah shifted uncomfortably under his scrutiny. "If that shadowy group has thrown in on the side of independence, there might well be hope for our rebel cause, yet." Proudly, Mr. Adams continued, "My Boston cousins started this *cause,* and my brother is encamped with General Washington out at Valley Forge." Tears came to his eyes, though his voice was deadly serious. "What can we do to help?"

Sarah swallowed her own tears. Until that moment, the mission to gather intelligence against the British had just been a test of her readiness to be an operative. Seeing this family's commitment to gain the liberty she had grown up with made her understand the stakes of the game she was playing.

"Simply watch, listen, and learn, as I'm sure you already do. Remember what you see and hear, but write nothing down. When I bring my eggs in next week, just tell me what you have learned. Can you do that?"

Mr. Adams nodded. "Many a quartermaster orders his unit's provisions from me and others I know whose leanings match ours."

"Often paying little or nothing at all!" Mrs. Adams said with venom.

Mr. Adams agreed, "There aren't many loyalist businessmen left in Philadelphia. When I go to the docks to claim shipments, I usually count the number and types of ships in the river."

Sarah could see the enthusiasm on their faces, which worried her.

"Please don't do anything out of the ordinary. The English have their own spies, you know." She let the import of that word sink in. "There will be no trial if they suspect you."

Like all patriots, the Adamses already knew the danger of their situation.

"Of course," Adams replied. "The redcoats think of us as stupid provincials. A wide smile and a hearty 'God save the King!' keeps them thinking that way."

Sarah smiled and nodded. "Just be safe." She nodded to Eliza. "You have a lot to live for. I'll see you next week."

A chorus of "Thank-you" and "God bless you" accompanied Sarah into the street outside.

79

PART IV

Father Dan
Present Day

*The importance of intelligence concerning our enemies'
displacements and movement cannot be overstated.
Philadelphia, and New York especially, need penetration.
The King's forces sit comfortably within the city, while the
Navy lays at anchor in the harbor. They have the advantage
of freedom to prepare and execute their plans for this
Spring's campaign, while we can but react blindly due to our
lack of foreknowledge concerning their intentions.*

— G. Washington War Journal
Valley Forge
December 1777

Chapter 14

Revelations

F ather Dan blessed himself as he closed his mouth. His eyes still reflected his shock, though. "You just snapped his neck?"

"Well, yeah. I wasn't going to let him get away with it."

"But you were just a girl."

Liz scoffed and John jumped in. "Yes, a girl who trained for years to protect herself and others. Perfectly justified and executed."

Liz bristled a bit at John's condescending tone, as if she didn't need his justification of her actions.

Dan was thoughtful for a few seconds. "I suppose so. I'll pray for you."

This time, she laughed out loud. "Seriously, Father? That was just the first time. If you're going to pray for me, you had better get some kneepads."

John chuckled, but Dan blessed himself again. Guilt was an emotion Liz couldn't afford and had left behind many decades before. Her job, if not her history, required her to compartmentalize each of the personas she had worn over the course of more than two centuries. Although the end results more often than not were something to be proud of, the means she had used to reach those ends were just as frequently best forgotten. But Father Dan's reaction to her first, and most justified, kill disturbed her. It wasn't guilt she felt but, rather, disappointment at his disapproval of what she considered to be one of her most heroic moments.

Her tone was indignant as she said, "You may not approve of my actions, but the Adams family definitely felt differently."

John tried to smooth the tension rising in the room. "Father, I told you when you accepted this assignment that what you learned about our order might be…distasteful to you."

His words had the opposite effect.

"Distasteful? Pouring over your archives has caused me many sleepless nights praying for your souls…and my own. I didn't *accept* this assignment. The Holy Father gave me no choice in the matter. This place, its history, and what it represents, has tested my faith in ways I never could have imagined. Every day, something new chips away at the bedrock of my beliefs. I fear soon my vocation will rest on nothing but rubble and sand."

Liz and John exchanged a look of raised eyebrows. Dan, abashed at his outburst, gulped down his brandy. Liz opened her mouth, probably to offer a snide comment, but the look from John closed her mouth again. Dan wondered how he would handle whatever other revelations were in the story she had yet to tell.

John's next words came out barely above a whisper. It took a moment for him to recognize his use of the mesmerizing tone that she knew could lull his target into some kind of trance.

"Father…Dan…our operatives, and Elizabeth especially, often need to ingratiate themselves to some very bad, even evil, people. That means they need to act the part. No, 'act' isn't a strong enough word. They need to *become* the person they are pretending to be." He looked at Liz, who nodded solemnly. "We must forgive them their transgressions in service to the Greater Good. You may well hear, or discover, details that will test you even further. I will remind you, though, of the command your Holy Father gave you to treat *everything* learned here as being under the seal of the confessional. I would offer that forgiveness of those confessed sins is part and parcel with that command."

John's soothed murmurs had only a partial effect. Dan slowly turned to look John in the eye before said, "Absolution, John, needs to be *earned*. Earned by sincere repentance." He turned to Liz with a fierce look. "Do you *repent*, Sarah Louise Harkin?"

Eyes wide with shock, Liz just returned his stare until Dan finally nodded, expressing his sorrow without words.

Chapter 15

The Wrapping

The strip of cloth stretched across the entire length of the workbench. Dan stood back about ten feet so he could take in the full length of it. At over fourteen feet long, at least a foot hung over each end of the table. Despite its length, it was about four inches wide.

The cloth was a very finely woven linen in a herringbone pattern. One edge was a finished weave, but the other appeared to have been ripped from a larger cloth. The ragged edge showed some signs of unraveling but, given its age, it was remarkably well-preserved. That age, confirmed by any number of analyses, was two thousand years. Dan scanned through the lab reports from centuries of analysis.

The herringbone pattern was typical of fine cloth woven in and around Jerusalem during the first century. It would have been owned by a wealthy person or family, perhaps to cover a banquet table. Other evidence—pollen and grit found within the matrix of the weave, the progressive yellowing of the fabric that was documented over the years—all pointed to its origin and use in Jerusalem in the time of Jesus Christ.

That was the empirical evidence, the physical attributes of the wrapping. Add to that the provenance of John's ownership of the cloth and the precious artifact it protected since the thirteenth century. The miracles that relic had performed, granting extended and even seemingly eternal life to Liam, The Enclave's founder and a long line of its operatives, were undeniable as Dan sat and chatted with Liam, now John, and Sarah, now Liz, daily.

Dan shifted his attention to the other artifact on the table, a simple piece of wood about two feet long, rounded into a knob on one end and with a jagged, splintered point at the other. He ran his hand reverently over its smooth surface. Its tight, straight grain showed wear close to the knob end, where a hand had gripped it over and over again.

Dan imagined the Roman legionnaire, Longinus, hunkered down behind a wall of shields, thrusting the *lancet* tip, lost some time during the centuries, into onrushing attackers. Abhorred by the imagined violence, Dan turned his thoughts to when the lance was used to make sure a crucified rebel was dead. Lifting the relic off the workbench, he closed his eyes and let his fingers feel for the subtle grooves of the legionnaire's grip. He had prayed over that most-sacred relic many times, but was always disconcerted that his fingers didn't match the ancient Roman's grip.

Before returning the lance to the table, Dan turned it to find the section at the fractured end where a wedge had been cleanly cut from the wood. The bed of the cut, deep within the lance, still looked fresh, although John had said he took the sample almost four centuries before. A tiny piece of it, looking as fresh as if it had been removed yesterday, still rested in the Vault, ready for more testing.

The species of the tree that birthed the lance remained a mystery, despite the testing done over the decades and centuries. And the Carbon-14 testing made no sense, placing the exterior surface at several thousand years before the emergence of human history, while the interior samples showed a much younger, even contemporary date.

Gently laying down the lance fragment, Dan leaned over the strip of cloth John called the Wrapping. While it was true that it came into Liam-John's possession as a way to hide and transport the lance, Dan's intuition told him it had a purpose separate from, and perhaps as important as, the relic it packaged.

"I don't even know which way is up," he murmured as he bent down until his nose was inches above the cloth.

Visible on the fabric was a series of light brown markings barely discernable from the age-discolored linen itself. Dan's impression, backed up by descriptions of the Wrapping over the centuries, was that the symbols had faded, getting lighter and lighter, while the base linen that held them darkened with age.

He turned to the computer with its gallery of photos, X-ray images, CAT scans, fluoroscopy pictures, and every imaginable electromagnetic spectral analysis. He enhanced the contrast on one of the visible light images until it looked like what he imagined the cloth to have looked like originally.

The expertly and tightly woven herringbone pattern disappeared into a bleached white, and the faded beige symbols darkened to a deep brown. They stood out against the starkness of the cloth like print on a modern magazine page. The similarity didn't end there. Each symbol—there were dozens spaced evenly along the Wrapping's length—was a perfectly formed set of horizontal and vertical lines, some of which crossed, while others stopped where they met at right angles. If Dan hadn't known they were placed on the linen at least a millennium before its invention, he would have thought a modern printing press made them.

Besides the obvious time discontinuity, the marks themselves could not have been printed, even by hand. Rather than being made by ink, paint, or some other pigment, only the fabric's topmost fibers were discolored, as if scorched by some unknown physical process.

To Dan, a polyglot fluent in over a dozen languages, the symbols, though barely visible after perhaps twenty centuries, were clearly some sort of language. But, despite his study of ancient languages that dated back to predecessors of Egyptian hieroglyphics and Sumerian cuneiform, he couldn't make heads nor tails of the markings.

"I've never seen anything like these symbols," he said to the otherwise empty room.

And none of his research, including an extensive search through every library with a linguistics research department on the planet, had yielded any hints.

With a sigh, he gingerly moved the broken wooden lance to the cloth. Though he suspected he couldn't hurt the lance itself, given its regenerative powers, his concern was for the much more fragile cloth with which he wrapped it.

Once he had folded the cloth over the lance lengthwise and used the rest to wrap a spiral around its length, he placed it back into its climate controlled secure drawer. With another sigh and a lingering look, he plopped down in front of his bank of computer monitors, hoping to make more progress on his other research agenda.

Chapter 16

War Journals

S ometimes I feel like an archeologist when I delve into these archives." Father Dan's comment elicited the desired look of interest from John and Liz. They sat again in John's office a week after their previous tense meeting. Dan shook his head as he continued, "I solved a mystery last night that no one even knew existed."

The interested looks turned to confused curiosity. Dan beamed as if he rather liked the feeling of knowing something about this tale that neither John nor Liz did.

"It is well known among historians that General George Washington was a habitual diarist. He wrote daily from the time he was a British officer fighting the French in the west of Pennsylvania and New York until the day he died at Mount Vernon. *Except*," he paused for dramatic effect, "during the American Revolution."

To his surprise, the only reactions he got from John and Liz were faint, knowing smiles. Frowning, he continued anyway, "Why would an inveterate diarist fail to record his thoughts during what he surely knew were the most important and impactful years of his life? The habit of recording everything of his daily activities, even whom he had dinner with, would have been nearly impossible to break. And the fact that he resumed his daily entries *the day after* the British surrender surely meant he didn't actually break that habit. Still, there were no known diaries of his while he commanded the Continental Army. That is, until last night!" he concluded triumphantly.

Teasingly, Liz asked, "So what do they say?"

Dan looked sheepish. "I don't know. They're just a jumble of numbers and random words. It's some kind of code, I think—"

Liz and John looked at each other and burst out laughing. Thoroughly confused, Dan's face flushed as their laughter slowly died down. They clearly didn't understand the significance of his find.

"But…"

John interrupted Dan with a raised hand. He turned to Liz and said, "You tell him."

Smiling, Liz said quietly, "The reason no one knew about Washington's war diaries is because I stole them from Mount Vernon as soon as the war was over. As I'm sure you figured out, that jumble of numbers and words means the diaries are enciphered." She chuckled. "The good General loved his cyphers."

Dan was stunned. "How—why—did you steal such historically important documents?"

Liz said, "That was a later operation of mine. It was fun. I can tell you about it sometime over a beer."

John explained, "Enciphered or not, there was no way we were going to leave evidence of our deal lying around for anyone to find."

Shocked, Dan asked, "Deal? What deal?"

Again, John and Liz looked at each other, seriously this time. John nodded to Liz.

"That brings us to the next phase of my story, how I became a full-fledged operative. And it contains a clue that just might help you crack the code."

PART V

Benjamin Tallmadge and Sarah
Winter 1777

Today may have been the strangest and possibly most
hopeful day of this noble endeavor. It seems an
outside agency, perhaps and hopefully a most
providential one, may have taken up our cause.

— G. Washington War Journal
Valley Forge
December 1777

Chapter 17

Invitation

C aptain Benjamin Tallmadge was a rising young officer on General Washington's staff. A classmate at Harvard and close friend of the late lamented spy Nathan Hale, Benjamin's commitment to the rebels' cause was cemented when the British captured his older brother William, serving under George Washington during the campaign of 1776. William disappeared into one of the prison ships anchored in New York harbor, never to be seen again.

The British powers, comfortably ensconced in their palaces and manor houses in faraway England, had no idea how their mistreatment of the King's own subjects had turned the once loyal colonists into rebellious traitors ready to die in order to gain freedom for their families and neighbors. Captain Tallmadge was one of those touched directly by Britain's cruelty.

General Washington saw the bright mind behind the young officer's zeal, and consequently gave him increasingly more delicate and dangerous tasks, all of which Benjamin excelled at. As Commander-in-Chief of the American armies, Washington saw the value of timely information gleaned from behind the enemy's lines in both Philadelphia and New York.

Philadelphia was the birthplace of what Washington thought of as a *noble revolution* and, as such, had an important symbolic value to the rebel cause. Recapturing that city would provide a much-needed boost to his army's flagging morale.

Symbolism aside, Philadelphia had little strategic value, tucked as it was at the top of the Delaware Bay between the Delaware and Schuylkill rivers, only one of which, the Delaware, was navigable.

Unlike Philadelphia, New York, the other major city held by the British was the strategic jewel of the whole Eastern seaboard. Midway between the northern and southern colonies, its large deep harbor served as a secure port for the British fleet. Those ships could move troops to anywhere along the coast in a matter of days, rather than the weeks it took to march overland, as Washington was forced to do.

Although they remained hunkered down in the city during the winter, Washington suspected that the British commanders were planning a campaign northward from New York up the Hudson River. If the British could take control of the river, they would split the colonies in two, isolating New England from their cousins to the south. The fort at West Point, located some fifty miles up the Hudson, and firmly held by the Americans, was all that stood in the way of the British plans.

Fully understanding the importance of timely intelligence, Washington had tried several spying operations, all of which were abject failures. Nathan Hale's demise at the end of a hangman's rope was only the most public, coming as it did, but two days after he had sneaked into the city in the guise of an itinerant teacher from Long Island. Whether it was his Connecticut dialect, or his lack of local knowledge, he was easily exposed and then summarily sentenced to a traitor's death.

Washington knew he needed a different approach, and he hoped that the young Captain Tallmadge might find one that worked before it was too late.

In contrast to these serial failures by the rebels, the information coming to The Enclave by way of Sarah's confidants in Philadelphia was consistently timely and accurate, though much less useful than if it had come from New York. The model that was working in Philadelphia—a network of informants embedded into the daily life of the city who reported through a courier with a legitimate reason to come and go on business—was one that The Enclave had employed for centuries. Abraham knew the same model for a spy network would work in New York, if they could show the American rebels its effectiveness.

The missing pieces of the puzzle for an effective spying operation in New York were a trustworthy spymaster who could build a network in New York as Sarah had done in Philadelphia, and a method of securely relaying the gathered intelligence to General Washington.

Information from Abraham's own spies within the Continental Army officer corps pointed to Captain Tallmadge, a native Long Islander on Washington's staff, to be the logical choice to build a New York spy ring. Not surprisingly, General Washington, being a keen judge of the officers and men serving under him, had come to the same conclusion.

But teaching Benjamin, and indeed Washington himself, the techniques they were going to need would be a delicate operation, and the next phase of Sarah's development. Abraham decided it would be best to start with a demonstration of those very skills.

Being an early riser, as usual, Benjamin Tallmadge rose before the two other junior officers with whom he was billeted in Valley Forge during the bitterly cold winter of 1777-1778. As he rekindled the banked fire in the room's fireplace, he noticed a sealed, folded slip of paper leaning against the candle on the room's small table. He was shocked to see his name, *Cpt. B. Tallmadge*, written in a clear hand just below the wax seal.

He took a few minutes to get the fire going again while his curiosity and anticipation grew. Finally, when the fire was going, he unsealed and read it by the flickering light.

Cpt. Tallmadge,

*On Friday next, if you find yourself at
the Rising Sun Tavern on the high
road between Germantown and
Philadelphia at noontime, purchase
the remaining eggs from the farm lass
walking past. Do so, and you may
ensure the success of both your new
assignment and the historic endeavor*

you have committed your life and honor to. Tell no one about this note and burn it before your companions arise.

The note was signed with a highly stylized 'E', and its presence and the few short sentences it contained sent a chill down Benjamin's spine. Who had placed this note in his room without disturbing its three sleeping occupants? How did 'E' know him? How did this mysterious 'E' know that he was always the one to light the morning fire? More importantly, how did he know that General Washington had been trusting him with secret missions of late? And, most bizarre of all, why on earth should he buy leftover eggs?

From Monday to Friday morning, Benjamin stewed over these and many other questions. Because of his innate trustworthiness and implicit loyalty to the General, Benjamin had no intention of obeying the note's admonishment. He kept the note in the pocket of his coat, refusing to burn it and intending to show it to the General in private.

The timing was difficult, however. Although he had several private meetings with Washington over the next several days, each time he held back, suspecting that if he discussed the note, even in the privacy of General Washington's office, there would be no farm girl walking past the tavern on Friday.

The thought that the note was bait for a trap set to capture him was foremost in his mind. That possibility had to be weighed against the unspoken evidence of powerful forces at work behind the simple missive. The access to his quarters and the knowledge of his role on the General's staff spoke of clandestine abilities that could prove very useful to the struggling rebellion. So it was, that after Friday morning's staff meeting, Benjamin asked for a private word with the General.

When they were alone, and before Benjamin could say a word, Washington spoke.

"You have been quite distracted the past few days, Captain. Do you have something to tell me?"

Feeling ashamed that he had been keeping such a secret from the one he thought of as *The Great Man*, Benjamin drew the note from the inner pocket of his coat and handed it to the General.

"I found this note in my quarters Monday morning, sir."

Washington read the note quickly and turned a quizzical expression to Benjamin.

"Why didn't you come to me with this immediately?" His tone had an edge to it.

"Sir, if the writer of the note knows the nature of the assignments you have been giving me of late, I had to assume they would know if I shared it with you before now."

Looking sidelong at his Captain, the General thought through the logic. Nodding, he came to a decision.

"I concur. You did the right thing waiting until your departure to this tavern was imminent." He paused a moment, deep in thought. "This note tells us many things in its few lines. First, as you surmised, the author has a spy in our camp. But a benign one, I would warrant. Perhaps operating for a previously neutral party."

Benjamin nodded, and Washington continued, "Second, this third party, whomever they may be, has revealed their existence to us," a small smile tugged at the General's mouth, "or, to you, at least. We can assume that means they may lend their support to our cause."

Washington met Benjamin's eyes, and his piercing look conveyed the full impact of his next words.

"They may be willing to support us *if* they think us worthy of their help. You, Captain, will be how they judge us."

Tallmadge had already followed this train of thought, and Washington could see that he had in the set of his shoulders. Benjamin's voice was calm and steady, though his heart was pounding.

"That is assuming, General, that the note is legitimate and not bait for a trap."

Washington was silent for a moment. "That is a possibility, of course, but if they already have a spy well placed enough to know the things this note implies, why would they need to compromise *you*?" Benjamin's eyes got wide. "No offense, son."

Washington's benign smile tried to smooth the ruffled feathers. The comment stung, but even to his own ears, his response sounded a bit too abrupt.

"What are your orders, sir?"

The General walked to the fireplace and tossed the note into the flames.

"You will do exactly as they told you to do. This may be the opportunity to achieve what we have been striving for—good intelligence that we can act upon."

"And if their spy correctly surmises from my lingering with you in private this long that I have revealed this secret to you?"

"Then they will know precisely where your loyalties lie, and that they can trust you to act accordingly—as I do."

Those simple words, spoken with absolute conviction, erased the previous hurt feelings, and filled Benjamin with pride and love for his Commander-in-Chief.

snapped to attention and saluting smartly, he said, "I'll report back to you immediately, General."

Washington returned the salute just as smartly, then placed his large hand on the smaller man's shoulder.

"I have the utmost faith in you, Son."

Chapter 18

Germantown

That first meeting between Sarah and Benjamin went as smoothly as possible. Benjamin, out of uniform and disguised as a gentleman traveler, ate a light lunch in the Rising Sun Tavern in the Germantown settlement. The establishment catered to traveling merchants, lawyers riding the circuit, and others wanting to avoid staying in occupied Philadelphia. The floors were well swept, the tables were clean, and the pewter shone.

After a surprisingly good meal, Benjamin paid his fare and sipped his mug of hard cider until the clock in the hall struck twelve. Casually, he rose and stretched before strolling out the door into the low autumn sunlight.

Standing by his tethered horse, Benjamin bent over with his back to the breeze to light his pipe. When he had it going, he drew a deep draught and watched the smoke drift away down the road on the breeze. Through the haze, he saw a pretty young girl approaching with baskets slung over her arms.

Not expecting such a young girl, he hesitated as she drew abreast of him on the road. But when he saw her eyes flick from his face to one of the baskets she carried, he realized his mistake and stepped forward.

"Excuse me, Miss. Were you able to sell all of your eggs this morning?"

Hesitantly, with a seemingly nervous look back at the tavern, Sarah stopped, but stayed in the middle of the road.

"No, sir, I still have a few left. Would you like to purchase them?"

Seeing her apparent shyness, Benjamin stayed at least an arm's distance from her.

"I believe I would, if I may."

"I have six, sir. That will be two pennies for them all."

"Two pennies? That seems pretty steep. I'll give you one and a half."

He reached into the purse at his waist and drew out one large and one small copper coin.

"That'll do kindly, sir. Do you have a handkerchief to wrap them in? You don't want to break them until you make it home."

Benjamin handed over his handkerchief and watched carefully as Sarah wrapped the six eggs with care. He detected no sleight of hand that may have slipped a message into the bundle.

"There you are, Sir. I know you'll enjoy them, as they are as fresh as can be. If you like them, I come by here around this time every Friday."

Benjamin, a little confused and still waiting for the exchange of some secret information, was stunned when Sarah just smiled and continued on her way up the road. But, playing his part, he tapped out his pipe before putting it in his coat pocket, mounting his horse, and following Sarah up the road. As he passed her, she looked up and, smiling, gave him the tiniest nod of her head. The meaning was quite clear. *Move along, we're done.*

Doubts filled his mind all the way back to his quarters at Valley Forge. What had gone wrong? Why was he returning empty-handed? He feared the embarrassment of telling the General that his mission was for naught.

With disgust, he spilled the eggs from his handkerchief onto the worktable in his room.

At least I came back with some very expensive eggs, he thought ruefully.

But that thought just made him feel like Jack from the fairy tale about the enchanted beans.

There's no goose laying golden eggs in this story, though. But then a thought struck him. *Wait, golden eggs?*

Feeling even more foolish, and remembering the girl's warning about not breaking them *until he was home,* Benjamin realized how carelessly he had dumped out the fragile eggs, setting them spinning on the tabletop.

Luckily, none had spun off the table, despite his reckless handling of them. In fact, all but one had quickly stopped wobbling and sat still. One, though, was still slowly spinning.

Taking that one in his right hand, and one of the other eggs in his left, he set them both spinning with a twist of his wrists. The one from his left hand wobbled a few times and stopped. But the one from his right smoothly spun merrily around.

That one was hard-boiled.

Catching the still spinning egg, he lifted it so he could examine it closely. Turning it over in his hand, Benjamin saw a nearly invisible seam running around the fat end. With his pocketknife, he pried off the end cap, and saw that the egg's yolk was missing. Delicately, he pulled out three sheaths of very thin paper that were folded twice and rolled into a scroll.

The paper was covered front and back with what appeared to be the tiniest lettering Benjamin had ever seen. Markings filled columns from edge to edge. A block of text occupied the bottom right corner of the back of the last page. Straining his eyes but still unable to read the script, Benjamin turned away to find a strong magnifying glass.

One of his roommates, Captain Leavenworth, fancied himself a naturalist. His current hobby, on which Benjamin thought he spent an inordinate amount of time that would have been better spent on strategy and tactics, was collecting the many species of insects found in the Pennsylvania woodlands.

At last, his stupid obsession will prove useful, he thought as he took Leavenworth's glass down from the shelf where he kept it, along with his latest batch of specimens.

Under magnification, the purpose of the miniscule script became clear. The columns were words arranged alphabetically, paired with sequential numbers. Seven hundred and sixty-three word-number pairs were listed, along with a pairing of individual letters and numbers with corresponding random letters. At the end of the list were instructions on how to use the cipher, including special instructions for expressing tenses, conjugations, and plurals.

The artifice needed to make such thin paper, and to write such tiny, yet crystal clear text was beyond Benjamin's understanding, but he knew immediately the importance of it. Those slips of paper held an entire codebook. But, more than that, he held in his hands a contract between himself and some unknown group who were obviously very skilled and experienced in the art of intelligence gathering—in other words, *spying*.

Resisting the urge to rush to General Washington with the news, Benjamin instead took out his own pen and paper. With Leavenworth's glass in one hand and the pen in the other, he set about copying out the codebook.

Chapter 19

The Chase

After the episode in the alley, the Adams family proved to be a wealth of information. Mr. Adams's gregarious nature easily engaged the occupying officers in revealing conversation, and his reports included tidbits gathered from those seemingly innocent exchanges. Adams also kept track of which commanders ordered what provisions and where they were delivered, details that indicated planned troop deployments and their movement.

One wintry day in late January was no exception. When Mrs. Adams went into the office at the back of the store to fetch the copper coins she owed Sarah for her eggs, she casually left her account book open on the counter. Within a few eye blinks, Sarah scanned and committed the week's transactions to memory. When she lifted her eyes from the page, though, she felt Eliza's light touched at her elbow.

"We just got in some pretty bonnets. Would you like to see them?"

This was their agreed upon signal that there was urgent information which Sarah needed to hear. As they made their way between the stacks and shelves of dry goods, Sarah responded in code with a hint of embarrassment.

"You know I can't afford them, though." *How important is this information that you can whisper and not write down?*

"You should try them on, anyway." *It is of utmost importance—life or death!*

In the corner of the store that held bolts of fashionable English fabrics and the notions needed to make them into ladies' dresses, Eliza took a lacy bonnet down from its shelf. She scanned the store to make sure no one would overhear them and placed it on Sarah's head. Leaning in to tie the bonnet's ribbons, Eliza whispered directly into Sarah's ear.

"The filthy redcoats know about your meeting today with the rebel officer. They even know the time and place of it."

Eliza stepped back and looked at Sarah appraisingly, holding up a hand mirror.

"There, isn't that the prettiest you ever saw?"

Turning the mirror back and forth to make sure no one had come within earshot, Sarah smiled and mouthed the words, *Thank you.*

Sarah never visited the Adams store again, and they ever knew the critical role she would play in the events to come—events that changed the course of world history—nor how important their own role was. Such was the reward for the risks they had taken, anonymous, silent heroism that no one else, not even Eliza Adams's descendants, would ever learn of. The role her family played in the American fight for freedom would remain uncelebrated, just as it was with so many other hidden heroes of that Revolution.

Sarah reviewed in her head details of the day's plan as she hurried, as inconspicuously as possible, toward the rendezvous place. It crossed her mind that her proctors from The Enclave may have deliberately compromised her operation as an ultimate test of her resourcefulness. She accepted this possibility, and the added risk to herself and the rebel Captain Tallmadge to whom she had been delivering her intelligence.

They had placed themselves in harm's way by choice, and they knew the consequences if exposed and captured. Her chief concern, however, was for Eliza Adams and her family and all the other assets she had recruited. It was imperative that their identities remain secret.

Sarah's briefings about the British prison ships were chilling, especially what happened to the women who were sent there. The rape Sarah had rescued Eliza from in that alley in Philadelphia would be a summer picnic compared to what she would face on board one of those floating hell holes.

The few who survived their sentences—all of whom were men, since no imprisoned woman ever emerged from her captivity—told horrible tales of starvation while chained in the holds of the ships, breathing air fouled by the effluent of the sick and the stench of rotting corpses. Confirmation of the horrific stories came when the emaciated bodies of the dead floated ashore.

She banished those thoughts from her mind by resolving to forfeit her life before revealing her sources of intelligence. She had already made that commitment to The Enclave years previously, so extending her loyalty to those she had personally recruited came naturally to her. All this she decided as she walked purposefully, but with no sign of panic, toward the Rising Sun Tavern.

The tavern had served as a place to meet Sarah's counterpart, Captain Benjamin Tallmadge, twice before.

That was too much of a pattern, she realized.

Situated just outside of Philadelphia town, it was a convenient and cheaper place for those traveling to Philadelphia from New York or Boston to spend a night or two. It also lay just outside the British guard posts on the Germantown Pike, which was the main thoroughfare into Philadelphia from the north. It was an excellent location for one, or at most two meetings. But three Friday meetings had proven excessive.

Passing her normal stops along the way, she knew full well that this was the last time she would set foot on the cobbles of ballast stones that paved Philadelphia's streets. She also knew that if she didn't intercept her young Captain before he arrived for lunch at the Rising Sun, it would be his last day of freedom, and perhaps hers as well.

Walking briskly and avoiding suspicion by smiling to passersby, Sarah left the confines of Philadelphia town proper. Then, gathering and lifting her skirts, she picked up her pace almost to a run. The tavern lay about a half mile along the road to Germantown, and she covered the distance as fast as her long skirts would allow.

Rounding the last bend in the road, she slowed down to take stock of the situation at the tavern. All seemed normal there. Horses stood tied up to the left of the low doorway, and the sign with a bright orange half sun swung lightly in the breeze. Although no British soldiers were visible on the road, Sarah knew suspected they lurked somewhere nearby.

Keeping her steps purposeful but unhurried, she glimpsed movement in the brush to the right of the road. Her trained ears picked out the distinctive sound of branches scraping leather and the stamp of a horse's hoof. Being more accustomed to boldly strutting in formation down the middle of the road, neither the horses nor their British riders understood the importance of silence while lying in ambush.

Passing their hiding place, she could even hear their murmured voices, though not their words. Their tone, though, was familiar to any young woman in British-occupied territory. Pretending to notice their presence, she quickened her steps. A particularly loud comment on the fit of her dress drew a barked command for silence from the troop's commander.

The location of the British ambush told Sarah three things. First, the British did not know of her part in the rendezvous. Otherwise, they would have ridden out to capture her, rather than just leering and speculating on her virginity. Second, they had not captured Captain Tallmadge yet, so there was still a chance that she could warn him. And, third, given their hiding place in an overgrown ditch alongside the road, the British cavalry would take precious seconds to extricate themselves from their position before they could give chase on the road.

Being earlier than usual for their clandestine meeting, Sarah wasn't sure where Benjamin was. Had he arrived yet? Was he still inside having his lunch? Her mind flew from possibility to possibility as she scanned the horses tied to the hitching rail, looking for Benjamin's.

To her relief, at the far end of the row, she recognized the white patches running from the pastern and fetlock up along the cannon on a horse's hind legs. To her even greater relief, she also saw pipe smoke billowing above the horse's back.

Looking to the ground beneath the smoke from thirty or forty yards away, she could just make out a pair of dusty boots among the horse's hooves. Not knowing Benjamin's habit of having a smoke while awaiting the pretty young egg seller, the redcoats didn't realize that he was right under their noses.

Sarah snatched one egg from one of her baskets, then dropped them both, along with the remaining unsold eggs so she could hitch her skirts up around her knees while she broke into a run. Her sudden bolt sparked action from the ambushers, and behind her she heard a rustle in the bushes and the commander's barked commands as the British struggled to climb from the ditch onto the road. Whistling like a herdsman summoning his charges to milking time, Sarah desperately signaled a warning to the Captain.

Her warning whistle and the loud curses and shouts from further down the road brought Benjamin out from among the startled horses. The sight of Sarah running full tilt toward him, and the British horsemen, who were emerging from their self-imposed trap, jolted him into action. Quickly, he unhitched and turned his horse into the road, but hesitated mounting as Sarah was still several steps away.

When she yelled, "Get on!" though, he jumped into the saddle. As Sarah reached the horse's flank, he reached down, and they clasped each other's forearms and, together, they hoisted her into position behind him.

With her skirts now around her waist, she perched on the horse's croup and wrapped her arms around the young Captain's waist. Without needing to be spurred on, the horse broke straight into a gallop as the first balls from the British pistols as the balls whistled past. With her heart pumping adrenaline-saturated blood, Sarah felt her consciousness leap to a new level of awareness.

Time seemed to slow down. With eyes focused forward on the road ahead, her ears heard bark exploding as pistol balls thudded into trees alongside the road. Raising her left hand to get a better grip on his coat, she felt Benjamin's heaving breath and pounding heart.

The gunshots paused, either because the British had exhausted their loaded pistols or, more likely, because they were holding back until they had closed the gap. Germantown lay less than a mile ahead, and Benjamin's steed was young and strong, but loaded with two riders, it steadily lost ground to the cavalry chasing them. For several minutes, the only sound Sarah heard was the thundering of the slowly approaching hooves. When she could see the first houses and barns on the outskirts of Germantown, she snuck a peek over her shoulder.

The British commander, riding a beautiful dappled gray at the forefront of the pursuers, raised his cocked pistol from mere yards behind them. A shot rang out, though no flash came from the raised weapon. Instead, the commander's horse stumbled and nearly unseated him as a patch of red blossomed among the gray of the mount's neck.

As if on signal, a fusillade of musket shots rang out, sending a barrage of lead from barns and the stone fences that lined the road, bringing the pursuers to a halt. With shouted curses, the British horsemen spun their mounts about and raced back toward Philadelphia as Sarah and Benjamin entered Germantown.

Captain Tallmadge, bewildered, slowed their mount, and Sarah leaned even closer to him and spoke directions directly into his ear.

"Right here, past two streets, then turn left."

After those turns, first off the main street, then onto a busy market street, Benjamin slowed the horse to a walk. Two more turns brought them to an area of stables and commercial warehouses.

Sarah whispered in his ear, "Stop here." Benjamin reined the horse to a halt. "I have vital information for you."

Astounded by the calm, matter-of-fact tone of her voice, he tried to swivel in his saddle, but she hugged him even tighter and wouldn't let him turn. With his own senses still on full alert, Benjamin felt the press of Sarah's breasts against his back and her hot breath tickle his ear. Then, to his astonishment, she slipped a hand into the pocket of his coat.

"As before, here is a message for your General." He reached his own hand into his pocket and caught hers as she withdrew it. Instead of drawing back, however, Sarah gently squeezed his fingers, then pulled her hand out and hugged him tighter.

"I have more than that for you." Her breath in his ear, the now unnecessary tightness of her embrace, and the lilt in her voice made the Captain wonder if she had intended the double *entendre*.

"Obviously, this operation is finished, but you must understand that they were targeting you directly?" Benjamin nodded his agreement before she continued. "The British command knows who you are, and they have circulated your description among their sentries and patrols. Even this proximity to your enemy is no longer safe for you."

The Captain puffed out his chest. "Your concern for me is much appreciated, Young Lady, but war is a dangerous business," he said indignantly.

To Sarah's ears, that sounded like false bluster. She leaned back, breaking contact, and eyed him skeptically.

"True, but danger can be managed. Taking unnecessary risks proves nothing more than how foolish you are."

Benjamin's shoulders fell as the bubble of his bluster burst. Finally able to turn in his saddle, he looked at Sarah with a fresh perspective and a new awareness. In a few simple words, and throughout their recent escape, this 'Young Lady' had demonstrated more poise and wisdom than most of his compatriot officers. When he met her eyes, though, the smile she flashed at him took the sting out of her words.

"I also bring good news," she said as she swung her right leg over the horse's tail and slid down his flank to the ground. "The British will abandon Philadelphia in the Spring. They are already making preparations to sail north." She let that bit of news sink in while she stroked the horse's neck. "The egg in your pocket also bears favorable tidings."

Benjamin felt in his pocket and found the hard-boiled egg, still intact, despite the rigors of the chase.

Sarah walked to the horse's head, stroked his forelock, and looked into his large, wet eyes. "Hello, my hero. What is your name?"

Benjamin offered a smile at the compliment, but then blushed when he realized she was referring to the horse.

"Oh, his name is Anemos. It's Greek and means…"

"'Wind.' Excellent choice." She looked up at him as if to said, *I'm not a country bumkin*. Looking back at Anemos, she continued, "You are well-named, my hero. Keep your partner safe."

She met Benjamin's gaze with fire in her eyes and a teasing smile. "You can take me for a ride any time, Captain." This time, her grin left no doubt that her double *entendre* was deliberate.

With a swish of her skirts, Sarah left Benjamin speechless and disappeared down an alley between two buildings.

Chapter 20

Operative Sarah Harkin

Y ou set me up." Sarah's voice was matter of fact, her anger held in check. "Did I pass your test?"

She gathered her skirts and swung her leg over her horse's back. Abraham held the bridle while she dismounted. He and Garrison had met her as she and her protective squad rode into The Enclave's main square. Though only about ten miles as the crow flies from Germantown, they chose their circuitous route home to throw off any pursuers, whether British or American, and it had taken the entire afternoon and into the early evening.

"Well, you made it home in one piece." Abraham scanned the other arrivals, who had all continued at a walk toward the stables. "As did everyone I see, so I would say you passed with flying colors." Abraham looked to Garrison for confirmation. A grunt was his only response. "I'm sure your Master Trainer," his gaze lingered on the gruff Garrison standing next to him, "will have some words of wisdom for you in your debriefing." Another grunt.

Sarah was sure he would.

Using her training, she took a deep breath and let it out slowly while examining her thoughts, emotions, and physical feelings. As it was supposed to, the mental self-examination exercise brought a clarity of thought, and her anger disappeared. She was left with the realization that the fury she had initially felt, which had cooled to a low simmer on the long ride home, and which, after her moment of self-reflection, she dispassionately held up for examination, was not caused by the danger that the exercise had placed her in. Rather, it surprised her to find that the root of her upset was the risk that Captain Tallmadge had faced.

Her self-assessment took only a moment, and to an untrained observer would have seemed that Sarah was simply catching her breath. Abraham, however, recognized this most basic lesson taught at The Enclave's Operative School, and smiled. Garrison simply nodded, but that alone showed his approval, as well.

"Tell me." Abraham commanded, as he led the horse toward the stables.

Sarah had heard those two words countless times during her years of training. They told her to voice the result of her internal mental exercise.

"I understand that a test under fire was essential for you to assess my readiness for an assignment." She looked to Garrison, who again simply nodded. Sarah continued in a flat voice, "Placing Captain Tallmadge in such a risky situation seemed unnecessary to me, however." Both Abraham and Garrison kept their eyes forward as they walked along the darkening street toward the stables. "Of course, he is an officer of the rebels, and should have known the risks involved in our..." she paused, "relationship."

Sarah caught Abraham's nod despite the gathering dark. He said, "You have read the report on your young Captain. He is no drawing room officer."

Garrison spoke for the first time. "Indeed, not. He has been blooded and has bloodied others in previous engagements. And each time, as he did this time, he has performed admirably."

"Quite honorably, I would say," Abraham added.

Abraham's comment brought back to Sarah the thought she had been mulling over during the ride home.

"Yes, he took quite a chance waiting for me and taking me on as his—and Anemos's—burden." She couldn't keep the admiration out of her voice.

The tone of her voice made Garrison glance at Abraham, who raised his eyebrow, showing that he had noticed the tone as well. "Anemos? 'Wind', is his horse?" Sarah nodded. "A clever young man, also."

Abraham picked up the thread. "There is much to admire in the young man. I am sure General Washington is equally impressed. I expect we will hear of a newly minted Major in the next few days. When we do, it will be time to move to the next phase."

They had reached the gate to the paddock where a boy of about twelve years old stood patiently. Abraham handed the bridle to the waiting groom, but Sarah laid a hand on his arm, holding him there while she stroked the horse's forelock. In response, the stallion, whose high spirit matched Sarah's and who, because of this, was Sarah's favorite, bent his head and nuzzled her chest. She hugged his long head and whispered something in his ear, to which the horse nodded and snorted what sounded just like a laugh. From a pocket of her gingham dress, she withdrew a piece of carrot and offered it, open palmed, to the steed. With a slurp of his lips, he gulped the treat and snorted his thanks while the groom led him away.

Realization dawned on Sarah as she watched the horse disappear into the gathering gloom. "So, you were testing *him*, also."

"Of course, Sarah. We—you—must know whom to trust as we proceed."

She wondered what the next phase of this 'endeavor' would be. But that was not the time for that discussion. All she wanted at the moment was a hot bath, a plate of dinner, and her warm bed.

Sarah learned of her first operation the following day. Two masked operatives roused from her bed well before dawn and led her, hooded, into a windowless log building deep in the woods. A hand on her shoulder and a poke in the back stopped her and brought her to ramrod attention. Her senses, at first muddled from sleep, by then revealed the rustling of heavy fabric and the scent of burning tallow.

The operative at her back pulled the hood from her head. She stood in a room lit by candle sconces sparsely spaced high on the side walls. The two operatives who had escorted her took their sentry positions on either side of the room's only door.

At the other end of the flagstone floor stood what appeared to be an altar. Behind it stood Abraham, wearing a red robe with a rope intricately knotted at his waist. Behind him and to his right stood Garrison, also robed, but in brown, who held a cloth bundle reverently.

Abraham signaled Sarah to approach the altar. When she stood before it, he intoned, "Hear ye! Hear ye! Before us stands a candidate for admission to the rank of Operative." Abraham paused and, from under his hood, his eyes bored into Sarah's. Raising his voice, he called out, "Is she worthy?"

In response, the operatives at the door and Garrison from his post in the corner shouted, "Huzzah!"

"Is she worthy?"

Louder now, "Huzzah!!"

"Is she worthy?"

At the top of their lungs came the final reply "Huzzah!!!"

A small smile appeared on Abraham's shadowed lips. "Having been judged worthy, let us invest this candidate with the vestments and kit of an Operative."

The operatives guarding the door left their posts, and each carried a bundle forward. One carried folded clothing and the other a small pack. With small bows, they laid their parcels on the altar.

Placing his hand on the bundle to his right, Abraham said, "This suit and mask of silk ensures your anonymity while on assignment." He placed his left hand on the pack made from the same fabric. "And this kit contains the tools you will need."

The two operatives took positions a step behind and to the sides of Sarah.

Abraham continued with eyes fixed on Sarah's, "Candidate, you must decide. Are you willing to leave your past life?"

Abraham paused long enough for Sarah to respond. "I am," she said without hesitation.

"Are you willing to live a lie as someone else for as long as it takes to complete your mission?"

Her hesitation spanned a single heartbeat. "I am."

"Understand, Candidate, that this is a decision that will span lifetimes." Sarah cocked her head, not understanding. Expecting her confusion, Abraham continued, "The greatest secret this order has kept for centuries is about to be revealed to you. It will bind you to The Enclave forever. Are you willing to accept this secret and keep it under penalty of death, and thereby leave your childhood behind?"

Firmly, knowing full well that her world was about to expand beyond the confines of the life she had lived until then, Sarah responded, "I am!"

Nodding, Abraham turned to Garrison, who walked forward with his own parcel, which he handed to the Grand Master. Abraham laid the bundle of linen cloth on the altar and meticulously, reverently unwrapped it, revealing a broken piece of a wooden staff.

Taking it in his hands, he raised it to eye level and explained in a more conversational tone, "This humble-looking, broken lance, yielded by the Centurion Longinus, pierced the side of Jesus Christ. Its miraculous power has kept your Master alive for more than five centuries." Sarah gasped as Abraham let the import of his words sink in. A moment later, he continued. "And it has resurrected many fallen Operatives. From this sacred relic," he turned the staff in his hands until a bare spot at the broken end was visible, "we have carved for you a cross for your own resurrection."

Garrison drew from inside his robe a small wooden cross, tipped with silver and strung on a leather thong. Abraham took it and held it in front of Sarah.

"When death is imminent, when there is no hope of escape, remove the silver tip," he pulled the silver from the end revealing a sharpened point, "and thrust the cross into your neck where you can feel your beating heart. Push it in to the hilt. It must remain embedded in your flesh for your resurrection to complete."

Sarah stood shaking with excitement and a wonder she had never felt before, which Abraham clearly saw.

"Speak your questions, Operative."

Sarah swallowed and tried to keep her voice even. "I have many, Master."

Abraham smiled and placed the thong over her head while Garrison and the two operatives stepped forward to shake her hand and slap her on the back.

"Of course you do, *Operative* Sarah Louise Harkin."

PART VI

Amy
Present Day

Faced with certain death at the hands of the insertion team sent to execute them, the Operatives Jennine and Francis Sullivan, undercover as Deborah and James Washington, used their Enclave-issued comms to signal their GPS location and initiate their extraction protocol. We can assume from the scene that the Recovery Team found that, given the remote location, and the overwhelming force they faced that both Operative Jennine and Operative Francis made the conscious decision to sacrifice their own chance at resurrection to give their daughter Amy a chance at life. The bullet wounds Amy suffered were clearly fatal, however, the intervention of her parents, by inserting both of their Operative Crosses into her carotid arteries on either side of her neck. It was through this heroic act that they preserved the life of their daughter, Amy Sullivan. Amy's subsequent resurrection procedure at The Enclave facilities in Pennsylvania was successfully completed. As expected, Amy has no memory of her parents' intervention, the attack, her death, or resurrection. Her physical development has progressed normally, and her mental acuity is significantly advanced for a child of her age.

— After-Action Progress Report, re: Amy Lori Sullivan

Chapter 21

Nightmares

Apiercing scream echoed across the sleeping Enclave. "Aimley. Aimley! *Aimley!*" Dolores Warner shook her foster child violently, but Amy continued screaming.

As Dolores drew her hand back to slap her awake, the girl's eyes flew open and her face contorted in terror, partly from the nightmare and partly from opening her eyes to the sight of the large Mrs. Warner poised to strike her.

Dolores dropped her hand.

"My Lord, girl. You'll wake the whole neighborhood. Stop with this nightmare nonsense."

The nightmare images faded. *And just how am I supposed to do that?* Amy thought. She kept the sarcastic thought to herself, however, and said meekly, "I'm sorry, Mrs. Warner. I—I'll try."

She let a single tear roll down her cheek while thinking, *If I knew how to do that, don't you think I would?*

Dolores was unmoved by the tear. "You'd better. Mr. Warner has work in the morning. If you don't keep quiet, you'll be sleeping in the basement again."

With that, she turned and marched out of the room, slamming the door. Amy waited for and heard the click of the deadbolt on the *outside* of the bedroom door.

Nightmares—night terrors, really—were much more frequent when she first arrived at The Enclave, relegating her to a bed in the Warner's basement at night. The recurring dreams of the night men with guns shattered her life became routine enough that she recognized them for what they were while still asleep. Dreaming lucidly that way allowed her to wake herself before the screaming started. Occasionally, like that night, a new nightmare snuck through. Unlike the others that faded away like an early-morning mist, that night's still burned in her memory.

Mom and Dad whispered in her ears, "I love you," right before they murdered her.

She was sleeping in a strange bedroom when her parents rushed in a moment before the tall men dressed all in black appeared at her bedroom door. Mom and Dad gathered her into their arms and whispered that lie before the agony blossomed in her neck. As she watched her blood soak the blanket, her parents covered her with their bodies just as the bad men's guns spat fire. With eyesight going black, Amy felt her parents stiffen from the impact of the bullets, then slump away, leaving her exposed to the next barrage.

Amy recovered from her physical wounds and awoke from the induced healing coma, but her emotional wounds ran much deeper. The scars that formed over her bullet wounds marked her as *different* to The Enclave's residents. The scars that never fully covered her emotional wounds caused her to question everything, including her very existence, further isolating herself from those who were comfortable in their simple, everyday lives.

With an understanding of Amy's trauma few could match, John placed Amy with the Warners when she had physically healed. His rationale was that they would appreciate a companion since their two children had both left for college and then decided to live their lives outside The Enclave.

This was not a well-thought-out choice on John's part, however. Not being operatives, he couldn't tell them the complete story of Amy's injuries and recovery. Anyone who saw the track of scars across her chest would question how she survived, though. Such questions only served to fuel the Warners' suspicions that The Enclave was more than just a quiet escape from the outside world. He had not known how Mr. Warner had handled being an empty-nester—by drinking himself to sleep each night. Nor had he thought through how Dolores's feeling of abandonment would transfer itself to the quiet, mysterious child who offered no opportunities for bonding with her foster family.

As Amy lay in bed staring at the ceiling and afraid this new nightmare would come again if she fell asleep, she, instead, calculated the number of nights, counting leap years, until her eighteenth birthday—her own Independence Day.

Chapter 22

Bullies

L iz walked along a path that wound through the village and out along the edge of the wooded acres. The Enclave encompassed roughly ten thousand acres in what is now Chester County, Pennsylvania. But its provenance dated back to a land grant issued to the Order by King James I of England in 1604, a full seventy-seven years before William Penn founded Pennsylvania in 1681. That precedence gave The Enclave a unique status. Although incorporated as Enclave Borough within Chester County, its special status meant that, for the most part, it existed outside the jurisdiction of the United States.

Similar to The Vatican, which is fully encircled by Rome but is itself an independent country, or the semi-sovereign tribal lands within the United States, The Enclave was an autonomous self-governing region. Unlike The Vatican, however, which announced its existence in the most opulent ways possible, The Enclave kept a very low profile. Few residents, other than John and his most-trusted advisors, even knew of their unique position. That list included Fr. Dan, since he found the original vellum document, signed with King James's royal seal, in the Archives.

Liz broke into a slow jog as she passed the last row of houses. Beyond lay several hundred acres of farmland. Leaving the village behind, she picked up the pace as she passed out of view. Just as John kept their independence secret, Liz kept hidden the physical capabilities she had developed and honed over more than two centuries.

Once out of eyesight of the village, she broke into a sprint as the path skirted the cleared fields, then dipped into the woods. She kept up a world-class pace over the rough ground for her route's six mile length, which circled the open farmland along paths and game trails through the forest. Only when she emerged back within sight of the village did she slow to a normal long-distance pace.

Lost in her own thoughts as she jogged behind the village school where the younger kids were out on recess, Liz was past the fenced schoolyard before the commotion in the schoolyard caught her attention. Looking over her shoulder, what she saw brought her up short. A group of girls stood in a circle, laughing and cursing at something on the ground.

Intuition told Liz that the "something" on the ground was really a "someone", and she had a pretty good idea whom that someone was. When the biggest of the older girls drew back and spit on the poor girl on the ground, Liz sprang into action.

Without even thinking, she took two long strides and launched herself at the chain-link fence surrounding the playground. Grabbing the top bar, she sliced her palms on the sharp welds of the fence, but kept going, vaulting over it in one bound.

Landing at a dead run, she burst through the evil circle and saw exactly what her intuition had feared. Amy lay curled in the fetal position on the ground. Her clothes were torn, and blood seeped from scrapes on her knees and elbows, but worst of all were the gobs of spittle hanging from her tangled hair.

"*Get back!*" The command issued from Liz of its own volition with such force that the older girls literally staggered backwards.

Bending down, Liz gathered Amy into her arms and held her tightly while the young girl sobbed into her shoulder.

"You *evil* little brats! How dare you treat Amy like this? You all should be ashamed of yourselves."

"Hey, you can't speak to these children like that." Two teachers came running around the corner of the school building. "Those kids aren't yours to order around."

Liz spun to face the newcomers, and the hatred in her eyes halted them in their tracks.

"Where the hell were you when this child was being abused? Look at her and look at this ring of bullies who assaulted her. You're the ones responsible for putting a stop to this behavior."

The older of the two teachers gathered her wits and launched her own counterattack.

"How dare you speak to us like that? *You people* don't belong here, and you certainly can't order us around."

Liz's anger boiled into rage, a silent killing rage which she barely kept in check. She squeezed her hands into fists, so the pain of her lacerated palms could clear her head.

Blood squeezed through her fingers and dripped to the ground. Her voice when she spoke was barely more than a whisper, but it cut into the adults like a knife to the heart.

"If it wasn't for *people* like me, you high and mighty hypocrites never would have been born. This Enclave would have died out long, long ago. If I had my way, there would still be a Work Camp, and I would send you two there tonight."

The younger teacher looked on in confusion, but the older one, who had heard the rumors of the long history of the Order and its operatives, staggered back as her hand flew to her mouth.

Liz continued in the same low, but powerful voice, "As it is, your days of spreading your hate and prejudices to the next generation are done. You'll both be scrubbing toilets tomorrow."

Hugging Amy even tighter, Liz walked past the teachers, who parted in fear at her passing. The only way out of the playground was through the school building, but they met no resistance as Liz carried Amy through the halls to the front entrance. The other teachers who had heard the confrontation outside stood in their doorways as they passed. Most hung their heads as Liz looked at each accusingly. Some, though, met her eyes and silently nodded their approval.

Chapter 23

A New Beginning

This isn't the 12th century, John."

The argument had been going on for several minutes. Liz, John, and Dan were in John's office. John sat behind his desk and Dan occupied one of the chairs facing him. Liz, too upset to sit still, paced back and forth across the thick antique Persian carpet while Amy waited in the office's anteroom with Karl Coolbaugh, Head of Security.

John struggled to keep his voice level against a rising tide of frustration. "The Enclave residents are necessarily iconoclastic. They've been indoctrinated to distrust outsiders. You, of all people, should understand that."

So far, Dan had kept his silence, but he leaned forward, ready to jump in if the argument got out of hand.

Liz's tone dripped with bitterness. "Oh, I've felt the abuse, resentment, and mistrust, believe me. You didn't tolerate it when you recruited me in this very office. But this isn't the 18th century either. If what happened to Amy today had happened down the road in Kimberton, your two *teachers* would be in jail right now."

Dan nodded his agreement, but John was undeterred. "You don't know the whole story. Aimley—"

"Don't call her that!" Liz's anger boiled over.

Her outburst, however, left John with a look of bewilderment, so Dan finally spoke up, "Her name is Amy, John, not 'Aimley.'" John still looked confused, so Dan continued, "'Aimley' is a rather derogatory nickname."

Liz cut him off. "It's short for 'Aimless Amy'. Why would anyone let an orphaned eleven-year old be called 'aimless'? I've heard how much trouble she gets into, but of course she's misguided, rudderless. She was ripped away from her old life after her parents died and thrust into this pit of prejudice and superstition." Spit flew from her lips. "Instead of giving her support and nurturing, you placed her with a miserable, resentful bitch and her drunkard husband. How did you expect her to react?"

John, abashed, turned to Dan for support with a look of helplessness. Dan just gave him a rueful shrug, and he turned back to Liz.

With arms and hands spread in a placated gesture, John said, "I understand now that the Warners were a terrible choice as foster parents. We—no, I—had hoped I could heal all of them at once. I can see that was a monumental mistake."

The regret and remorse clear in John's words had a calming effect on Liz. She rubbed her bandaged hands together lightly, wincing at the dull ache the gesture produced.

"Broken people can't fix each other, John. At least not while they're still broken."

Dan watched the exchange with a thoughtful look, as if the spark of an idea glowed in his mind, but he kept silent and let it smolder.

John took a deep breath and met Liz's gaze. His voice when he spoke was full of regret.

"Amy's parents didn't die during a home invasion robbery like most people believe." He paused, as if hoped Dan would pick up the story but, after a moment, John continued. "Her parents, Bob Sullivan and Julie *Harkin* Sullivan," Liz raised a quizzical eyebrow, "were murdered by members of a drug cartel during an operation."

John paused, waiting to gauge Liz's reaction. It came immediately.

"You sent married *parents* out on an operation?"

John shook his head and held up a hand. "They weren't parents, or even married when they went out. It was Bob's third operation and Julie's second."

Now Liz looked perplexed, yet a ray of hope shone on her face. "Had they ever…"

"No, neither of them had been…resurrected."

Her shoulders slumped, and the look of hope vanished. Liz asked, "Where was their handler?" Her right hand went involuntarily to the wooden cross at her throat. "Why didn't they use their…"

Dan finally spoke up, a new resolution in his voice. "Bob and Julie slipped away with Amy for a weekend getaway. Apparently, they failed to elude the cartel killers who were following them. When the family was asleep in the house they were renting in the Poconos, a cartel assassination team slipped in and killed both Bob and Julie."

Liz's sharp intake of breath was almost a gasp. "When Carlos, their handler, responded to their emergency signal, he found *all three of them* riddled with bullets, but Amy was still…alive. He brought her straight here. To the outside world, officially, she is still 'missing.'"

Liz knew the implication—they were too far gone to be resurrected, unless… Reflexively, her hand went to the missing cross at her throat. "So, they couldn't use their crosses, or whatever it is you give new Operatives these days?"

Dan and John exchanged looks, trying to decide who would continued. Finally, Dan dropped his chin to his chest, a quiver in his voice. "We still issue operatives nondescript wooden crosses like yours. And yes, Bob and Julie lived long enough to use them. But…" He swallowed the sob that threatened to escape as a choked gasp.

Liz looked from one to the other as a horrible realization crept into her heart. "No. No."

"Yes." John was near tears himself. "When Carlos found them, both of their crosses were buried to their hilts in Amy's neck and she was in the throes of resurrection."

Liz buried her face in her hands while tears rolled down John's face and Dan cried unabashedly. "Oh, my…God."

Wiping his cheeks with a handkerchief, John said, "Carlos sedated her, of course, then rushed her here. Her injuries were extensive, but she did heal. Her body did, anyway."

"Does she know?"

Both men shook their heads, but it was Dan who answered. "She doesn't remember the attack or anything until she woke up here in the hospital."

Liz looked doubtful. She remembered her own visits into the netherworld between death and rebirth. Dan continued, "As you well know, though, the physical scars take a long, long time to disappear. The ones she carries from the six gunshot wounds still show on her chest and torso. Needless to say, this has fueled speculation and rumors."

A few moments passed silently until Liz finally asked, "So, what happens now?"

John, clearly out of his element, just shrugged, but resolve was back in Dan's voice.

"She needs a new guardian, obviously. This time, though, it must be someone who can nurture her and someone she can bond with." He looked for some sign of recognition from Liz, but got nothing back. "She *needs* someone who understands what she has been through, who can explain to her what her nightmares mean, and what her future holds." He saw a hint of understanding in her eyes as she shook her head slowly. He stared into her eyes as he continued. "Someone who will take her away from this place back into the outside world…"

Both Liz and John could now see where Dan was going with this argument. Neither of them liked it. John leaned forward with his hand up in a stop sign, but Liz beat him to the punch.

"Oh no. I know where you're going with this, Father. Very clever, but I'm not capable of taking care of a *kid*."

"Finally, something we agree on." John looked at Liz in solidarity. "Liz is an active Operative. She can't be burdened with a child."

"*Inactive*, remember? And don't call her a burden, John." Liz looked annoyed despite her opposition to Dan's idea. "No child is a burden." Her tone reflected her long-festering resentment toward John.

Before she could lash out further, though, Dan interrupted with a calming voice. "You came to her rescue today, and from what I saw when I got here, she practically had to be peeled away from you. Sounds to me like you two have already bonded." Liz opened her mouth, but no objection came. "And there's another thing. As John said, Amy's last name is Harkin. That should ring a bell, I believe." Liz looked wary but nodded. "It turns out Amy is your great-to-the-ninth niece. Directly descended from your younger brother, James."

Liz shook her head. "I never had a brother named James."

John spoke up. "Your mother was pregnant when you went to finishing school down south."

"I'll be damned."

"Look, we have to finish your life story for the Archives. Let's move Amy in with you until we're done, then we can discuss this again."

Liz and John knew exactly what Dan was doing, but a trial period certainly made sense, and it was clear Amy couldn't go back to the Warners. They reluctantly nodded in unison.

Dan smiled. "Great. I'll tell the Warners. I'm sure they won't have any objections."

He stood and opened the office door. Amy leaned forward in a chair with hands folded in her lap, her feet swinging a few inches above the carpet. She snapped back when the door opened unexpectedly.

Giving her a warm smile, Dan gestured for her to join them in the inner office. Reluctantly, Amy climbed off the chair, and with back ramrod straight, entered the room. Before Dan followed her, Karl laid a hand on his arm. When Dan looked back, Karl nodded to Amy, then touched his ear and gave a shrug, saying without words that she may have overheard at least some of the previous conversation.

Mouthing, "Thanks," Dan closed the door.

He ushered Amy to his chair, but she stepped away to stand next to Liz. Liz, clearly pleased, smiled.

"How much did you overhear?" Dan asked gently.

Amy gave Liz a sidelong glance, then turned to him. "You want me to live with her," she nodded toward Liz, "instead of the Warners."

Dan nodded. "We think you'll be more…comfortable with Ms.—"

"You can call me Liz," Liz interjected. "And I'm excited to have you as a houseguest."

Amy tuned slowly to Liz. They held their appraising stares for several heartbeats. Finally, she nodded. "Okay."

Chapter 24

Black Magic

L iz and Amy opened the gate in the picket fence in front of the Warner house. On the ground lay a pile of clothes, shoes, and a few toys. The clothes were rolled into a ball of wrinkles. The shoes were worn and of all different sizes. Most of the toys were broken.

Liz walked up the sidewalk, her disgust plain on her face.

"It looks like Mrs. Warner emptied my dresser and closet," Amy said with a hint of humor and no care for the state of her wardrobe.

Liz snorted. "I'm not surprised." She lowered her voice and tried to keep the growing anger from her voice. "I guess Father Dan already told her what's happening."

Amy just shrugged and looked dubious.

Liz looked down at the small pile of detritus that represented all of Amy's worldly possessions. "Why don't you fold these clothes and pair up the shoes?"

"But they're all dirty."

"I can see that. But if they're folded, they'll be easier to carry." Liz took a deep breath. "I have to talk to Mrs. Warner."

Amy's eyes got wide, and she quickly set to work folding the dirty clothes. Liz climbed the steps and crossed the porch to the front door. As she raised her hand to knock, the door flew open.

"Get that junk off my property."

Two things were clear from her tone of voice. Mrs. Warner had been watching through the door's sidelight, and the junk she was referring to was not the pile of clothes.

Liz kept her voice level despite the color rising up her neck. "First of all, it isn't your property. It is The Enclave's. You are just squatting here temporarily. Second, if you hadn't just thrown Amy's things in a pile, we would have been gone by now."

Warner poked her forefinger into Liz's chest, and Liz stiffened. Warner's voice rose in pitch, "Just get out. We don't want your kind around here."

Warner drew her hand back, ready to poke Liz again. But before she could, Liz grabbed her wrist and twisted it painfully backwards.

Leaning in, she whispered, "If you know anything about *my kind*, you should know two things." She bent Warner's wrist even further, eliciting a whimper. "First, The Enclave wouldn't exist without my kind, and second, if you ever lay a finger on either me or Amy again, you won't be squatting in this nice house. You'll be lying in a hospital bed."

Liz released Warner's wrist, who stepped back and began rubbing it. Her eyes narrowed as she said, "We know about you. You and the others like you...like *her*." She pointed at Amy. "We don't know what black magic you use, but we know it's evil and we're determined to drive it out of this town."

Liz was astonished, but her face broke into a sarcastic smile. "You foolish old woman. Are you living in the Dark Ages? What an idiotic thing to say, to believe."

Liz shook her head and turned away, but halfway across the porch, she spun back around and yelled, "Boo!"

She got the reaction she was hoped for as Warner stumbled backwards into the house. Liz laughed loudly as she descended the steps to where Amy waited, arms loaded with at least half of the clothes, toys, and shoes. Liz bent and kissed the top of her head before picking up the rest of the neatly folded clothes.

"Amy, let's go home."

Liz stood in the anteroom, waiting for John to open the door to his office when a click and the whisper of well-oiled hinges startled her. A portion of the wall to her left swung inward. When Dan stepped through the opening, he found Liz crouched in a defensive stance.

Raising his hands, palms facing outward, he said, "Whoa. It's just me."

Liz relaxed. "So, you have your own secrets around here." Dan shrugged in response. "Secrets. That's what I'm here to talk about."

John opened his office door and stood aside to let the others enter. Closing the door again, he said, "We've always had secrets, Elizabeth. What concerns you now?" His tone indicated he wasn't happy being interrupted.

Picking up on his tone, Liz replied sharply, "What you think are secrets aren't anymore."

The remark had its desired effect.

"OK, you have my attention." John sat behind his desk. "Report out."

Liz fixed her gaze on the wall and, in a neutral, near-mechanical voice, she related her encounter with Dolores Warner. When finished, she turned back to John with raised eyebrows.

John just sat silently with a deep frown on his face, so Dan asked the obvious question. "How much do you think she knows?"

"I don't think she knows anything. What she and her ilk seem to have observed or somehow figured out is that I am older than I look."

"She said that?"

"No, but her reference to 'Black Magic' shows…"

"Let's not jump to conclusions," John finally spoke. "She could have been referring to any number of activities we engage in."

Liz shook her head violently. "Don't patronize me, Abraham." Using his historical name caught both John and Dan by surprise. "People live a lot longer in this age. Some who live here have seen me come and go at least three or four times. And what about all the other operatives?"

Her question led Dan to asked another one. "How many operatives are currently active?"

Liz nodded. She wanted to know the answer, as well, but John wasn't ready to give out that information.

"That is proprietary. Neither of you need to know who or how many."

"John, I can just search the archives and have an answer in a few seconds," Dan said.

John's shoulders sank. "Damn computers. We currently have five active operatives and six on leave, including you, Elizabeth."

Dan looked surprised by the number, but Liz nodded. "Have you replaced Amy's parents?"

John shook his head. "No, and I'm not sure I will. I don't have any candidates at this point."

Dan was thoughtful. "And Amy, of course." Both Liz and John looked surprised, so he continued, "She's been resurrected. She may not be a trained operative, but The Enclave needs to watch over her. We owe her that much, at least."

John turned to Liz. "Do you think she's an operative candidate?"

"Oh, wow. I wouldn't condemn her to that kind of life." She paused, but when no response came from either of the others, she continued, "The training and discipline would certainly be good for her. I don't know her well enough to know if she has what it takes to get through it all, though."

When Dan spoke, he was clearly reluctant. "She is very bright, very creative, and very self-motivated. If her impulses aren't channeled toward a worthy goal, they will find their own goal, which might not be so 'worthy'."

John nodded, having reached a decision. "Okay. Elizabeth, since she'll be living with you for a while, I'd like you to evaluate whether she would make a worthy candidate for operative training." Liz started to object, but John cut her off. "Consider it your next assignment, Operative Elizabeth. You wanted a new one. Now you've got one."

All three were silent for a moment, then Dan spoke. "That still leaves the problem of the Warners and their gossip."

John waved his hand dismissively. "We've had rumors and gossip before. I'll have Karl remind folks that The Enclave is more than just a sleepy borough in rural Pennsylvania. We exist for a reason, and the work we do is very important, which makes it very secret. Spreading rumors and gossip runs counter to the very existence of The Enclave."

Liz wasn't convinced. "That may have worked in the past, but what about people who want The Enclave to be just a sleepy village?"

John's expression darkened. "Well, we've dealt with those folks before, too."

His tone told both Liz and Dan that the discussion had reached its conclusion.

PART VII

Major Tallmadge
Winter 1778

We were so close, but now I fear our best chance at gauging our enemy is lost. Still, there is cause for hope, if the last secret message can be believed.

— G. Washington War Journal
Valley Forge
February 1778

The two days that have just passed must be the strangest and most eventful of my life. So momentous were they that I am reluctant to recount them, even in this enciphered journal. O, Glorious Day! All hail this mighty endeavor's greatest friend, le Marquis de Lafayette.

— G. Washington War Journal
Valley Forge
March 1778

Chapter 25

Promotion

T he message egg that Captain Tallmadge brought back to General Washington did indeed hold good news, although the General could scarcely hope to believe it while he awaited confirmation from Mr. Adams and Mr. Franklin, Congress's emissaries to France. The egg's note said that through their ministrations and the continual letters of encouragement sent back to France by the Marquis de Lafayette, King Louis XVI had formally committed France to the Americans' cause. As was always the case, the note was signed with the flourishing '*Æ*'.

Benjamin's account of the Germantown escapade, reported to Washington in his private chambers upon his return to camp, was concise and unembellished, leaving no hint of the excitement, nor the danger of the close encounter. Several other eyewitness accounts from Germantown patriots, which had filtered back to Valley Forge over the next several days, were considerably more hyperbolic, causing Washington to summon Benjamin back to his headquarters.

While awaiting Benjamin's arrival, General Washington paced about his office like a caged lion. Glancing out the window, he saw a horse and rider approaching at a gallop from the fields where Captain Tallmadge had been drilling his men. The General stopped and fixed his gaze on the rider, gathering his thoughts for the coming interview.

The Captain's actions showed several facets of his character. His courage under fire was obvious and well-known to all who had witnessed it firsthand, as the General himself had. What impressed him the most about this latest action, however, were the decisions Benjamin had made under the most stressful of circumstances.

By all accounts, other than Benjamin's own, he could have bolted while Sarah was trying to outrun the British cavalry, leaving her to her fate. But he had not. In fact, he nearly lingered too long, not through indecision, but rather to save his confidant. His sense of responsibility and loyalty to this stranger, with whom he had had only exchanged pleasantries a few times, was most admirable in the General's eyes.

Even more impressive, though, was Benjamin's unconscious recognition that he should defer to Sarah's direction as they made their escape. By his own humble admission, he had followed her commands from her initial warning whistle until she calmly left him alone on the backstreet in Germantown. In Washington's view, letting those lead who know the situation better than you do was a fine quality in a commander. So it was that, as Captain

Tallmadge dismounted and tied Anemos to the rail, the General made his decision.

Seating himself behind his desk, and clasping his huge hands with forefingers extended thoughtfully to his lips, Washington listened to Benjamin's boots on the stairs, then the hallway. He suppressed a smile as they paused for a heartbeat or two before there came a knock on the office door.

"*Entre.*"

Benjamin strode into the small room, snapped to attention, and saluted smartly. After Washington lazily returned the salute and with a wave of his hand indicated the Captain should stand at ease—the General found such formalisms tiresome in private company—Benjamin relaxed a little.

"Sit down, Son. We have much to discuss." Benjamin took the proffered chair and Washington continued. "It seems you left a good deal out of your report on the 'Germantown Chase', as I hear it is now being called."

A faint smile tugged at his mouth, which he tried to cover by leaning his tall frame forward and placing his elbows on the desk. Taken aback, Benjamin didn't notice the smile or the teasing tone.

"I assure you, General, that I reported all the facts directly to you that very day."

Having gotten the desired response, the General allowed the suppressed smile to spread across his face.

"That is exactly my point, Captain. You reported only the facts and left out all the juicy details!"

Jaw working like a fish out of water, Benjamin stammered out a reply. "I didn't…I did not think the General would be interested…"

That was more than Washington could take, and the laughter he had been holding back burst forth in a loud guffaw.

"My Lord, Son, I'm just jesting you. I would have thought much less of you if you had embellished your report with how pretty the girl was, or how close the pistol shots came as they whizzed past your ears. You correctly left it to others to weave those details into the story."

Blushing, but relieved that the dressing-down he was expecting was simply a joke, Benjamin acknowledged his hero's praise with just a nod.

With a more serious countenance and tone of voice, the General continued, "The truth that is at the root of the stories now circulating among the officers and men is self-evident. At every stage of Friday's event, and under the most stressful of circumstances, you made the right decision and took what must have been the only correct action. The rescue of our wonderful spy, and the selfless deference to her more informed knowledge of the situation, shows to me what I have suspected for quite some time."

Benjamin held his breath awaiting the wisdom of the Great Man, but after a few seconds it became clear the General wouldn't continued without prompting. So, taking a deep breath, Benjamin asked, "What is it that you have suspected, Sir?"

A smile returned to Washington's lips. "I have suspected, and you have proven, that your duties should be expanded, *Major* Tallmadge." Holding up a hand to forestall any protest, Washington continued, "The duties I am assigning you bring with them dangers that few on my staff, indeed in this entire army, have faced or will ever face. Having good intelligence about the enemy is a key component in any winning strategy, and despite the more common opinion held by many of my officers that spying is ungentlemanly and thus somehow unfair, we both know that it is absolutely essential." Benjamin nodded vigorously as Washington continued, "The lives of the men we command matter much more than any notion of 'fair play.' War is not playtime or some social event. Salon sensibilities do not apply when the lives of these men—fathers, brothers, and sons—and the very existence of this fledgling nation hang in the balance."

Both men rose from their seats, and Washington came around his desk while Benjamin stood at rigid attention.

"Major Tallmadge—Benjamin—I am entrusting you with the task of building a spy ring that will supply me with the intelligence we need to tip the balance of this war in our favor."

Benjamin somehow stood even taller and snapped another sharp salute. This time, the General drew himself up to his full height, and slowly, formally returned the salute in kind, then extended his hand, which Benjamin clasped in both of his.

"There are many preparations to make, Major. What will you do first?"

"Well, Sir, with the information that the British will abandon Philadelphia, New York will become the focus of the conflict here in the North. From New York, the British can launch assaults anywhere along the coast. They could march north up the Hudson River to cut off New England from the rest of the colonies, or they could march south into New Jersey to regain what they lost this past year."

The General nodded. "Exactly my thinking. Knowing the deployment of defenses, the distribution of munitions stores, and the readiness of campaign supplies in and around New York will be key to success." Washington thought for a moment. "Knowing whether to mount an attack on the city itself, or to respond as quickly as possible to British sallies to the north or south, is crucial. Prior knowledge and situational awareness will be critical."

It was clear that Benjamin had come to the same conclusion when he responded. "With the British leaving Philadelphia, intelligence operations must focus squarely on New York." Washington nodded his ascent as Benjamin continued, "We have learned from both the failure of my good friend Nathan Hale, and this latest exercise in Philadelphia that good useful intelligence can only be gleaned by operatives who are integrated into the everyday life of the area in question. Also, the collected information can only be carried from that area of occupation to our agents in the field by someone who has a legitimate reason to come and go and to socialize with the operatives, just as our young farm lass did."

Washington had been nodding throughout Benjamin's recitation, and he broke in.

"I have learned something else very important from the accounts of the Germantown Chase," this time there was no joked in the reference. "The source of the musket shots that issued from the barn and stone wall on the outskirts of Germantown is a mystery, even to the local residents. None of the patriots in the town claim to have any knowledge of who might have fired them. Clearly, though, whomever counter-attacked knew of your mission in advance, and where expertly placed to repel any pursuit." Benjamin looked confused, yet intrigued by this bit of information, but kept his silence.

Not getting a response, Washington continued, "Despite many inquiries, the identity and origin of the ambushers who laid in wait, turned the pursuers about in such a timely fashion, then disappeared afterwards, remains a mystery. The only plausible explanation is that they were there to protect the young girl, the spy."

The General let Benjamin absorb these revelations, but Benjamin had already reached the same conclusion. "Clearly, the group that has been feeding us information and whom we know only as 'E' is well-organized and highly skilled," he said.

In their subsequent discussion, which stretched throughout the afternoon, Washington and Benjamin tried to puzzle out how their operation had been compromised. Several options presented themselves. First, they realized that the regularity of his visits to the Rising Sun Tavern, timed as they were to coincide with Sarah's trek home, could have raised suspicions. It was easy to conclude that his appearances at the tavern, only when the courier happened to pass by with leftover eggs to sell him, could have led a loyalist to alert the British.

Also, although Washington and Tallmadge told no one else about Benjamin's clandestine meetings, his regular departures from camp, followed a few hours later by his return and a hurried meeting with the General, could have alerted a British spy within Washington's own officer corps.

Such a possibility chilled the General's heart, but though he knew it to be distinctly possible, he refused to raise the specter of suspicion among his cadre of officers. He knew the background, and many of the families, of his staff. Though no man can see into another's heart, the Great Man believed in the loyalty and goodwill of his officers, and indeed of his entire army.

As they discussed other possible sources of the intelligence breach, Benjamin was chagrined. "I should have known that establishing such a pattern was dangerous. Meeting at the same time each week was so *foolish*."

Washington was more sanguine, understanding that spy craft was more of an art than a science.

"It was not foolish, Son. Is it not true that many traveling merchants take their lunch at that same tavern every week? Even several times each week?"

Benjamin nodded. He did indeed see many of the same faces each week. Still, the guilt he felt from his lack of foresight exposing the young girl to so much danger showed on his face and voice.

"Sir, perhaps it was not foolish, but it was certainly amateurish. We must become much more professional." Washington nodded and Benjamin continued, "But now our connection to this mysterious 'E' is broken, just when we need it most. How do they know the things that they know?

Details about the enemy's activities in Philadelphia, and the intentions of the French? Their sources of information must be widespread and well-placed."

"All you have said is true, but how do we know we can trust them?" Benjamin's response was cut short with a wave of the General's hand. "Only you and I—and whomever *they* are—knew of your meetings with their agent. And yet, there was a squad of the British lying in wait for you." Again, Benjamin tried to interrupt, but Washington plowed on. "Not only was there a squad of British, apparently there was also a counter ambush laid for them. Perhaps the purpose of the operation was not to feed us intelligence, but rather to lay a trap for the British."

The General paused for breath, and Benjamin jumped in. "With due respect, General, I have to disagree. A proper ambush would have been set along the road just north of the tavern, and the trap would not have been sprung until they fully enfiladed the cavalry. As it was, the shots that halted the pursuit came from in front of us, and from a distance that was not optimal. To my eye, inexperienced as it may be, it was clear that they were defending us, and just in the nick of time." Washington considered this as Benjamin continued, "Besides, my contact—I don't even know her name—was more than just a courier and was always in more danger than I. Perhaps the operation had a deeper purpose than we know. Their preparation implies as much. She and her people were in total control and fully prepared, including having rescuers perfectly positioned at Germantown."

"But that itself seems suspicious to me. How did they know that particular meeting would go badly?"

Benjamin had already thought this through. "I would bet that they were ready every time we met. They could have come and gone every week with no one knowing, just as they did this last time. That kind of preparation does not surprise me, given what little we know of them."

Satisfaction dawned on Washington's face as Benjamin made his arguments. He nodded and said, "I agree. But our discussion is moot, is it not? We have no way to contact them, and you certainly cannot go back to Germantown."

This time, it was Benjamin's turn to nod, but he had no more ideas, and no more to add to the discussion. Most disappointing, of course, was losing the opportunity to have such a conduit of useful information. But, overlaid over that disappointment was his personal disappointment, kept hidden from the Great Man, that he would never see that brave young woman, or feel her breath on his ear, ever again.

Chapter 26

A Midnight Visit

T he operative was clothed all in black, with a hood that fit tightly across the forehead with folds that swept behind the ears, forming stiff cups that afforded maximum sensitivity to the sounds of the forest. A mask covered the face from just below the eyes and hung loosely to the chest. The fabric was so finely woven that it made no sound as the operative's head swiveled from side to side, examining the forest clearing on the riverbank. A horse stood as silently, so well trained that he would stand without a sound all night and all the next day, if necessary. Only at the next nightfall, if his master didn't return, would he make his way, riderless, back to The Enclave.

Most of the snow was gone from the clearing, leaving behind a soft loam of pine needles, rotting leaves, and waterlogged deadfall branches. The trek through the sodden forest was easily accomplished in total silence, as would the rest of the operative's duties this night. Previous scouting missions had revealed the sentries' patterns and tendencies, and so it was known that the soldier who walked this section of the perimeter liked to hurry past the river so he could sit and smoke his pipe before climbing back up the hill to his checkpoint.

Lying on the soft ground under the cover of low-hanging hemlock branches, the operative watched as the sentry trudged past, heading upstream and making no effort to disguise his presence or motion. His lack of any attempt at stealth was a symptom of the general state of discipline that the rebel army had fallen into since the news of the British departure from Philadelphia had spread throughout the ranks.

Now would be the perfect time for a nighttime raid, thought the operative.

But the British, with their Old World notions of warfare, would never entertain such an "underhanded" attack.

They still don't understand that this rough country demands new tactics. Those of us born here know this in our bones, though. We share many sensibilities with these 'Americans.' We've made the right choice in backing the rebels' cause.

The operative watched as the sentry disappeared around a bend in the river.

Now Abraham needs to convince this General Washington to accept our assistance…but on our terms.

Rising silently and backtracking the guard's path along the river, within ten minutes the operative came within sight of the farmstead where Washington had made his headquarters.

Leaving the Major's summons was straightforward, as the operative had been inside his sleeping quarters before. Washington's junior officers, Major Tallmadge among them, were housed in a small guest house on the estate about one hundred yards from the main house. The rough clapboard siding was easy for the operative to climb using clawed gloves and boots made for the purpose.

As was their custom, the three men who shared the second-floor bedroom had left their single window open a few inches to provide some much needed fresh air. Light upward pressure proved that the window sash was still well-oiled from the operative's previous visit, so it made only the slightest sound as they eased it fully open.

Pausing before entering the room, but hearing no change in the breathing of the occupants, the operative slid in over the sill. Benjamin slept closest to the window on the operative's left. Three steps around the bed brought the small nightstand between the two beds on that side of the room within reach. The operative drew a folded note, addressed to *Maj. Tallmadge* and sealed with wax imprinted with the Æ sign of The Enclave, from a pocket and placed it on Benjamin's side of the table. Three more steps and the interloper returned to the window and silently slipped through it. Then, hanging by one hand, they lowered the sash to its previous position, and dropped lightly to the soft ground below.

Leaving the second note, the one addressed to *Gen. G. Washington*, was more difficult. The General's bedchamber, above the first floor meeting room in the stone walled headquarters building, was well guarded. Two sentries, who were much more alert than the one at the river, walked constantly around the headquarters grounds. In addition, Washington's aide, Jonathan, slept in an antechamber just outside his door.

The operative knew these facts and had incorporated them into the night's plan, so timing an approach between the circling sentries was not a problem.

Scaling the stone wall of the headquarters building, though possible, would take too long, with multiple sentries patrolling the grounds. Instead, they had decided during painstaking planning meetings that the best course of action was one that required more stealth than acrobatics.

After silently traversing the yard to the back porch, the operative tested the latch on the kitchen door. It lifted without resistance, and they knew The Enclave's contact inside the camp had helped prepare the mission, and the operative knew the intelligence the spy had gathered about the layout of the house, and the sleeping arrangements inside, was trustworthy.

A fire was banked in the winter kitchen's fireplace. The warmth felt good after the night's chill, but there was no time to enjoy it. A quick inspection in the dim glow from the embers revealed, as expected, a back stair leading up from the kitchen to the upper hallway. The operative took the stairs as quietly as possible, stepping confidently over the two steps which, the reports had said, would squeak under their weight.

The intelligence clandestinely smuggled to The Enclave included a sketch of the layout of bedrooms on the second floor. On the right side of the hallway, two closed doors led to guest bedrooms, one of which was currently occupied by the Marquis de Lafayette, and the other by his valet and *aide de camp*. Immediately on the left was a room that Washington used for small, private meetings, including those with Major Tallmadge, which had become more and more frequent. The backup plan called for simply leaving the summons in this unoccupied room, but with a bit of arrogance, the operative continued on confidently.

Only the remaining door off the hall, also on the left side, stood open. The operative crossed to it and looked into a room that was originally a nursery, but was now occupied by the General's personal aide, Jonathan, who snored lightly.

The operative took three silent steps across the room to the closed door leading to Washington's bedchamber, then froze in place, a shadow among shadows, as Jonathan stirred in his bed and rolled onto his side. When his breathing became regular again, a quick examination of the inner door revealed, as expected, that there were no hinges on this side, the door being hung to open into the room beyond.

Disappointed but not surprised that the General wanted the privacy of a closed bedroom door, the operative knew it would almost certainly squeal like a piglet when opened. With the hinges inaccessible to the oil pouch tucked in another pocket, there was no chance to deliver the note directly to the General. Reluctantly, the operative pulled the second sealed note from the same pocket as the first and slipped it under the door.

Within a minute's time, the operative crouched in the shadows of the back porch and waited for the sentry to pass before returning to where the horse waited patiently, and where the operative would lie hidden throughout the day.

When General Washington arose and discovered the note on the floor just inside his bedroom's threshold, his first assumption was that Jonathan had slipped it under his door during the night. This assumption turned to astonishment, however, when he flipped it over and saw the wax seal imprinted with the '*Æ*' symbol. It took but a moment for him to grasp the import of the mere presence of the note there in his inner sanctum. The security of his headquarters had been thoroughly compromised and an unknown person—a potential assassin—had stood only feet from him while he slept.

Still, amid the growing anger and humiliation, Washington felt a tingle of excitement, and his rational nature overcame those initial emotions. What better way for them to prove that they do not wish him harm?

The General carried the sealed note to his writing desk and slid one drawer all the way out. Setting it on the floor, he reached his long arm deep into the void and withdrew his copy of the codebook. After ripping open the seal, his astonishment quickly grew as he translated the missive.

> *We hope the information we have*
> *given you, as well as all of our*
> *previous actions, dispose you to trust*
> *us when we tell you our organization*
> *would like to assist your fledgling*
> *rebellion. If you desire the assistance*
> *of our far-reaching and quite capable*

*resources, send the Major alone on
foot at midnight two days hence to the
clearing by the river where your men
are fond of fishing. Tell him to prepare
for a long night's ride and a full day's
meeting, followed by another night's
ride back to your headquarters. Tell
no one else of this summons and burn
this note and its translation
immediately.*

℈

The General's initial reaction was to summon Benjamin to discuss the implications of this offer, but if the Major came rushing to headquarters, rumors would fly through the camp. Better to wait for the Major to attend the morning staff meeting and discuss the matter with him afterwards.

Satisfied that the next day's *tete-a-tete* would remain secret, he took pen to paper and wrote an order to cover Benjamin's absence, sending him on an inspection tour that would take at least the whole of the following day. He then pulled down his copy of Samuel Johnson's *A Dictionary of the English Language* and took from another hidden drawer his secret war diary. The war diary was written using a numerical substitution cipher of his own devising. The cipher used the summed page, entry number, and grammatical form—one for noun, two for verb, and so on—of the word in

Johnson's *Dictionary*. He then added that base number to the sum of the day, month, and year of the diary entry.

After much practice, he had memorized many common words' base values, so he had but to add those values to the sum of the date and his key to encrypt most of the words he used in his diary entries. Enciphering the translated note was trickier, but his quick mind made quick work of the task.

Tossing the original and the deciphered copy into the room's fireplace, Washington waited to be sure it curled and ignited before opening his bedroom door. The squeal of the hinges alerted Jonathan, who had already laid out the General's breakfast in the meeting room next door.

As he sat down to his morning meal and the stack of letters, commissions, and other paperwork he would have to work through that day, he thanked Jonathan, then dug into his normal breakfast of cold venison, hard cider, and a boiled egg.

Chapter 27

Good News

As February became March, preparations among the Revolutionary Army encamped at Valley Forge turned to the upcoming Spring campaign. Major Tallmadge was drilling the squad of cavalry who would become his own corps of dragoons in the open field they rather jokingly called the Grand Parade Grounds. They were practicing a flanking maneuver against the Second Pennsylvania regiment, slogging through the trampled ground, wet from the melting snows of the harshest winter any who suffered through it could remember, when a courier arrived with a summons from General Washington.

Leaving his Sergeant Major in charge, Benjamin set off at a gallop, wondering what news could be so urgent to summon him from the training ground. Perhaps the General had also been contacted again by the mysterious Enclave. The note, found on his nightstand that morning, had simply instructed him to await orders from the General. At the crest of the hill, he turned Anemos west and followed the main road through the encampment, descending toward the Schuylkill River. Washington's headquarters lay on the banks of the slow, shallow waterway.

His heart quickened at the thought of seeing the young farm girl again, and he urged Anemos on even faster. His hope for another encounter with Sarah was dashed though, as he approached the headquarters building and saw the collection of horses tied up outside. This had the look of a hastily called meeting of Washington's full staff and all of their subordinate commanders.

Benjamin swung his leg over and dismounted as Anemos slowed to a walk. Handing the horse off to a waiting groom, he dashed up the flagstone walk, and leaped up the steps to the stone building's wide porch, which he crossed in two long strides.

Washington's personal aide, a young corporal named Jonathan, threw open the front door at Benjamin's approach, and took his doffed hat as he crossed the threshold. Jonathan nodded to the home's parlor off to the right of the front door. At twenty by twenty-five feet, the parlor was the largest room on the first floor of the house that now served as the General's headquarters.

General officers and their subordinates filled the room, milling about. Many of whom nodded to Benjamin as he entered. He sidled along the near wall that separated the parlor from the center hall, listening silently to the whispered rumors. The snatches of murmurs that he picked up told him that no one else seemed to know the purpose of the meeting.

Almost as if his arrival was the cue Washington had been waiting for, the General, and a much shorter man dressed in the pale blue of a French army officer, entered the room through a second door at the far end of the wall against which Benjamin now stood. A hush immediately fell over the assembly.

"Good afternoon, Gentlemen." Washington surveyed his officer corps until he found Benjamin, with whom he locked eyes for a moment before finding and nodding to his more senior general officers. Murmurs of greeting and nodded heads were exchanged in return.

"I bring you some much needed good news today." Somehow, as if by magic, the tension in the room eased. Benjamin himself felt his own body relax, and a weight seemed to be lifted from his shoulders.

"We have known for two weeks that the British are preparing to abandon Philadelphia." Most of the general officers who were privy to that tidbit of information simply nodded, while the more junior officers' faces lit up with surprised smiles. It did not go unnoticed by the politically astute in attendance that Benjamin was one of those who simply nodded.

"But I am also pleased to tell you that regaining our newborn nation's capital is not the only—or the most important—news of the day."

At this, even the general officers' faces registered their surprise. Benjamin, who recalled every word of the notes received from The Enclave's pretty young operative, immediately realized that the General's obvious good mood could only mean one thing, and his face broke into a broad, knowing smile. This, too, caught the attention of those concerned with the pecking order of the officers within the room, and especially by those most concerned with their own advancement.

Washington seemed to be enjoying the suspense his cryptic words had created, and a sly smile tugged at his normally stern features.

"We had previously received intelligence," with this, he looked directly toward Benjamin, and many heads turned to follow his gaze, "that France's King Louis XVI would soon throw his support to our cause." A general stir ran through the gathering. "I am very pleased to tell you that just today we have received confirmation that the unceasing efforts of our dear friend, the Marquis de Lafayette," Washington grasped the shoulder of the Frenchman who stood at his side, and gave it a hearty brotherly shake, "and the tireless work of our emissaries, led by Mr. Franklin," the General reached into a pocket of his coat and withdrew a rolled parchment document which he raised above his head, "has resulted in the signing of a Treaty of Alliance between France and our newborn nation."

Bedlam broke out among the assembled officers as they embraced their neighbors and pounded each other on the back. Soon shouts of "Huzzah!" and "Hurrah!" could be heard even on the road outside. One by one, each of the officers made their way forward and gave hearty handshakes to Washington and Lafayette.

The General let the celebration go on for a few minutes before raising his hands and calling for their attention.

"Gentlemen, please! This is truly a momentous occasion, and could well save our noble cause, but only if we take the utmost advantage of our French cousins' support. We must redouble our efforts to prepare our men for the upcoming campaign." Again, heads nodded throughout the room, as the mood became more subdued. "All junior officers, go and spread the morale-boosting news among your charges, but do not let their emotions get the better of them. We still need to maintain our good discipline. Would my general officers and immediate staff please remain?"

Major Tallmadge, along with the other junior officers, shuffled toward the hallway until Washington's voice boomed over the noise of boots on the plank flooring and the clamor of excited voices. "Major Tallmadge, I asked my immediate staff to remain."

Confused, Benjamin stopped in the doorway and looked back over his shoulder, causing a logjam of bodies. The smiled on the faces of the others confused him even further until one of his friends, a Major Smith, who was ten years his senior, poked him in the ribs and said with a smile, "Get back there where you belong, you young fool!"

Recognition and embarrassment dawned on Benjamin's face as Jonathan pulled him through the doorway and led him down the hall to the doorway at the other end.

The planning session lasted well into the evening. A supper of cold meats and cheeses had stilled some grumbling stomachs and Washington's leadership had kept the normally headstrong commanders working together. By the time they needed candles to light the room, the beginnings of a plan had emerged. When the weary officers at last left for their own quarters, each had an action plan to refine and prepare for.

A gentle hand on his arm, placed there by General Washington, told Benjamin to stay behind as the others filed out. During the meeting, the General had made Benjamin's position official by naming him assistant to General Charles Scott, whom he also named as his Chief of Intelligence.

When they stood alone in the room, Washington gathered up the maps and papers strewn across the room's worktable. He looked sidelong at Benjamin.

"Tell me what you think of your new assignment."

Benjamin collected his thoughts for a moment. "I appreciate the confidence you have expressed in me, General." He hesitated, reluctant to said more.

Washington expected his reticence, so was ready with the next prod. "But you wonder why I made General Scott, and not you, Chief of Intelligence?"

"No, Sir. I am certainly not senior enough for the position. An assignment of such importance deserves the attention of a general officer."

Washington was uncharacteristically frank. "Pshaw! We both know what your objection is." He looked expectantly at Benjamin, who remained silent. "Go ahead. Say what is on your mind."

Ordered to express his opinion, Benjamin had no choice. "Well, General, I am not convinced that General Scott is the, ah, wisest choice."

A playful smile tugged at Washington's lips. "Yes, General Scott's has expressed his views on the use of spies very publicly. He hates the very notion of sneaking about stealing secrets from the enemy. I have myself heard him say it is 'ungentlemanly' and 'beneath the dignity of an officer'."

"He has made such statements to me directly, also."

"Which is why you will report directly to me any information of import that *your efforts* generate. File regular, innocuous reports through General Scott, but funnel all interesting information to me."

With raised eyebrows, Benjamin nodded as understanding dawned. "So, General Scott is, ah, my *beard*?"

Washington threw his head back and laughed uproariously. "Yes! Oh, that is rich. The stiffly formal General Scott as your *beard*."

Both men let loose peals of laughter. When they caught their breath, Washington continued, "When the British learn, as they assuredly will, that General Scott is my official Spy Master, they will believe that they can operate with little threat of disclosure. This may well loosen their discipline, which will make the job of *your* spy network easier."

Benjamin's face clouded. "But, when The Enclave learns, *as they assuredly will*, of General Scott's appointment, they may not believe in your commitment to gathering intelligence."

Washington smiled a knowing smile. "I suspect that when they learn, *as they assuredly will*, that you are General Scott's assistant, they will see the ruse for what it is. Remember, Ben, that unlike the British, they have already come to know of your abilities and commitment. I have no doubt that if they are serious about helping our cause, they will welcome with this turn of events."

Benjamin nodded his assent to Washington's plan, but his innate humility prevented him from full acceptance, at least until he could prove to himself that he deserved the tremendous responsibility the General, who was the wisest man he had ever met and whom he thought of as a second father, had just placed firmly on his shoulders. That weight which had lifted from his shoulders earlier in the day now came crashing back tenfold.

"I have your first assignment in your new role, Major," Washington said. He then related the contents of the summoning note.

Chapter 28

Rendezvous

Major Benjamin Tallmadge crouched just behind the tree line along the edge of the riverside clearing. Creeping with the utmost care, it had taken him most of an hour to cover the half mile or so from his quarters to this hiding place among the trees and ferns. He came early, hoping to learn something of this mysterious Enclave by observing whomever he was meeting as they approached. Convinced he had left no sign or sound of his passage, he lay in wait in the bushes.

When the cold nose of a horse touched the back of his neck, however, he let out a short yelp of surprise and stumbled forward into the clearing. Spinning around, he stared slack-jawed at a horse and its rider, dressed all in black and wearing a black mask and cowl. The horse and rider slowly walked out of the woods. Behind them trailed a second saddled mount.

The skill it had taken for two horses and a mounted rider to approach within arm's length of him completely undetected amazed him. When he had recovered his wits and began to speak, whether to ask a question or to declare his admiration, the rider raised a gloved hand, palm facing him.

The message was clear—there would be no conversation this night. Instead, the rider drew the spare horse forward, which Benjamin swiftly mounted.

The operative then tossed him a black hood, still holding his horse's lead line. The Major looked at the hood in his hands, then up at the silent rider waiting stock still. With a shrug, he pulled the hood over his head and leaned forward, resting his head on the horse's withers as they started off at a quick walk.

He estimated they had ridden for perhaps a half-hour when his horse pulled up short. He had tried to track their twists and turns while blindfolded, but had quickly lost his bearings. The ride was slow, but Benjamin kept his head down to avoid low-hanging branches.

With his horse stopped, he raised up and sat tall in the saddle, stretching his back, when his hood was yanked off.

They stood in a clearing, but the height of the surrounding trees prevented most of the ambient starlight from illuminating the scene. His escort tucked the hood into a belt, turned the horse, and rode off down a game trail at a near-gallop. Benjamin kicked his heels into the horse's flanks and followed into the blackness.

Hours later, as the Eastern horizon was brightening with the coming dawn, the riders emerged into another clearing. This time, though, they were not alone. Three more black-clad riders awaited their arrival. Without a word, two outriders flanked Benjamin, and another brought up the rear as they all proceeded at a walk along a much wider path.

The path widened into a road and the riders kicked their horses up to a trot as the road curved out of the woods and along an open field ready to be planted with corn. The next field was freshly tilled and Benjamin could smell the earthy richness of the soil as they trotted past. Soon, though, those pleasant smells gave way to the scent of manure spread on the third field they passed. Rather than being unpleasant, though, Benjamin smelled the richness of it, noting the health of the cows in the quality of their shit.

By the time they trotted past the pasture with at least fifty head of cattle, some milk cows and some beefy Herefords, Benjamin realized he was being given the grand tour in order to impress him. And it certainly did.

He wondered how big this Enclave was, and what they would show off next.

They answered his unspoken questions when the group rode into The Enclave's village. To Benjamin's eyes, the stone buildings looked old. Older than any other buildings he had ever seen. Old, but well maintained. Most were constructed of hewn fieldstones, though some were of an older timber and stucco style reminiscent of illustrations he had seen in collections of Shakespeare's plays.

There was already evidence of activity, despite the early hour. Benjamin smelled baking bread, which caused his stomach to emit a loud rumble. He looked to his escorts in embarrassment, but none gave any indication that they had heard. Instead, they rode silently down the main street of the town.

The shopkeepers and tradespeople who were out and about barely noticed their passing, as if a collection of horsemen dressed in black from head to toe, surrounding an officer of the Continental Army passed through their streets every day.

Or, they have learned to studiously ignore such processions, he thought.

As if to confirm this thought, a young girl of about six and her older sister emerged from the side yard of a house carrying empty water buckets. The youngster stopped short, gaping at the impromptu parade, but her sister, without even a glance at Benjamin, turned the girl's head to avert her gaze and led her by the hand toward the town well.

As the morning brightened, Benjamin and his escorts followed the street to where it ended at the front garden of the largest building he had yet seen in the village. The three story cut stone structure was as wide as the Pennsylvania State House in Philadelphia, where the colonies had declared their independence, and like that building a bell tower topped it with a large clock face. Several windows on the first and second floors glowed with candles and firelight.

At the garden gate in front of that obviously the most important building in the village, the operative who had met him at Valley Forge dismounted and signaled him to do the same. Without a word, his escort offered something in their palm to their horse—an oddly familiar gesture to Benjamin—after which the other escorts led their horses down a side street to the stables.

Still without speaking, his escort led him through the garden gate, up the half-story steps to the large oaken double doors. There a liveried doorman cum butler met them and, with a nod to the operative, led Benjamin into the dark interior. When the door clicked shut behind him, Benjamin looked over his shoulder and saw that his companion since midnight had not entered.

With a shrug, he followed his new, but also silent, escort down a central hall paneled in oak. Benjamin took mental notes of everything he saw, even the richly woven, no—embroidered—tapestries that hung above the wainscoting.

After passing several closed doors on each side, the butler led him into a large meeting room. A newly laid fire burned in the hearth at the far end, giving off a warmth that was quite welcome to Benjamin after the night's journey. A long table occupied the center of the room, with ten arch-backed chairs arrayed on each side and matching armchairs at either end.

The room was also wide enough to accommodate similar chairs lining the walls. Two windows flanked the fireplace, and two doors were set in the side walls three-quarters of the way down the room.

To his surprise, Benjamin saw that before the farthest seat on the left side of the table, a full breakfast of steaming eggs, sausage, and biscuits with gravy lay steaming on a fine china plate. The butler walked the length of the table and pulled back the chair in front of the meal, clearly inviting Benjamin to sit and eat. The luscious smells of the breakfast laid out on the table elicited another protest from his empty stomach. With another shrug, he took his seat. But when he turned to offer his thanks, the butler was nowhere to be found.

Although astounded by everything he had seen, his empty stomach wouldn't let him ignore the spread before him. It smelled absolutely delicious, so tucking the linen napkin into his collar and lifting the heavy silver knife and fork, Benjamin enjoyed the best meal he'd had in months. When the plate was clean, he leaned back and sipped hard cider from a silver goblet.

The mystery of the vanishing butler was solved when he felt a push of air as the door behind him swung silently open. He could hear the clatter of dishes and kitchen activity through the open door.

The butler stepped forward to retrieve his plate and silverware and finally spoke. "Master Abraham will be with you shortly."

Again, before Benjamin could thank him or ask anything, he disappeared into the kitchen and the door swung shut.

Benjamin didn't have to wait long until the door in the wall opposite from where he sat opened and three people strode into the room. First was his mysterious escort of the night before, still hooded and dressed in the tight-fitting suit of black clothes. The fabric of those clothes was dull and seemed to absorb the flickering firelight. The operative circled the table and took up a position directly behind him.

Next through the door came a large man who gave Benjamin the distinct impression that he was not one to be messed with. He stood behind the chair directly across the table from where Benjamin, who had risen at their appearance, stood.

The last person through the door was a small, very young-looking man. He walked to the head of the table to Benjamin's left and offered his hand in greeting.

"Welcome, Major Tallmadge. My name is Abraham, and I am the author of the notes you have been receiving of late."

Several things about the man struck Benjamin. First was his age. He didn't appear to be over twenty years old. Second was his stature, which seemed to be that of an adolescent not yet grown into maturity. Third, but most impressive and apparent with but a moment's study, was the unmistakable air of command and leadership that he possessed.

"Let me introduce Mr. Jonathan Pierce, who is responsible for keeping our small community here safe and secure."

The man across the table simply nodded without offering his hand.

"Please take your seat. We have much to discuss."

Before doing so, though, in order to break the spell of total control he seemed to be under, Benjamin turned to the operative standing behind him.

"And this fine fellow who has been my silent companion these last several hours?"

Abraham, who had already sat down, smiled. "Our operatives live normal lives like everyone else here in The Enclave, but when called to duty, they use their extensive training to remain silent, invisible, and anonymous." He nodded to Benjamin's chair. "Please."

The strangeness of the encounter was getting more and more confusing. But Benjamin knew there were powerful forces at work, and that he had best be very cautious.

The weight of responsibility felt heavy on his shoulders. He was somewhere out in the wilderness as the sole representative of his fledgling nation and completely at the mercy of this mysterious, yet well-organized group. The thought alarmed him, but he did his best to keep his face neutral.

"Major, I am sure this entire episode, from the first note you received in your quarters at Valley Forge, until this moment, has been very confusing." Benjamin simply nodded as Abraham continued. "You must be wondering whom could this strange group of people who call themselves an Enclave be, and why are they offering to help your nascent revolution? To put your mind at ease, allow me to relate a brief history of our group.

"This village is the most remote outpost of an organization, which we call The Enclave. Our order has operated for many centuries across the continent of Europe and beyond with a mission to learn and hold dear the world's secrets. Those secrets could be the mundane and tedious— certain politicians' unusual sexual proclivities, for example. Or they could be historically profound. We believe that you and I, and all the inhabitants of this vast, unexplored continent, are on the cusp of a turning point in history.

"Frankly, in our collective memory of centuries of intrigues and power struggles, we have never seen a time when the rich and powerful, alongside the common folk, have united in one goal—freedom. Our group applauds your efforts and would like to offer our help and support for your cause."

Benjamin, whose heart rate had steadily raced during this speech, smiled broadly. "From the information you have provided us and the skills you have demonstrated so far, it is clear to General Washington and myself that your aid would be a great asset to us." He paused, almost hesitant to said what was necessary. "On behalf of General Washington, I thank you wholeheartedly for your offer. I must ask, however, what you stand to gain in return?"

He spread his arms to include the whole of the village. "You sit out here in the wilderness isolated from whichever power ends up ruling this land. And," he nodded to both the man across the table and the operative at his back, "you certainly seem able to take care of yourselves. So, I fear I have nothing of value to offer you in return."

Abraham glanced at the man named Pierce on his left, who spoke for the first time. "The very existence of our group has remained a closely guarded secret—a secret that we maintain with the utmost care."

Pierce's eyes bore into Benjamin's. The message and the implied threat were crystal clear. This meeting and everything that he learned there must remain secret. Benjamin felt a bit like a priest hearing confession.

When Pierce saw the recognition of this fact in Benjamin's eyes, he continued. "There have been times in our history when our existence has become known to those in power. Those episodes have invariably ended in loss of life—on both sides—not to mention the disruption to our organization and its members. We want to avoid similar situations in the future."

"I am afraid I don't understand what you are driving at."

Abraham answered in a hushed voice, "We believe that, with our help, General Washington and the collection of wise and erudite men in your Continental Congress will establish on this continent a new *kind* of nation. Not a monarchy with its rigid class structure, but rather an egalitarian society based on the freedom of the individual men and women who hold in their hands the power to make for themselves and their families the best life they can. In such a society, we believe The Enclave will remain a safe place for us to live and do our work."

"But surely your isolation so far from civilization will keep you well protected."

Abraham smiled as if teaching a lesson to a small child. "My dear Major, your provincial thinking is endearing, but wrong. This land, so full of resources and so empty of people, will fuel expansion and the growth of your thirteen colonies until the entire continent, regardless of its vast extent, will overflow with farms and cities." His voice dropped to barely a whisper. "And it will completely encircle this Enclave of but ten thousand acres."

Ten thousand acres! The Enclave's size amazed him. Nevertheless, Benjamin had nothing to offer.

"I am still at a loss as to what I, a poor Major, could possibly do to help you."

Abraham chuckled. "Ah, Benjamin. You, of all people, have the ear and confidence of your great General. What we wish, nay what we need, is his guarantee that after he accepts the mantle of leadership of your new nation—whatever form that leadership takes—he will ensure our sovereignty and safety for generations and centuries to come."

Taken aback at the enormity and audaciousness of their demand, Benjamin sputtered "But, but—"

Abraham held up a calming hand and smiled. "I know what I say seems ridiculous to you now. But when this war is won and your Congress decides what form of government will rule over this land, it will be obvious who should lead it. General Washington will then have the power to grant us this land in perpetuity." He nodded toward Pierce. "We have drawn up just such a document that you will convey back to Valley Forge this evening. If you can convince your mentor to sign and seal it, leave it where our Operative met you last night." Abraham's smile faded, and his voice became deadly serious. "We believe in, and are putting our faith in, General Washington's absolute integrity. If he signs it, we believe it will be so."

Abraham's speech gave Benjamin a chance to gather his thoughts.

"Assuming what you believe actually comes to pass, and the General becomes our national leader, how do you know he will have the power to create a separate nation within our borders?"

"If he agrees to do so now, I have the utmost confidence that he will do so then."

Benjamin nodded in turn. He also had a total belief in George Washington's integrity.

"So, how do you propose to help us?"

Abraham smiled at Benjamin's tacit agreement. "Oh, we have quite a plan for that!"

The return trip was a reverse of the first. Benjamin followed the still-silent operative for several hours before they stopped and they again hooded him for the last leg of their journey. After a winding ride hunched over his horse's mane, they stopped where he could hear the rushing of the river. He straightened, expecting to feel a tug on the hood covering his head. Before it was pulled off, though, he felt warm breath on his ear and heard a faint female voice whisper, "A pleasure riding with you again, Sir. Say hello to Anemos for me."

As recognition and astonishment dawned on Benjamin, Operative Sarah, no longer anonymous, ripped the hood from his head and galloped into the dark woods.

PART VIII

Amy
Early Autumn, Present Day

The child, Amy Lori Sullivan, continues to exhibit unruly and self-destructive behavior. Her antisocial behaviors and abrasive comments have led to her being ostracized, teased, and borderline bullying by her age peers. Similarly, her teachers report that she is often disruptive in class, often showing off her grasp of the material and belittling other students who may be progressing at a slower rate. This has led to frequent and increasingly harsh punishments by the school's faculty and administration.

Most telling are the child's frequent night terrors that disrupt not only her sleep, but that of her hard-working foster parents. Mild, age-appropriate sleep aids have been prescribed, although there is some evidence that the child pretends to swallow the medication, without actually doing so.

All indications are that this child suffers from Post Traumatic Stress Disorder, due to the violent death of her parents by automobile accident that also severely injured the subject. Although the child claims to have no recollection of the accident, nor of the substance of her night terrors, subconscious scarring is the most likely explanation for her behaviors.

— Psychological Assessment of Amy Lori Sullivan,
Samuel Stevens, PsyD, LCP

186

Chapter 29

Bonding

Amy sat on the floor of the small apartment, drawing in a notebook while Liz paged through a travel magazine. A documentary about the Civil War played on a television in the background. Amy had been very distant ever since leaving the Warners and Liz tried to make her feel comfortable and safe, but despite her age, she had very little experience with children. To her, most children were a tangled mess of illogic and emotions. By contrast, Amy's reticence was soothing, but also somehow disconcerting. So, after Liz's attempts at conversation had resulted in one-word, noncommittal answers, she gave up and let things settle into side-by-side solitude.

Meanwhile, the television droned on. Periodically, Liz would mumble, "They got that wrong." Or, "That's not what happened."

Finally, after several comments like that, Amy turned to Liz. "How do you know so much about the Civil War?" There was a faint hint of accusation in her tone.

Liz pointed to a stack of books on an end table. "I read a lot."

"About what?"

Liz put down the magazine. "Just about anything and everything. Science, math, biographies, but especially history. I love history."

Amy turned around, her drawing forgotten. "What's so interesting about history?"

Liz smiled. "History is the story of us. It's the story of every person, everywhere."

Amy's voice was barely above a whisper. "Even mine?"

Liz's breath caught in her throat. She slid down onto the floor next to Amy.

"Yes, Little One. Yours, too. But yours is just getting started. I have a feeling your story will be a long one with lots of adventures."

Amy smiled for the first time since moving in. She turned back to her drawing and said, "Like yours."

Liz gave her a long look as she continued drawing. Finally, she said, "What makes you say that?"

Amy shrugged, but didn't look up from her notebook. "You just seem…old." Liz laughed lightly and Amy continued. "I mean old*er*. Older than you look. The way you argued with Mrs. Warner, and with Mr. John. And how you *know* things."

She finally looked up and met Liz's eyes. Liz tried to keep her face a neutral mask while she tried to decide how far to let this conversation go. Her first inclination, borne of two centuries of subterfuge, was to quickly change the subject. But something told her to let Amy's inquisitive mind have free rein. So, she simply raised a questioning eyebrow.

Thus prompted, Amy asked, "Are you a witch?"

The question set Liz laughing, but when she saw the scowl on Amy's face, she asked, "Why would you think I'm a witch?"

"Mrs. Warner...she said 'Black Magic'..."

Recovering from her outburst, Liz frowned. "Unfortunately, people fear things they don't understand. And, some people like Mrs. Warner, see evil forces lurking behind everything that their limited education never taught them."

Amy frowned in response. "You mean she's ignorant of facts about you, so she acted...ignorantly toward you."

"You could say that, but I think it goes deeper. This place is so isolated from the outside—the *real*—world that people who've lived her their whole lives are...unsophisticated."

"You mean they're *ignorant*." Amy smiled mischievously.

Liz laughed again when she realized how she had been manipulated by Amy's wordplay. "Well played."

"What is it about you, and 'others like you' that Mrs. Warner is afraid of?"

Liz looked deep into Amy's innocent eyes. This was the crux of the conversation that she would normally avoid at all costs. But given what the girl had been through, she deserved more than a casual brush-off.

"I spend a lot of time away from The Enclave," she began. "And no one other than John, and Father Dan, I guess, knows where I go or what I do when I'm gone. Mrs. Warner is old enough to have seen me come and go more than once."

Amy leaned back and studied Liz's face. "And you never get—no, you never *look*—older."

Liz kept her face neutral. "There are a lot of treatments to keep women looking younger than they actually are."

Her explanation rang hollow to her own ears, but Amy nodded slowly, either accepting the excuse, or allowing to let the half-truth stand.

Deciding it was time to change the subject, Liz asked, "What are you drawing?"

When Amy turned her notebook, Liz's mouth fell open. Filling the page were sketches of Liz, each one a perfect likeness. Her eyes widened in wonder when she realized the sketches showed her with different hairstyles and clothing from different historical periods and could very well have been exactly as she had worn them.

"OK, how many windows are in the office building behind us?" Liz and Amy sat on a bench in the central square of The Enclave's village, enjoying their lunch. The "office building" Liz referred to was an eighteenth century tavern whose upper two floors had been converted to administrative offices a hundred years before.

Amy squeezed her eyes shut and scrunched up her face as she pictured the building she had walked past a thousand times.

"Six single windows on the third floor, four double windows on the second and a...I don't know what you call the one that bulges out of the front of the tavern."

Liz nodded. "Good. That's called a 'bay window'. But you forgot one."

Amy shook her head vigorously. "No, I didn't."

"What about the one in the door? Hmm?"

"But that one doesn't count anymore—"

"Yes, it does. Someone could be watching us right now through it."

Amy shook her head more slowly and a small smile crept across her face. "Actually, they can't," she said smugly, and it was Liz's turn to look confused as Amy continued, "Last Halloween, I snuck out and soaped the whole thing, and Mr. O'Reilly has never cleaned it off."

Liz chuckled and looked over her shoulder. Sure enough, the setting sun reflected pure white where she expected to see dark windowpanes.

"So you sneak out at night?"

Her tone was gentle, but Amy gasped as she realized she had revealed one of her closely held secrets. She dropped her head and hunched her shoulders, expecting a tongue lashing—at least.

"I'm sorry, Ma'am. I've only done it a couple of times, and never since I moved in with you."

She peaked out from under her bangs to see Liz smiled at her.

"And I hope you never have to sneak out on me. But if you feel like roaming around the village in the middle of the night, check with me first." Amy looked at her sideways with a raised eyebrow. "I might want to go with you."

They both laughed out loud. "You would do that? Have you done that before?"

"Oh, you have no idea. Someday I'll tell you a funny story." Amy looked at her expectantly, but Liz shook her head and continued, "That's a story for when you are older—much older."

Rather than being disappointed, a hopeful look flashed across Amy's features. Liz's offhand comment gave Amy hope they would still be together when she was much older. From the faraway look in Liz's eyes, she suspected her older guardian might feel the same way. At least, she hoped she did.

Chapter 30

Bareback Mountain

Y ou really grew up here?"

"I really did."

There was a hint of fall in the air as Amy walked alongside Liz on the hiking trail. She kept her head down, eyes fixed on the trail, intent on keeping her new boots out of the mud. Buying them had been an excursion out of The Enclave to the giant mall in King of Prussia. Amy listened intently as Liz explained that the thick woolen socks they also bought would keep her feet warm even if they got wet. Liz laughed when Amy swore she would never even let the boots get smudged, let alone wet. As Liz's first gift to her, she hugged the box to her chest all the way home.

As they rounded a large puddle on the trail, Liz nudged her with her hip, knocking her off balance. Amy's right foot flew out to catch herself, and landed right in the middle of the puddle, splashing mud all over her boot.

Aghast, Amy looked up at Liz with tears in her eyes. "I...I'm sorry."

The tears disappeared when Liz smiled and chuckled. "Amy, they're hiking boots, not dancing shoes." She lifted her own right foot, clad in well-worn and mud-stained leather. "We water-proofed them before we left, and we'll clean them up when we get back. OK?"

"OK," said, relieved.

"Good. Now, let's put them to good use." With that, she ducked under low-hanging branches and set out off-trail.

Within a few yards, Liz turned onto a game trail that switched back and forth as it climbed toward the ridgeline that ran atop a string of hills bisecting The Enclave's land. Amy was wide-eyed as Liz pointed out the animal sign that they encountered. There were deer tracks and scat. Also buck rubs—bare spots on tree trunks where male deer rubbed the velvet off their antlers. Further along, they found smaller tracks made by a fox alongside the splayed tracks of a bird, probably a grouse, that it was hunting. The prize, though, was a set of large footprints made by a mountain lion on the prowl.

When they finally reached the top of the hill, Liz turned south and led Amy through the woods to a rocky clearing about a hundred yards wide. Running down each side of the ridge were meadows which, Liz knew, were a riot of colorful wildflowers in the Spring. In the early autumn, though, it was the blaze of red, gold, and orange foliage that gave the place its color.

"I used to call this place 'Bareback Mountain'." Liz's voice was hushed and almost reverent. She reached down and took Amy's hand. "Follow me, but be careful on the rocks."

She led Amy over the field of boulders for about twenty yards, then gingerly started down the far side of the hill. Just under the crest, a shelf of rock protruded out from the hillside, forming an overhanging shelter about ten feet deep. As Liz lowered herself to her knees to look inside, Amy dropped into a crouch and walked right in. She turned from the back of the space as Liz crawled in as well.

"How did you know about this place?"

"I used to come here when I was your age. This was my secret place."

Liz sat down next to Amy, who snuggled close and whispered, "Now it's our secret place."

Wrapping Amy in her arms, Liz let her silent tears dampen the girl's unruly mop of hair.

The hike to the secret cave wasn't Liz and Amy's only clandestine excursion. They had a mutual fondness for sneaking about the village late at night. For Amy, it was a thrilling way to act out against the constraints of being a foster child. For Liz, it was a way to relive the short period of her life when she wasn't bound to John and The Enclave.

Liz made sure she limited their midnight raids to childish pranks, like imitating racoons by dumping trash cans, or soaping windows at Halloween. The secrets they shared formed a strong bond between ancestor and child. But they also encouraged Amy's deep-seated, hidden desires for payback.

Chapter 31

Revelation

God, she's a handful, Liz thought with a little internal smile.

They moved out of the one-room efficiency Liz was assigned when she arrived into a more spacious two-bedroom apartment. The move sparked a change in Amy. Out of the oppressive environment at the Warners, she was immediately thrown into close quarters with Liz. Neither situation made her feel at home. But their new digs, including a bedroom that she wasn't filling instead of one of the Warners' fleeing children, felt like a fresh start for both of them. It only took a day or two for Amy to come out of her shell. After a week, the two were inseparable.

One evening, as Liz was finishing the dishes—the bandages were off her hands after her leap over the chain-link fence, but she still felt the healing itch—she watched Amy writing at the kitchen table.

Liz had taken over Amy's education too, insisted that she shouldn't have to go back to that "viper pit" of a school. She was still discovering the young girl's abilities, continually impressed by her innate intelligence.

"Amy, these dishes need to be put away."

Without a word of complaint, or a roll of her eyes, Amy dragged her chair over to the counter. For an eleven-year-old, she was relatively small, so she had to stand on the chair to reach the upper cabinets. As Liz dried the two plates and two glasses, she handed them to Amy, who carefully placed them in the empty spaces on the cabinet shelves.

After she returned to the kitchen table, Amy said, barely above a whisper, "What does 'resurrect' mean?" She sat very still, looking down at the school workbook.

Liz snapped her head around but tried to keep her voice neutral. "Where did you hear that word?"

Amy just shrugged.

"I guess I have to tell John to upgrade the soundproofing of his office," Liz said sarcastically.

Amy just shrugged again, so Liz hung up the dish towel and sat down next to the girl.

"Well, it means to repair something that is broken."

She paused, looking for a reaction. Amy looked at her expectantly. Liz plunged ahead.

"It also means to bring someone who has died back to life."

Amy dropped her eyes and looked thoughtfully down at the table. "Did I die?"

Liz sighed, not knowing how to have this conversation with someone so young.

"When your parents…died, you were hurt in the accident very badly. It took a long time for you to recover."

Amy stood up and pulled her shirt off over her head.

"What are these round marks on my chest? And the matching ones on my back?"

Her tone was challenging, and Liz guessed that Amy already knew the answer when she continued. "I'm remembering things…in my dreams." She swallowed a lump in her throat, but she was determined to find out the truth. "There wasn't a car accident, was there?"

Looking Amy straight in the eye, Liz shook her head. "Your parents didn't die in a car accident. They were killed by some very bad men. Men that they were trying to stop from doing their bad things. When those bad men shot your Mom and Dad, they shot you, too."

Holding her gaze, Amy asked evenly, "Then why didn't I die, too?"

Liz swallowed hard. "The last thing your parents did before they died was…save you." Amy absorbed this silently, so Liz took Amy's hand in hers. "Your parents, your Mom and Dad, were heroes, Amy. Never forget that, and never, ever let anyone tell you otherwise."

Amy dropped her gaze and she let her tears flow. "I really miss them."

The pain in the girl's voice was too much for Liz. She knelt next to the chair and gathered the sobbing girl into her arms.

"I know you do, Honey. But they want you to be happy. I know that."

When her sobs subsided, Amy mumbled into Liz's chest, "You're like them, aren't you? You fight bad people, too?"

"Sometimes." Liz kissed the top of the girl's head. "That's our secret mission."

After a moment while she absorbed that revelation, Amy asked, "You're not going to leave me, too, are you?"

Unable to answer, Liz just squeezed her even more tightly.

PART IX

Sarah
Summer 1779

— *Culper Ring Codebook*

Chapter 32

The Mission

I told ya, Miss Sarah, to let me take care of that."

The middle-aged maid took the dress from Sarah's hands and hung it in the ornately carved armoire. Annie's sliver-flecked black hair was pulled back into a bun at the base of her skull. Her dark skin shone with a sheen of sweat.

"Oh Annie, I'm not used to having someone do everything for me."

Annie's tone hardened. "Well, you had better get used to it, Missy. You're a lady now. The lady of this fine house. The wife of a very successful merchant, not the daughter of a backcountry sharecropper, no more."

Sarah nodded, slightly chagrined. They cut her finishing school lessons short because of the rebels' pressing need for intelligence into British plans for the war. Instead of completing her training, Sarah traveled to South Carolina to meet her 'husband', Charles Webster. Together, they sailed north with their 'maid' Annie to New York under the protection of a British Navy convoy. Rather than trying to pass Sarah off as a sophisticated Southern lady with all the habits of someone born to privilege, her cover story was changed.

Her persona for this operation was that of a Southern country girl—not a stretch other than the accent—who was married off by her widowed father to Charles, a wealthy man more than twice her age. Her father needed a new draft horse and, with two other daughters at home, it seemed to him a good deal.

The notion that she, or any woman, could be married off in exchange for a *horse* infuriated her, but Sarah vowed to use that as motivation in her new role. Charles and Annie were, of course, members of The Enclave themselves and veterans of several operations.

"Why don' you make sure the workmen put the furniture where you want it, Ma'am," Annie suggested.

"And get out of your hair, right?" Sarah smiled, and Annie chuckled.

"You're payin' those men a pretty penny, Ma'am. You should make sure they' doin' their job right."

"Of course." With that, Sarah left the large bedroom that she would share with Charles, crossed the wide hallway, and descended the winding staircase. The crew of five large men were carrying the dining room furniture through the double front doors.

"Put the sideboard against the inside wall, there. Make sure you center the table and arrange the chairs five to each side. The armed chairs go on the ends."

Her instructions really weren't necessary, and two of the workmen exchanged a glance. Other than her young age and her Southern drawl, this job was no different from dozens they had done before. The influx of Loyalists to British-held New York was becoming a flood.

Unlike the way the British treated suspected rebels within New York—confiscating their property and even throwing them in prison without a trial—Loyalists in the rebel-held areas were generally tolerated and treated kindly. Still, those who were loyal to the English crown felt much safer within the bosom of the British army.

Charles, a smart businessman and merchant, saw an opportunity to provide tobacco, leather goods, hams, and salted pork, along with all manner of other consumables to the encamped army and anchored navy. At least that was their cover story. The Enclave's large landholdings in Virginia and the Carolinas provided the materials and capital for this ruse.

While Sarah and Annie oversaw the unloading of their household goods, Charles was off somewhere, obtaining proper storage space for his ship's cargo.

"Be careful with that box! It has our china in it."

With a grunt, the foreman set the crate down gently next to the breakfront standing in the corner of the expansive dining room.

"Beggin' you pardon, Ma'am," he said as he straightened up. Sarah faced him but remained silent, so he continued, "I imagine you'll be needin' staff to run this place." He paused but seeing no reaction, pressed on, "My wife and sister used to cook and clean for the, ah, *rebels* who owned it last." Sarah's raised eyebrow was her only reaction. "I was thinkin' maybe they could come by to present their *bona fides*?"

It took a moment for Sarah to realize that her new position came with responsibilities that she had no idea how to handle. Feeling overwhelmed, but feigning confidence, she replied, "Yes, of course. Have them come by tomorrow and speak with my maid, Annie."

The man's head jerked in surprise. "The *niggra*, Ma'am?"

One thing Sarah had not gotten used to, nor indeed felt at all comfortable with, during her brief stay in the South, was the treatment of slaves. The very notion of one person owning another was so foreign to her upbringing at The Enclave that she bristled internally at the man's words. But she kept her external demeanor neutral.

Raising her chin, she spoke haughtily, "Annie will handle the day-to-day management of the household. Your wife and sister must speak with her, and if she thinks them suitable, I will be happy to hire them—on a provisional basis, of course."

Confused, the man nodded. "Of course, Ma'am. Very good, Ma'am."

As he went back to the task at hand, Sarah resolved to fight the urge to defer to Annie—at least in public— despite the black woman's greater experience.

Sitting at her writing desk, Sarah withdrew the codebook from the hidden compartment in the back of the top drawer. The four responses to the shopping lists she had carefully prepared lay on the desk, ready to be opened. The lists of items her new home needed all contained the number *355* somewhere among the many items listed.

355 ounces of salt from Reginald Stevenson's spice shop. A summary line showing a total of 355 items of linens from Ian Stewart's shop. A similar total number of ribbons, bows, and yards of fabric from Miss Sally's millinery. And finally, 355 party invitations from James Rivington's print shop.

The number 355 was the entry corresponding to the word "Lady" in the codebook she had slipped into Major Tallmadge's pocket. At Major Tallmadge's insistence, and to preserve the greatest secrecy, she had only been told that her contact among the mostly ineffective spy ring he had already assembled in New York was a shopkeeper. Likewise, Major Tallmadge told that shopkeeper to expect contact from a well-placed "Lady" who would identify herself via the corresponding entry in the codebook they now shared. These four shops were the last ones on her list. If none of them were her secret contact, she would have to think of a new ruse to make contact.

Always eager to gain a new client, the responses from the various shops had come swiftly after Annie delivered the lists. Three were innocuous replies thanking her for her business and providing the cost and timetable for delivery. The fourth, however, was much more intriguing.

My Lady, Mrs. Webster,

    It pleased me to receive your order for 355 invitations to your housewarming party. As you provided no date for the affair in your note, I will leave a space for you to write in the date at a future time.

> *The cost of your order, My Lady, is 1
> pound, 9 shillings and 7 pence.*
> *Finally, My Lady, I host a coffeehouse
> at my shop on each Tuesday and Thursday.
> You and your husband, Mr. Webster, are quite
> welcome to join the festivities. It would be a
> good way to meet those loyal to The Crown in
> an informal setting.*

> *Regards,*
> *J. Rivington*

Sarah was pleased with the invitation to the coffeehouse. She knew, through the gossip network that Annie had already established, that members of the British officer corps were frequent attendees. But she was disappointed that she would have to concoct more shopping lists. Still, something about Mr. Rivington's note nagged at her. He used the word 'Lady' no less than three times in the brief note, but there was no reference to her code number other than reiterating her ordered. The only other numbers were the price quotation, which seemed quite exorbitant to her. Still, he mentioned getting to know "those loyal to The Crown." That would certainly include British officers.

Getting ready to write another note to cancel the order because of the steep price, Sarah paused, still puzzled. There were twenty pence per shilling and twelve shillings to the pound. Her quick mind did the arithmetic. One pound, nine shillings, and seven pence added up to exactly 355 pence.

Smiling, Sarah composed a note accepting his terms and promising to attend the coffeehouse at their earliest convenience.

Chapter 33

The Culper Ring

With the staff dismissed for the night, Sarah, Charles, and Annie sat alone in the house's upstairs study. Despite the mid-summer heat and humidity, the windows throughout the house were closed and latched. The three sat sipping their glasses of hard cider poured from a pitcher that Annie brought up from the cool depths of the cellar. As the stoneware pitcher sweated in the heat, droplets ran down its sides to collect on a lace doily.

The fine oak paneling reflected the light of the single candle off its highly polished surface. The three sat in the corner farthest from the room's lone window, out of sight of any neighbors who might be suspicious of Annie's familiarity with Sarah and Charles.

"So, you've found your contact. That was a clever approach." Charles took a long draught from his glass and reached for the pitcher to refill it.

"Yes. It can't be a coincidence that the obviously exorbitant price he quoted added up to 355 pence." Sarah sipped her cider much more judiciously than Charles.

Annie nodded. "I agree, and the scuttlebutt among the other domestics in town is that Mr. Rivington's coffeehouse is a favorite spot among the British officer corps."

"I've heard the same thing," Charles agreed. "The question now is how to cultivate a source of information among them."

That was Sarah's task, and one for which she was thoroughly trained. She sat up straighter and spoke. "There must be a Major among them who is lonely and in need of feminine companionship."

Annie and Charles exchanged glances, perhaps not thrilled with how eager Sarah seemed to be to apply her lessons of seduction. Charles's response was not enthusiastic.

"Well, we need to get the lay of the land first. Surely a quick attempt to bed a high-ranking officer would draw unnecessary suspicion."

Sarah pursed her lips but didn't reply.

Instead, Annie said, "Besides, a Major most likely avails himself of the company of the many whores—excuse me, 'courtesans'—who have set up shop around town."

Sarah realized this was another lesson from her more experienced colleagues, so she waited silently until Charles picked up the thread.

"Agreed. A junior officer would be a better target. Their more meager means would keep them away from the high-priced companions of their betters. Also, their position in society would prevent them from using the cheap whorehouses the common soldiers frequent."

Annie nodded vigorously, agreed with Charles's logic. "And if they are missing their pretty, young wife at home, then someone else's even prettier and younger wife, who is a little rough around the edges, would be very appealing."

Sarah blushed, more at the compliment than the sexual implication. Her training these past few months included lessons in the arts of seduction. Still, the thought of actually putting her training into practice made her nervous. She took a sip from her warm cider to calm herself before turning to Charles and speaking.

"We must keep a lookout for such a young, married, junior officer, then."

Charles nodded. "But also one who can provide useful information once you have caught him in your snare." His leering expression gave Sarah a chill, and a thrill.

It took nearly two weeks to make all the arrangements for the Websters' housewarming party. The printer and Sarah's newly acquainted rebel contact, James Rivington, was very helpful during the preparations, though he was not at all what Sarah expected.

James published a fiercely loyalist newspaper, *The Royal Gazette*, which spewed vitriol at the "filthy rebellious traitors" every week. Though obviously an excellent cover for a spy working for those same traitors, it also had the effect of attracting British officers and like-minded citizens to his coffeehouse, where English brandy and local spirits loosened tongues, and gossip swirled like a nor'easter storm.

His acquaintances within New York society and among their British occupiers made up most of the guest list for the party. He also suggested ordering the bulk of the provisions for the party from his friend Robert Townsend, whose shop was next door to James's. Robert, known as R.T. to his friends, was a frequent contributor of local interest articles to the *Gazette*. Because of his close affiliation with James, many of the British officers frequented R.T.'s store and had their quartermasters buy much of their provisions there.

All-in-all, they were as deeply embedded within the loyalist society as simple shopkeepers could be. What they lacked, though, was inside access to the officers themselves, in whose eyes they would always just be common folk beneath their station.

Of course, this fraternization with, and vocal support for, the British made James and R.T. hated figures among the independence-leaning citizenry in New York who, of necessity, kept their heads down and their mouths shut.

Little did these patriots, or anyone else throughout the colonies, know the profound effect these men would have on the outcome of the war. Nor did many generations that followed understand. The impact these men, along with their fellow members of the famous Culper Ring of spies, Abraham Woodhull, Caleb Brewster, Austin Rowe, and the mysterious Lady 355 had, can't be overstated. They provided information directly to General Washington that saved the nascent rebellion at least three times and delivered the single most decisive piece of intelligence that ultimately won the Revolutionary War for the Americans.

Chapter 34

Major Andre

With the party in full swing, Sarah and Charles were completely immersed in their respective personas. Charles presented himself as a philandering drunkard more interested in chatting and dancing with the local debutants than his own wife. For her part, Sarah feigned being a slightly bewildered country wife thrust into a world for which she was ill-prepared. In reality, that wasn't too far from the truth, which made that part of her mission easier.

A flurry of activity at the main entrance to the ballroom drew Sarah's attention away from Quartermaster Lieutenant Reynolds, with whom she was chatting. A swirl of greetings surrounded two latecomers, making their way across the room toward the far wall where Sarah held court as hostess. Charles, noticing the disturbance, scurried toward her on an intercept course with the arriving couple. As the newcomers approached, the knot of revelers welcoming them fell away to reveal a tall man, in full officer regalia, and his striking female companion.

He wore a Major's uniform with ribbons and insignia indecipherable to Sarah, but impressive nonetheless. He doffed his plumed hat as he bowed a greeting to Sarah, although he kept his eyes fixed on hers, telling her without words that his bow was perfunctory and in no way indicated her station was equal to his. Straightening, he handed his hat to an aide, who trailed behind, then stepped to the side, presenting his companion.

She was stunningly beautiful with jet black hair coiffed into a complex arrangement that enhanced her statuesque height and framed her high cheekbones. Delicately applied makeup subtly emphasized her dark eyes and full, red lips. Her ball gown, made of the richest brocade and gold embroidery, plunged in front from her delicate shoulders to reveal a small birthmark on the dusky skin below her left collarbone. The gown's subtle shades of blue and purple blended perfectly with her skin tone. A gold pendant hung from a gold necklace. It was an odd design of beautifully carved and filigreed interconnected bars. Against the light brown of her skin, the pendant practically glowed.

The overall effect was magical and held everyone's attention as the woman nodded ever so slightly to Sarah, whose breath caught in her throat. She had never seen anyone so beautiful, and the Major, in his bright red greatcoat, white trousers, and sword, was but a complement to her presence.

Charles, who arrived at the same time, said a little breathlessly, "My Dear, may I present Major John Andre and Myra..."

Ignoring Charles, Major Andre interrupted, "Mrs. Webster, it is a great pleasure to make your acquaintance. May I present my companion, Miss Miira?" He pronounced her name as *Mee-rah*. "She has traveled a great distance to be with us this evening."

Flustered and feeling decidedly inadequate, Sarah stammered, "Ah, welcome to our home, Major Andre and," her mind raced to recall the strange name, "Miira." Recovering her wits, she continued, "Such a lovely name. Is it Egyptian, perhaps?"

Major Andre bowed again, and Miira flashed a smile that didn't reach up to her eyes.

"Well done, My Dear. You made a better attempt pronouncing my name than most of your colonial fellows."

"I would be most interested in learning about your home, Miss Miira. Perhaps you could join me for tea sometime?"

Miira raised an eyebrow and studied Sarah for a moment, then she nodded. "Very well." Then, turning dismissively to Andre, she said, "Come, Major. Let us dance."

As Miira turned fully away from Sarah, Andre offered a small nod and an apologetic half-smile at the obvious dismissal.

Sarah and Charles stood stunned as the two swept onto the dance floor. After a moment, Charles shrugged and went looking for another drink. It took another second or so for Sarah to realize there had been a third member of the late-arriving party who stood before her patiently.

When she pulled her gaze from the dancefloor and made eye contact with the young officer standing before her, he snapped his heels and bowed deeply.

"Mrs. Webster, I am Captain Leslie Alfred, Major Andre's *aide-de-camp*. It is my utmost pleasure to make your acquaintance."

Having recovered her persona after Miira's snub, Sarah smiled widely at the Captain. "Captain Leslie, it is indeed my pleasure as well."

The Captain, looking confused, said, "Pardon me, Ma'am, but my full name is Leslie Alfred. I am called Captain Alfred."

Sarah laughed lightly. "I am sorry, Sir. That is just my Southern ways sneaking out. In the Lowcountry down south, we often call our friends by their title and first name out of respect." She flashed her best flirtatious smile. "For example, everyone, even my cousins, refers to my mother as Miss Jane and my father as Mr. William. So, pardon me if I was too forward, but Captain Leslie just came naturally to me." She dropped her eyes, then looked up at him with a small smile. "I would be delighted if you showed me the same courtesy," she said a little breathlessly.

Leslie was delighted by Sarah's southern drawl and the hint of intimacy this upper-class lady showed him, a mere Captain.

"There is certainly no need to apologize, My La—ah, Miss Sarah. I consider it a compliment and hope we will continue to address each other thus in our future meetings."

Sarah smiled sweetly at his formality. "I most certainly will, my good Captain Leslie, now that we can call each other friends. And I hope I have many occasions to."

Trying to hide the rush of color to his cheeks, Captain Leslie bowed again and hastily withdrew.

Looking across the room, Sarah and Charles made eye contact as he gave her a subtle nod.

Chapter 35

Fishing

As the summer came to a close and the weather turned to blustery days and cool evenings, the Websters melted easily into New York society. A good harvest came in throughout the countryside of New Jersey and New York, and the smuggling trade that brought fresh produce into the town, bypassing the British occupiers and tax collectors, flourished.

While most of the smugglers brought goods into New York, Caleb Brewster plied his trade in both directions. Punishments for slipping past the British patrols on the rivers varied from confiscation to imprisonment, depending on the disposition of the commanding officer and his willingness to accept the readily offered bribe. For Brewster, a member of the secretive Culper Ring, the outbound trips were even more dangerous. He carried a steady stream of encrypted messages destined for Major Tallmadge and General Washington. Capture with such material meant either a life sentence in the hold of a prison ship or a summary execution. From the stories spread among the rebels by those few offenders of minor crimes who survived their sentences, a quick death at the end of a rope would have been better than a lingering death on the water.

He carried secret dispatches written in invisible ink to avoid detection, but both sides in the war knew the formula for the ink that, once exposed to the heat of a candle, became visible again. As Sarah prepared for her first mission, James Jay, a physician in England and brother of John Jay, the President of the Continental Congress and future Supreme Court Chief Justice, invented a new "sympathetic stain" that was undetectable without its matching chemical reagent. Through the machinations of The Enclave, James sent the ink, reagent, and their formulae to his brother, who immediately passed them on to Washington for use by his spies.

The undetectable ink meant the Culper Ring could write dispatches in the margins of books, between the lines of personal letters, and even across James Rivington's *Royal Gazette*—legitimate papers for Brewster to carry to his friends and relatives on Long Island or New Jersey. At least one of whom passed the subtly marked pages up the line and into the Major's hands. Despite an established pipeline for intelligence about the enemy's plans, until the Websters arrived little useful information made its way to the General.

While Charles feigned drunkenness most evenings and Annie gossiped with the other households' servants while at the market, Sarah sipped afternoon tea with the other wives. Many of them were feeling increasingly like captives within the besieged island of Manhattan. Sarah's invented stories of life in the rebel-held South also help foment displeasure among them. From the ladies' offhand complaints and comments about their husbands' dealings with the British, Sarah gleaned bits of intelligence. Those tidbits were but copper coins, though, compared to the potential wealth of information known to the British officers.

Those officers were eager for action, and the enforced idleness of garrison duty led to relaxed discipline. As a result, more and more of the contraband brought into New York by the smugglers was rum, wine, and whiskey, purchased by the army itself.

The experienced boatmen, sneaking past the British picket ships late at night, knew that if their cargo included any of those spirits, they were likely to be given free passage even if caught. Of course, their cargo would be appropriately "taxed," so they still avoided detection as much as possible.

The boredom and free-flowing spirits meant that the parties among the upper-class New Yorkers and British officers became more frequent. And, in order to meet the growing demand, James Rivington doubled, then tripled the frequency of his coffeehouses. Most evenings, a mixture of the social and military elite attended. As the music played and the drink flowed, the officers' tongues loosened.

It was at one of these *soires* that Sarah and Captain Leslie slipped outside in search of a quiet spot.

"Brrr. I'm not used to this northern weather."

Sarah shivered and rubbed her hands on her bare arms. Leslie gallantly removed his coat and hung it on her shoulders. His hands lingered a bit longer than necessary, so Sarah leaned back against his chest.

"The season has definitely turned," he said, pulling her closer with his right arm around her shoulders.

Sarah snuggled into his embrace and turned her face up with parted lips. Accepting her silent invitation, Leslie bent and kissed her lightly.

"Oh, my," Sarah sighed as their lips separated.

"Oh, my indeed. I have wished for that kiss since the day we met," Leslie whispered. "Please forgive my forwardness, but I wish for…no, I *need* more."

Without a word, Sarah turned in his arms, entwined her gloved left hand into the hair on his neck, and pulled his head down to hers. This time, the kiss was anything but light, and they each made their intensions clear with their tongues.

After nearly a minute that seemed mere seconds to Sarah, she drew back, stepped out of his arms, and slipped his coat off her shoulders.

Handing it back to him, she said, "Captain Leslie, I do believe I should like your company for tea sometime. Tomorrow, perhaps?"

Folding his coat over his arm and taking a deep breath to calm himself, Leslie replied, "I would be honored, Madam. May I escort you home this evening?"

Sarah smiled but shook her head. "That won't be necessary. Charles and I need to get home. He departs for Long Island on business in the morning." Leslie cocked his head. "Something about local hogs and smoked hams." Her hands fluttered as she shrugged. Then, placing a hand on his free arm, she smiled and met his eyes. "Tomorrow for *tea*, then?"

Leslie bowed deeply and Sarah returned to the party.

On the ride home in the carriage, Charles, having dropped his drunken act, said, "It looked like you might have sunk the hook."

Sarah gave him a sidelong look from her seat in the carriage. "Spying on me, are you?" Charles just shrugged, and with a small smile, Sarah said, "He's hooked, and I've angled him to the boat."

She left unsaid her plan to *land* him at tea.

PART X

Amy
Present Day

Liz—excuse me, "Miss Elizabeth" (why use 5 syllables when 1 will do?)—has "encouraged"—insisted is a better word—that I keep a journal to put my feelings into words so I understand them better. I think she thinks that by writing down my hate for this place, I'll stop getting in trouble. But every time I try, it just makes me so much angrier. I did get her to promise not to ever look at this journal, although like every other adult in this hellhole, I can't believe her. Why can't I? Because SHE'S AN ADULT IN THIS HELLHOLE!

Maybe that's not fair. She's been kind, at least, without being all fake lovey-dovey. She says she has my back, and she did get me out of the deepest part of this HELLHOLE, but we'll see...

— Amy's journal

Chapter 36

Clearance

The library's search bot returned a summary of its results to Amy's question.

The request "What does the number '355' mean?" is too ambiguous for a concise answer. There are many meanings of that number. I suggest you refine your query to a particular geographical region, time period, or other topical restriction.

The vague reply was particularly frustrating, since Google's results all pointed to either a short-lived female spy movie or the legendary Revolutionary War spy it was based on. A spy whose code name—code number—was 355. You'd think the library's AI would at least give those results back.

It was a typical response Amy got when she asked a question the adults in The Enclave didn't want to answer. Vague, deflecting nonsense. But Amy would not be deflected.

"Tell me how the number 355 relates to The Enclave's operations. Please."

The answer came back immediately.

I'm sorry, Amy, but you are not cleared for information concerning any Enclave operations.

Well, it was worth a shot. She shifted on the hard wooden chair and looked around the expanse of the library for inspiration. It felt solid and sturdy, even though its soaring vaulted ceiling seemed to float above the worktables, study carrels, and comfortable hearthside furniture far below. Amy's eyes followed the lines of the timber arches as they arced down from the peak to disappear into the side walls. The ancient design, perfected in cathedrals like *Notre Dame*, *Chartres*, and, most recently, *La Sagrada Familia*, leaped into her mind. The misdirection of the spindly columns separating the main floor—the nave in those sacred piles of stone—from the true genius of the architect—the succession of diminishing arches, each offloading some of the burden from its larger sibling. In those cathedrals, the effect was intended to convince the humbled attendants below of the power of God to suspend tons upon tons of stone miraculously without visible support.

Rather than humbling its occupants, though, The Enclave library inspired inquiry. That was its *raison d'etre*, after all. And inspire Amy, it did.

"Please tell me how the number 355 relates to Elizabeth deLeau."

This time, the bot chewed on her inquiry for a full two seconds.

I'm sorry, Amy, but you are not cleared for information concerning any Enclave operations.

Well, wasn't that interesting? Amy was preparing a more probing query when she heard the soft click of an electronic lock from under the second-story gallery. A moment later, Father Dan appeared from between the stacks of books. He came up short when he saw Amy staring at him.

"Oh, hi, Amy. What are you…ah…working on?"

She wanted to blurt out, "Where did you come from?" But she knew all she would get in response was more misdirection, if not an outright lie. She didn't think Father Dan had ever lied to her before, though. Still, she acted like having a priest appear out of thin air was the most natural thing in the world.

"Hi, Father Dan. I'm just working on a research project."

She kept her face neutral and her voice chipper. Dan, on the other hand, visibly relaxed.

"What are you researching?"

"Miss Elizabeth told me the pendant she always wears honors her great-something grandfather, who had a lifetime batting average of .355, but I can't find any Major Leaguer who hit that for his career."

Dan's face tensed a little, but he nodded as he took a seat at her worktable. "I couldn't find one either. You know, as stories get passed down through families, they often get…"

"Exaggerated?"

He chuckled. "I was going to say 'embellished,' but you get it. I suspect he played for a minor league team, not one of the majors."

Amy raised an eyebrow. "He hit .355 in the minors and didn't make it to the majors?"

Dan shrugged in response. ".355 in the minors, less than that in the majors? Or maybe he got injured. Who knows?"

She had thought of that, of course, and given baseball's fanaticism with statistics, she had expected some result from that line of inquiry, but got no results. Recognizing another deflection, she just nodded, and Dan relaxed again.

"You're probably right. I thought maybe it had something to do with whatever it is she does for The Enclave."

Her offhand comment took Dan by surprise. "What makes you think what she does for The Enclave has anything to do with that number?"

He immediately saw his error when Amy's face broke into a wide smile. "So she *does* work for The Enclave." She clapped her hands victoriously. "She won't tell me anything about her job, you know."

Dan's frown slowly turned into a wry grin. "I should have learned long ago not to treat you like a normal eleven-year-old."

She gave him a mock-hurt look. "Are you saying I'm not normal?"

Dan let a moment of silence pass between them, during which Amy's devilish grin faded. When he spoke, he was deadly serious.

"Amy, we both know you are special. You're smarter than most kids nearly twice your age. You learn things faster than your teachers can teach them. I suspect you've learned how you learn, which most people never figure out. That means you can teach yourself just about anything. But," he held up a warning finger. "You will soon reach a point where you will have to make some big decisions. You'll have to decide *how to use* your intelligence. Whether you'll write amazing software, paint beautiful pictures, compose symphonies, heal sick people, or build beautiful buildings," he spread his arm, "like this one." He paused a moment. "More importantly, you'll have to decide whether to do *good* things with your abilities, or not-so-good things. Will you *help others*, or just enrich yourself?"

Amy had held his gaze through his speech, but then she dropped her eyes.

"Why are there so many secrets surrounding this...*place*." Venom dripped from her last word.

Dan, who had seen and heard her hatred of The Enclave many times before, took her hand in his.

"I'm sure you know—or at least suspect—that The Enclave does very important work. Work that, by its very nature, must be kept secret for a whole host of reasons. Trust me when I tell you that, on balance at least, the work is for *good*. For the good of humanity across the world. I don't know specifics about Liz's role in that work, but I do know it has been very, *very* important."

Amy started to ask something else, but Dan held up his hand to stop her.

"Enough questions for tonight. I've said enough—probably too much—already. And it's late. Let me walk you home."

When Dan returned to the library after dropping Amy off at Liz's apartment, he hurried through the secret door under the gallery and down into the Vault. Before he even sat down, he called out to the air, "Searcher, Tell me how the number 355 relates to Operative Elizabeth deLeau."

The bot's response was immediate.

Certainly, Father Dan. Operative Elizabeth deLeau, nee Margaret Fisher, nee, ...

Fourteen names later, the bot continued.

...nee Sarah Harkin. During Operative Harkin's first operation in 1779, she infiltrated the British High Command in New York and integrated with the spy ring known as the Culper Ring. She operated under the code name "Lady," represented in the spy ring's code book by the number 355."

"Well, well, well," Dan mumbled. His fingers danced across the keyboard as he and the bot conversed long into the night.

229

Chapter 37

A Secret Discovered

Amy lay prone on the library floor reading her book. The shelves of books towered over her waif-like body. Ever since Liz gave her permission to spend as much time there as she wanted, the library had become her sanctuary. Sitting at a worktable under the high ceiling, or curling up on the carpeted floor deep in the stacks under the gallery, as she was then, was the only time she felt truly at home.

She had an ulterior motive this evening, however. Ever since Father Dan surprised her by appearing out of nowhere from under this gallery, the question of where he had come from burned within her. Earlier in the day, as she approached the library for her daily alone-time, she saw Dan enter ahead of her. When she arrived, though, he was nowhere to be found. Finding his disappearance to be as mysterious as his earlier appearance, she decided to hide out and await his reappearance.

She picked a spot where, by peeking between books on the lowest shelf, she could see the spiral staircase that led up to the gallery above. Leaning a little to her left, she could also see along the display cases of historical artifacts along the library's inside wall.

Four hours later, however, and already late for her curfew, she closed her book, resigned to having missed this opportunity, but resolved to try again. The thump of the book closing was echoed by the distinctive soft click of an electronic lock.

Amy held her breath as she watched one of the display cases and a portion of the wall behind it swing soundlessly open. Although she couldn't see into the room beyond from her position, she clearly saw Father Dan stick his head through the secret door. He looked left and right surreptitiously, then stepped fully into the library. Dan reached behind the display case, which swung back into position with just another mechanical click.

With another look around the silent room, he climbed the winding stairs to the gallery and out of Amy's sight. But she heard another, conventional, door open and close. Given the layout of the building, she knew John's offices lay beyond it.

She knew she should hurry home and face Liz's annoyance for missing curfew, but when choosing between doing what was expected and satisfying her curiosity, Amy always chose the latter.

So, on tiptoe, she crept up to the faux wall panel and slid her hand behind the display case. Her fingers met what she could feel was a keypad. Although tempted to try a few passcodes, she knew that, with Karl Coolbaugh's obsession for security, there was no way she could guess what was sure to be a random set of digits.

Satisfied that she had learned at least part of one of The Enclave's secrets, she gathered her books and hurried home. In her haste, though, she didn't notice the spyeyes mounted in the gallery's woodwork.

Chapter 38

A Secret Revealed

A my endured Liz's lecture on the importance of following rules like curfews, even though she could tell Liz's heart wasn't in it. Amy was sure her guardian had broken many more and worse rules than breaking curfew in her day. But she acted appropriately chastised and promised to *try* to be home on time from then on. Both parent and child knew how hollow that promise was.

"Okay," Liz said resignedly. "Get yourself to bed, Young Lady."

She opened her arms, and Amy came in for their nightly stiff, awkwardly formal, hug. Neither woman nor child was ready to express their growing affection. As Amy pulled away with a whispered "Good night," a series of staccato raps sounded from the apartment door.

After peering through the peephole, Liz opened the door to find Karl Coolbaugh standing there. He nodded to Liz, then looked past her to where Amy stood.

"I need to take the girl to see John," he said without so much as a "Hello."

Stepping between Karl and Amy, Liz said, "Why. What does he want with her at this hour?"

The Head of Security considered how to respond for a moment, then said, "There's been a security breach, and she," he nodded toward Amy, "is the cause."

Liz started to protest, but when Karl gave her a tilted nod, she knew it would be fruitless. Instead, she turned to where Amy stood silently.

"Come on Amy. Let's see what John—"

"No," Karl interrupted. "Just Amy."

Liz turned on him. "What do you mean, 'Just Amy?' You think I'm sending her to be interrogated without me?"

He frowned and looked decidedly uncomfortable. "You…you're not cleared for this discussion."

Liz barked a false laugh. "If this *discussion* involves Amy, then I damn well *am* cleared for it."

Having known Liz his entire life, Karl knew this wasn't an argument he could win.

"Alright, come along. Let John decide."

"Damn straight," Liz muttered as she held out her hand to Amy, who grabbed it like Liz was reaching out from a lifeboat while she was drowning.

Amy wasn't surprised to see both John and Father Dan in John's office. When Liz marched through the door holding Amy's hand, Dan turned to John with a wry smile.

"Told ya," he said. "Pay up."

John gave a rueful nod, and when Karl started to explain how Liz insisted on accompanying Amy, John held up his hand. "It's okay, Karl. The good father and I had a side bet. He won. We've got it from here."

The security chief hesitated at being dismissed so abruptly, but then nodded and left the room.

John then turned to face Liz. His voice was almost gentle. "You remember when you were about Amy's age and we had a similar meeting in this very room?" Liz gave him a wistful smile and nodded. "Well, it seems the Universe has come full circle."

He turned to Amy. "My Dear, you have figured out a secret that not even your...guardian?" He glanced at Liz, who shrugged. "That not even Liz knows. Father Dan tells me you've been asking about The Enclave's mission and the secrets we keep. Perhaps it's time for you to become a real member of The Enclave."

"She's too young, John," Liz barked.

But John just smiled and said, "Full circle...Sarah."

Amy, who was hanging on every word, looked up at Liz, whose face had gone hard as stone.

"Sarah is long gone, John." Her voice was cold.

"Is she?" he said. Then he turned to Amy, "How many times has she taken you sneaking around late at night?"

Amy's surprised look revealed enough without speaking, but she said, "Never—I don't know what you mean."

John looked to Liz, who nodded and turned to the girl.

"Amy, The Enclave has many secrets, and when you do its work, sometimes you have to tell many lies. But here, in this room, there is no lying. Here, only the truth can be told. Do you understand?"

Amy nodded, then turned to John. "Three times. Plus I've snuck out twice on my own."

The pride in her voice was reflected in Liz's surprised expression. John and Dan both let out laughs.

"Good girl," John said. "I won't lie to you, either. The secret doorway you found leads to the heart and soul of The Enclave. Not even Liz knows about it. It's a vault that houses all manner of documents, archives, and artifacts that stretch back to long before The Enclave was founded. We call it The Vault, and Father Dan will give you a tour of it, if you—both of you—would like."

Amy smiled, and her head bobbed up and down. Liz, with raised eyebrows, just nodded.

John and Dan stood and walked to a door set into the paneling of the outer office. As Dan reached behind a picture and entered his passcode, John said, "Please don't touch anything. The instruments and machines down there are delicate, as are any documents Father Dan may have left lying around." Dan looked annoyed, but just shook his head. John continued. "I'll promise you the same thing I promised your…Liz, many years ago, and Father Dan more recently. You can ask anything you want. I will never lie to you, but I may tell you that you aren't ready to hear the answer. Okay?"

Amy nodded quickly, and Dan pulled open the upper entry into The Enclave's Vault of Secrets.

PART XI

Sarah
Autumn 1779

*"I intend to visit 727 [New York] before long and think by
the assistance of a 355 [Lady] of my acquaintance, shall be
able to outwit them all."*

*— Letter from Abraham Woodhull (Culper, Sr.) to
Gen. George Washington*

Chapter 39

Seduction

*T*ea went as expected. At least as Sarah had expected, and probably as Leslie had hoped. After tea and cakes served by Annie, Sarah led Leslie on a tour of the townhouse, but they never got past the guest bedroom. Playing tour guide, Sarah stepped into the room and when Leslie followed, she closed and latched the door. What followed was a late afternoon romp that allowed Sarah to put into practice the lessons learned at The Enclave's "finishing school".

Lying together in the bed, Sarah ran her fingers through the ringlets of Captain Leslie's chest hair glistening in the setting sun.

"Charles will not be returning until tomorrow evening," Sarah whispered in his ear.

But rather than enticing Leslie to spend the night, the mention of Charles's name had the opposite effect.

"Oh, unfortunately I need to get back to headquarters," he stammered.

"Must you?" Sarah slid her bare leg over his.

Leslie leveraged himself up to his elbows.

"Yes, I'm afraid so. Major Andre will expect a progress report," he said as he slid sideways out of bed.

Sarah sat up frowning and let the bed sheet slide down to her waist.

"Not a 'progress report' on us, I hope," she said with mock concern.

Leslie turned back and Sarah saw that the sight of her nakedness had the desired effect.

"No, I assure you, My Dear, that will be our secret."

"It had better be." Sarah slid out of bed, stepped up to Leslie, and put her arms around his neck. She felt his desire burning between their naked bodies. "That would sully my reputation."

She rose up on her tiptoes to kiss him.

"I do need to get back," he said, but the earlier conviction was gone from his voice.

"Will Major Andre be at the mess?" She already knew that Andre took his meals in his quarters, often with his consort.

"No. He…"

Sarah planted another hard kiss on his mouth.

When they parted, she whispered, "Then why don't you eat here?"

Her hooded eyes met his, and she took his left hand in her right. Walking backwards, she pulled him back to the bed. Leslie followed like a lost puppy.

"What kind of 'progress report?'" Sarah asked, with her head on Leslie's chest and her leg entwined with his.

"Hmm?" A groggy Leslie asked.

"You said the Major would expect a progress report."

Leslie's eyes flew open, and he shot up to a sitting position, dislodging Sarah. "Drat! I completely forgot." He looked down at where Sarah lay on her back with her breasts exposed. "You are quite the distraction, My Dear."

Sarah gave him a pouting frown. "Am I just a *distraction*?" But her pout broke into a broad smile. "I'd be happy to *distract* you any time, my dear Captain. Now go write your report. I'm sure it is very important to the war effort."

Leslie snorted as he slid out of bed. "It is just a list of suspected rebel sympathizers. Not as important as some operations we have brewing."

Sarah's heart quickened, but she resisted the urge to probe too deeply. "Not anyone we know, I hope?"

She watched appreciatively as he dressed, and he dismissed her concern with a wave of his hand.

"Of course not. These are low-class dock workers and such who fail to appreciate the security and protection the new tax levies are providing them."

Sarah frowned and shook her head. "Ingrates."

"Exactly." Buttoning his shirt, he looked down at Sarah, who had pulled herself up to a cross-legged sitting position. "You are quite bold, you know. Not like the stuffy matrons I've met."

Pulling the sheet all the way off, Sarah met his gaze. "I'm not one of them. I'm just a young country girl trying to raise my station." She paused to let that sink in. "I think we have that in common, no?"

After a moment, Leslie nodded, but Sarah noticed his hand go reflexively to the gold band on his ring finger. She made a sound quite like a cat's purr.

"Both of our marriages are advantageous, I suspect. But an ocean separates yours, and decades divide mine. Let us ease our respective irritations."

He gave her a speculative look. "Without dislodging either's station?"

The bargain struck, Sarah gave a knowing nod and extended her hand. "Deal?"

Leslie took her hand as if to shake it, but instead raised it to his lips and caressed her knuckles with his tongue.

"Deal," he growled.

Chapter 40

First Intelligence

After their next "teatime," as Leslie got dressed, Sarah didn't coax him back to bed.

"Another 'progress report' for our dear Major Andre?" Sarah lay on the bed propped up on one elbow, but kept the sheet tucked tightly into her armpit. "It must be very important."

Leslie paused while buttoning his pants. "It is indeed." He looked down at his new lover, who was so willing to cuckold her husband. Thinking of clueless Charles gave him a twinge of regret, so he said in a conspiratorial tone, "Tell Charles not to take any colonial money on his excursions in the country." He gave a little chuckle.

"Why, I am sure he never deals with any *rebels*."

"No, but I have heard that some merchants in New York do. Anyway, tell him to stay away from it."

"I will, but whatever for?"

Sarah batted her eyes, and Leslie just gave her a wry smile while he continued to get dressed.

"Very soon the Colonial money will be worthless." He spun the desk chair around and sat down to put his boots on.

This sounded like the kind of information Sarah was hoping for, so she rose from the bed, wrapping the sheet around herself.

"How can it become worthless overnight?"

Leslie strained, pulling on his left boot for a few seconds. When his foot slid in, he continued, "It was Major Andre's idea. He bribed a worker at the rebels' mint in Philadelphia to turn over a set of printing plates and enough linen paper to bury the colonial economy."

He beamed at Sarah, who beamed back excitedly—for her own secret reasons.

"So you will print *faux* money!"

Leslie dragged his right boot over his foot. "Even better! We will print *real* money—indistinguishable from the rebels' own but backed by nothing but thin air."

Feigning confusion, Sarah said, "But won't that just give them more money to buy things with?"

Leslie smiled patronizingly and spoke as if explaining arithmetic to a small child. "No, My Dear. With a flood of *fiat* currency in circulation, everything will get more expensive, and the real money will buy less and less."

Sarah knew Leslie's explanation was flawed, but she clapped her hands, nearly dropping her bed sheet in the process.

"Oh, how clever. I bet it was really you who gave Major Andre the idea, was it not?"

Leslie blushed a little. "I admit, I was a party to the early discussions, and I did turn the traitorous printer in Philadelphia back to being a loyal subject of the Crown."

Sarah slipped out of bed and stood in front of where Leslie sat, dropping the sheet as she did so. Before Leslie could do anything but stare, Sarah straddled his lap and looped her arms around his neck.

"You are definitely going to be somebody important, Captain Leslie Alfred."

With that, she bade him goodnight with a kiss that was sure to linger in his thoughts and dreams until their next liaison, then she swept out of the room, leaving him alone in their love nest.

As soon as Sarah heard the heavy front door close behind Leslie, she went to the writing desk, drew paper, ink, and a quill from a drawer and began composing a shopping list for Robert Townsend's store. When she finished, she opened the top drawer, reached all the way in it to the back, and pushed a hidden latch. Half of the back panel of the drawer swung open, and Sarah withdrew from the secret compartment a phial of invisible ink and another quill.

At the top of the page, she wrote the following with the invisible ink:

39! 290 DGTA 737 LKMAW NRGZAY, 477! —355

Translated, the message read simply, "Alarm! British have Pennsylvania money plates, paper! —Lady"

When she finished, she rose from the desk and turned, only to find Annie standing in the doorway. She eyed Sarah appraisingly, who was wearing just her dressing gown.

"I assume everything went as planned?"

"Better than that, oh much better." She held out the shopping list. "Can you run this down to Mr. Townsend's shop right away?"

Annie's eyes opened wide in surprise. "Already?"

Sarah just nodded, but her look made Annie hurry for her coat.

Chapter 41

Crisis Avoided

Did you tell anyone that thing I told you last week?" Leslie was agitated, standing in Sarah's entry hall.

"What 'thing' are you referring to?" she asked innocently.

"The bit about the money," Leslie whispered.

"Oh, that. Just Charles—as you instructed me to."

Even more agitated, Leslie grabbed both her upper arms. "You didn't tell him why, did you?"

Sarah's well-honed reflexes took over. She jerked her arms free and took a step backwards into a fighting stance, her muscles taught and her mind ready for violence.

"Of course not! That drunkard would have probably shouted it to the world. I just told him that taking the rebels' money would reflect very badly on us and might tarnish our loyal reputation."

Leslie, untrained in martial hand-to-hand fighting, didn't recognize Sarah's posture. He relaxed a little but looked around the hallway as if suddenly realizing the conversation might be overheard.

"Maybe Charles figured it out on his own," Leslie said, although he didn't sound convinced.

Sarah felt him eyeing her suspiciously, so she resumed her Southern country girl persona, but remained prepared to fight. She reached out and laid her left hand gently on his right arm—his sword arm. Then she leaned in close and whispered, "Why are you so upset?"

The captain scanned the room again before leaning in himself and whispering back, "The Continental Congress has just announced they are canceling all the old currency notes and will issue new ones next month. It has also issued a warning to be on the lookout for newly printed or fresh-looking bank notes."

A thrill of victory flashed through her, but Sarah kept her voice confused. "Oh, my. What does that do to your printing scheme?"

"It is ruined! We have been running the presses night and day, but no one will take our bills now!" Sarah gave him her best sympathetic look but said nothing. "What is more, our contact in Philadelphia has been arrested, tried, and hanged for treason. The more than generous payment we gave him was confiscated and is now in the rebels' coffers." Leslie said this last with a note of finality.

Sarah tut-tutted and pulled him into her arms. "Would you like some tea? To take your mind off these troubles?"

Leslie paused for a few breaths before drawing back. "As tempting as your *tea* is, I must get back. Andre is livid. I only slipped out while he was interrogating his spies."

"Then be safe, My Love." Leslie gave a start at her words, then gathered her into his arms and planted a hard kiss on her mouth.

After he departed, Annie came out of her hiding place in the next room.

"Well played, My Dear."

Sarah beamed. "And we know for sure what we had suspected." Annie cocked her head questioningly. "Major John Andre is the English spymaster."

"Ah." Annie nodded. "And you have his aide 'in the boat'."

"Indeed, I do." Sarah couldn't keep the smile from her face.

Chapter 42

Miira and Peggy

The nighttime glow and the smoke of the bonfire burning worthless colonial currency caused quite a stir in New York and the surrounding area. When shards of burned banknotes began drifting down from the sky, Major Tallmadge got his confirmation that the counterfeit crisis was over. His note from northern New Jersey was simple:

> British burning old banknotes. Suggest we do
> same.

At the beginning of the campaign of 1780, General Washington assigned Major Tallmadge command of the Second Continental Light Dragoons, a small horse-borne scouting and probing force.

The assignment was made for two reasons. Having Major Tallmadge acting as a field commander cast doubt in the British minds, specifically Major Andre's, on Benjamin's role as spymaster. By posting the Dragoons along the Hudson in New York, though, it placed Benjamin much closer to the source of the flood of intelligence now streaming from the heart of the British command in New York.

His location meant Sarah's notes on the chatter and gossip she overheard, and most importantly on Captain Leslie's pillow talk was delivered to Benjamin and the General in a matter of days, rather than the two weeks or more that it had taken previously.

As the War dragged on, month after month, an uncertain normality settled over New York. The failure of the long-planned and expensive counterfeiting scheme left Major Andre's commander, General Howe, needing some good news to send back to England. With boredom affecting his troops' morale, combined with reliable intelligence that General Washington and his armies were, for the time being at least, ignoring New York, the British high command decided the time was right to sail the bulk of the army out of New York, headed for warmer climes.

Working his relationships with the Quartermaster General, and promising him good prices, Charles secured a place for his own ship in the naval convoy bound for South Carolina. He sailed south with the fleet to replenish his depleted inventory.

The southern campaign was a great victory for the British. They captured Charleston, South Carolina, but they didn't stay long. Leaving behind a garrison force, the Army re-embarked on the Navy's ships and, along with Charles, who had plundered Charleston and filled his ship to the gunwales, sailed back north to New York. All told, they were gone a total of four months, during which time Sarah, Peggy, and Miira spent many afternoons at tea, not always pleasantly.

Miira struck Sarah from the first time they met as a cold fish. Repetitive conversations over British tea did little to dispel that notion.

"Life has become so boring!" Peggy Arnold complained as she daintily lifted her teacup and saucer to her lips. Eyebrows raised on the faces of the other two women sitting at the table. "Oh, present company excluded, of course."

Peggy tried to cover her embarrassment by quickly taking another sip of tea.

Sarah and her other guest, Major Andre's consort Miira, exchanged a sidelong glance. It was Miira who replied as if speaking to a small child, "You do realize that there is a war going on, My Dear?"

"Of course, silly. My husband is out there in it." Peggy either ignored the tone of Miira's question, or more likely didn't catch it at all. Peggy was the pampered daughter of a wealthy and very loyal New York family. Strangely, though, she was also married to a General in the rebel army, one Benedict Arnold. Arnold, the Hero of Lake Champlain, had recently been given command of the strategic fort at West Point on the Hudson River above New York.

This put Peggy in a precarious position in New York society, now dominated by British officers and sycophantic Loyalists. She had few friends other than Sarah, who had cultivated a relationship with her as another outsider to the iconoclastic social scene.

Sarah's motives were more subtle, though. Given that Peggy had one foot among the upper echelons of the British officer corps and the other likewise placed among the rebels, Sarah figured she would make the perfect scapegoat should suspicion of a high-society spy emerge, which it undoubtedly eventually would.

Unfortunately, Peggy's apparent empty-headedness and confusion over the simplest political discussion made her a most unlikely spy. She was tolerated by Major Andre, mainly as a potential source of counterintelligence about the rebels.

This afternoon tea was requested by Peggy. Wanting to feel less like an outsider, she hoped that a friendship with Andre's companion would lead to better acceptance among her peers.

Changing the subject, Sarah turned to Miira.

"That is a lovely pendant you wear. Does it have a special meaning?"

Miira reached up with her right hand and fingered the silver bangle suspended by a finely crafted silver chain. The figure itself was like nothing Sarah had seen before. It was composed of a series of bars which met and intersected at right angles.

Holding the pendant out from her neck so Sarah could lean forward and examine it more closely, Miira smiled and said, "It is my name in an ancient language of my native land."

Her English was excellent, but Sarah could detect a slight, unfamiliar accent which was much less prominent than her own affected southern drawl.

"It's beautiful. What language is it?"

Miira let the pendant fall back to its place between her collarbones. She said a word that seemed to be composed of syllables completely foreign to Sarah and Peggy's ears.

"It is actually a dead language. No one speaks it anymore."

"Oh, like Latin?" Peggy's observation drew surprised looks from her companions.

"Why yes, actually," Miira replied. Peggy beamed and sat back in her chair, quite satisfied with herself. "Except that Latin is still spoken by the Roman Catholic Church."

She and Sarah exchanged a look that said they shared the same thought—how sheltered Peggy must be to not know that.

Holding Miira's gaze, Sarah asked, "What part of the world is your native land?"

"In the East," Miira replied a bit evasively.

Rather than pressing the issue, Sarah nodded and changed the subject again. To Peggy, she said, "It is certainly more…stimulating when the officers are around—again, present company excluded."

Peggy sighed her agreement and Miira, who had observed Sarah and Leslie's intimate conversations on several occasions simply gave her a knowing look, as from one mistress to another. She may have also noticed Sarah's greatly reduced intake of wine, and a slight plumpness of her cheeks, that had appeared recently. Indications that Sarah was keeping more than one secret.

"Tell me more about your homeland," Sarah asked Miira after an uncomfortably long silence.

"There is not much to tell, really. Desert, desert, desert."

"I've never seen a desert," Peggy said.

"Neither have I," Sarah agreed. "Do you ride camels there?"

Miira saw the honest interest in her two companions' faces, which made her expression soften into a smile.

"Some men do. Women are not allowed to, though."

"I can't imagine how one could even sit on that big hump in skirts." Peggy said, and giggled at her own comment.

Miira wasn't amused. "They use saddles on the camels, of course. But that is not why women do not ride." Seeing the other women's genuine interest, she continued, "You women here in the West do not know how lucky you are. A woman dressed as you do here would be stoned to death in the village square."

Shocked, Peggy gasped. Sarah was less surprised and wanted to learn more.

"What do you wear there?"

"In the strictest districts, women are covered from head to toe in a black hijab with only their eyes visible through a narrow slit. To go out in public exposing anything but one's eyes and hands is to risk death."

Peggy sat with her hand over her mouth. Sarah leaned forward, fascinated by Miira's words.

"But, why?"

"That is how the old men in charge interpret the *Qur'an*, the Muslim holy book. Women have no rights. They are their husband's property." Miira leaned in so she and Sarah were face to face. "Your slave Annie has more freedom than the richest woman in my homeland." Her voice rose, dripping venom. "You sit here in your fancy brocades and silks, drinking tea from halfway around the world, complaining about being bored." She turned her growing fury on Peggy, who practically cowered in her chair. "And your husband's rebels complain about paying taxes."

Sarah sat back, understanding much more about Miira for the first time. "And now you're here. It must be pretty refreshing."

Miira took a deep breath, immediately calming herself.

"My apologies, Ladies. Yes, I managed to escape to England." She turned to Peggy. "I will not further upset you with the details." She offered Peggy a small smile, then turned back to Sarah with a serious look. "I find these rebels' demands and this entire war like the whining of spoiled children. When your mother country reasserts control over these brats, I hope the 'spanking' will be thorough and complete."

The inference of these words for Peggy's husband and Sarah's secret compatriots was not lost on either of them. Peggy let out a gasp, and a long moment of silence followed Miira's rant. Sarah finally broke it without any attempt at humor.

"Well, it seems our tea is not the only thing that has gone cold this afternoon." She stood, forcing Miira to do so, as well. "Thank you, Miss Miira, for coming to my home this afternoon."

Sarah's dismissal of her was obvious. Without another word, Miira turned to find Annie standing behind her, holding her shawl. With an indignant sniff, she wrapped it around her shoulders, as she had wrapped herself in righteous indignation over Americans fighting for their freedom. Without another word or looking back, she proudly followed Annie to the front door.

Sarah watched as Annie closed the door and turned back to her. The look they exchanged carried an obvious message.

She is now our enemy.

Peggy's quiet sobs brought Sarah back to the present, and she turned to comfort her friend.

PART XII

Liz
Present Day

The Wrapping script has me baffled. I know there is a pattern to it—much more of one than most languages. In fact, it appears to be almost binary in its formation, and its signs appear to have been printed rather than hand-written. Of course, given the Wrapping's age, that is a ridiculous idea. The regularity and consistency of the signs, though, implies the use of some kind of stylus, ala cuneiform. But even with a stylus the writer must have had a very steady hand and infinite patience. The signs are clearly organized into words, making this an alphabetic script. Whether it is a phonetic alphabet or symbolic is a question. I'm leaning toward phonetic, as there seems to be a relatively limited number of distinct signs (letters) in the text (32 out of a total of 514).

Words seem to be assembled from letters sharing a common base line with a gap between words. No other punctuation is visible, although some words have "tails" at the ends of the baseline.

The text is written in a column, with up to five or six words per row. These could be modifier/object groups, or simply an efficient use of the available space (although there are rows that are sparsely occupied).

I've copied some of the most common letters in a word below.

Note that what I've drawn is much cruder than the Wrapping script, which appears to be almost printed, although it has faded and does not seem to use pigment that has penetrated into the cloth. The next step is to categorize the various letters and see how they relate to one another. There is a pattern here. I know it.

— Fr. Dan Koprowicz Research Notes

Chapter 43

Pendant

Wat exactly did her pendant look like?" Dan asked as Liz sat back and sipped her Blanton's.

She gave him an exasperated look when she replied, "That's what you got from that bit of story? 'What was she wearing?'"

John chuckled and Dan got defensive.

"No, of course not. The woman Miira sounds like a real femme fatale. It's just that languages are my thing, you know."

Liz shrugged. "I don't remember exactly. It didn't look like any language I had seen then or have seen since."

Dan thought for a moment. "Can you draw it?"

It was Liz's turn to think, but she took much longer. After almost a full minute, she said, "I think so. Give me a pen."

John pulled pen and paper from his desk.

Liz drew a figure, then crossed it out, drew another and crossed it out. Finally, after the third or fourth try, she spun the paper around so Dan and John could see it.

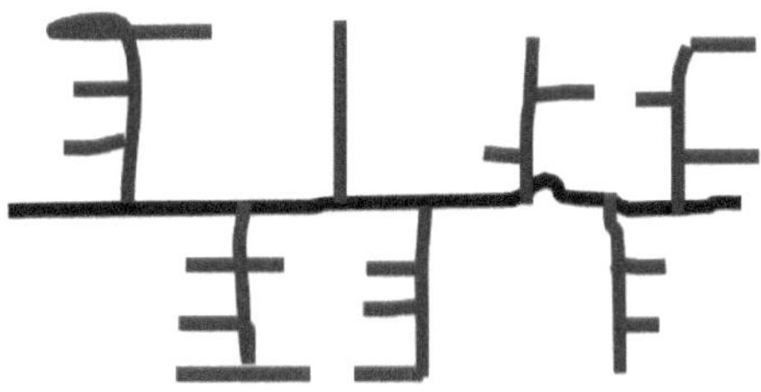

"Huh."

"That's it? 'Huh'?"

"Ah, well, it's not what I was expecting." Dan didn't sound puzzled. Rather, his tight voice hinted at suppressed excitement.

John leaned over the drawing. "That looks…familiar."

Dan shot him a warning look over Liz's head. Before John could say anything more, Dan spoke up, "Frankly, I was expecting Aramaic. That would have been out of use for several centuries by the time you met Miira."

"She did say it was a dead language. But you say it isn't Aramaic?"

Dan hesitated. He could lie and say he was mistaken, that it really was Aramaic, but that wasn't his nature.

"No, it isn't. I'm going to have to do some research. Let's call it a night."

Liz looked at John, who nodded. She shrugged and said good night.

As soon as the door closed behind her, John turned to Dan. "OK, what's up?"

Dan looked John in the eye. "There's a reason this symbol," he shook the paper with the drawing, "looks familiar."

John waited impatiently for Dan to continue. "Why?"

"You've seen it before. This is the first symbol on the Wrapping."

"The Wrapping? You mean the Lance Wrapping?"

Dan nodded. "I need to double check, but I'm positive this symbol is at the far left end of the strip of cloth, if you hold the selvage edge down."

"The first symbol on the left? So, you don't think the language is Semitic? Like Hebrew or Aramaic?"

"The symbol on the Wrapping is rotated ninety degrees." He turned the paper sideways. "Which means it should be read vertically, like a scroll. And it isn't Semitic. I think it was written with a stylus, like Sumerian cuneiform." He nodded to himself. "Yeah, I think it's older than Aramaic, or Hebrew. Maybe older than cuneiform."

John was skeptical. "That would put it five to seven thousand years old. We know the lance is about two thousand years old. Are you telling me the Wrapping is thousands of years older than the lance?"

"No, no. The language is older. That doesn't mean the cloth is."

John relaxed a little, but his voice betrayed his growing excitement.

"Will this help you read the rest of the message?"

"Maybe. It's a start, at least."

John took a deep breath and let it out slowly. "I've waited a long time for a *start*."

Chapter 44

Probing Questions

I can't believe you didn't believe me." Liz's voice reflected her irritation. "You had to have your lackey check up on me?"

"Now wait a minute, Elizabeth." John was equally irritated. "Father Dan did the research on his own. I approved the publication of the article, of course, but he does all his research completely independently. Besides, he's not my lackey."

Liz scoffed. "Sure, he's independent, until you drop one of your subliminal hints into the conversation."

John took a deep breath. "I would never do that with a friend. Plus, I hadn't even seen the good Father since we last met."

Liz just glowered at him until a voice came quietly from a darkened corner across the room.

"I'm sitting right here, you know." Dan's teasing tone was accompanied by a bemused expression and a slight shake of his head.

Liz's face flushed with embarrassment. "Father, I'm so sorry. I…I didn't realize you were sitting there."

"Obviously not. I've been called a lot of things, but never a 'lackey'…until now."

Liz's shoulders dropped and all the fight went out of her. Hanging her head, she walked over to where Dan was sitting and sat across from him.

"Please forgive me. Just being in the same room with John brings out the worst in me and I say things I don't mean."

Dan looked sideways at John as he sat down, as well. "He can have that effect on people."

John nodded. "Indeed. I could tell stories."

Dan turned back to Liz. "Of course, I forgive you, Liz. That's kind of what I do." His self-deprecating humor had the desired effect, and both Liz and John let out a little laugh. "I really wasn't checking up on you. I just found the story of the British counterfeiting plot fascinating, and I wanted to learn more about it." He took a sip from the glass in his hand. "Why are you so upset about this? I only used publicly accessible sources for the article."

Liz sighed. "I understand, Dan. I'm upset because Amy read the article and wouldn't stop asking me questions about it. Deep, probing questions. Like she thought I had firsthand knowledge."

"She's a smart, inquisitive girl. I'm sure she found the story as fascinating as I do."

Nodding, Liz said, "Well, if you think that plot was interesting, wait 'til you hear the rest of the story."

"I'd love to hear the stories of *all* of your operations, especially your first. Your after-action reports in the archives are spotty, at best. I believe the good you've done should be captured for future generations of operatives to learn from." He gave her a lopsided grin. "And so future articles I write about your exploits will be accurate."

She eyed the priest, realizing, finally, that she had been set up.

"Okay, Father. You win. She eyed the glass in his hand. We're going to need a lot more bourbon."

Chapter 45

Amy's Crash

Liz burst into the anteroom to John's office dressed in running shorts and sports bra to find Karl Coolbaugh, Head of Security, standing over Amy. The girl sat hunched over in a wooden chair against the wall.

Liz ran and knelt down in front of her. "Amy, what happened?"

Rather than answering, Amy broke into sobs and Liz turned to find John standing in the doorway to his office. Fr. Dan stood behind him, looking stricken.

"I'll tell you what happened. In here, please." By his tone of voice, Liz knew it wasn't a request.

Rising, she started to protest, which was her normal reaction to authority. "I can't leave her here."

"She'll be fine. In here," he repeated. "Now."

Liz looked to Coolbaugh, who nodded curtly, but kept his deadpan, serious expression. That told Liz this wasn't some minor infraction of the rules. She leaned over, gave Amy a quick hug and whispered, "It'll be OK, Honey."

Amy just shook her head, which filled Liz with a deeper sense of foreboding.

"She's coming in with me," she said.

"No way," John said.

Karl stepped forward to take Amy away from her, but she knocked his arm away with a backhand swipe while she pulled Amy around to her other side. Faced with a mamma bear defending her cub and rubbing his bruised forearm, Karl looked up to John, who just shrugged and turned back into his office.

Inside the dimly lit room, John sat behind his ancient desk while Liz settled Amy into one of the overstuffed armchairs. Dan just paced back and forth, in and out of the shadows against the far wall. Once Amy was curled up in the club chair, Liz stood in the center of the office, looking defiantly like she had been summoned to the headmaster of a very strict school—which is basically what had happened.

Trying and failing to keep the quiver out of her voice, she asked quietly, "What did she do?"

John looked at Dan, who stopped his pacing and faced Liz with his hands clasped behind his back.

"While you were out on your run, Amy took your keys and went for a joy ride in your car." He held up his right hand, palm out, as Liz opened her mouth to ask a question. "After terrorizing several people on the sidewalk by her erratic driving, she proceeded to plow the car into the fence around the school playground."

Liz gasped as John shook his head and Dan continued, "Thank God," he blessed himself, "the car is front wheel drive and it got hung up on the collapsed fence."

John spoke up, "She was still flooring the gas pedal when the teachers pulled her out of the car."

Liz couldn't believe what she was hearing. She spun to face Amy, who hid her face behind her pulled up knees.

John continued, "The bruises on her face are from hitting the steering wheel, not from the teachers—or the kids. Luckily, Karl had been alerted to her erratic driving and pulled up on the scene as they pulled her from the car. Otherwise, I'm not sure what would they would have done to her."

"Oh, my God. I know she's been harboring hatred for those kids and teachers—with good cause, in my opinion." She waved off Dan's objection before he could voice it. "But this. This is beyond anything I could have anticipated." She massaged the bandages that were still wrapped around her hands from her own encounter with that chain-link fence. "What happens now?"

John and Dan shared a look. Liz could tell they had discussed this already, but she couldn't tell if they agreed.

Dan spoke first. "She can't stay here, Liz. You must know that."

After a moment's hesitation, Liz just gave a slight nod.

John said, "As you know, we don't operate the Work Camp anymore. We rely on the local authorities for criminal offenses."

"You're not sending her to the locals!" Amy, peeking between her knees, saw Liz step forward and plant her hands on John's desk. "She's not going into the System."

"No, no, although that's certainly what the teachers and most of the kids' parents want."

Liz held her imperious position, leaning over John's desk.

"Where are you sending her?"

John shook his head. "I don't know yet. Another Enclave residence, I suppose."

"You can't just shuffle her off to be someone else's problem. She needs help, John. Sending her to another foster family will only cement her resentment against The Enclave."

Dan nodded his agreement. "What else would you suggest?"

Liz detected a hint of a suggestion in his voice but refused to acknowledge it. "How would I know? You know I've never had kids."

Her words dripped bitterness, leaving John abashed and Dan looking confused.

"Maybe it's time," Amy heard him murmur. A silent thrill ran through her, awakening a possibility she hadn't allowed herself to even hope for.

Chapter 46

Toxic Separation

Liz stood in the doorway and watched Karl Coolbaugh lead a sobbing Amy out of the anteroom to the secure rooms that served The Enclave as jail cells. John had insisted that they hold her there for her—and Liz's—protection.

"I'll pack a bag for us and join you in a little bit," Liz promised as Karl led Amy away.

When they were gone, she turned to John. "So what happens now?"

"I've already had to field calls from irate parents and teachers who literally want her head." Liz and Dan looked shocked, but John shook his head and continued with a smirk. "We don't do that anymore. Since no one was hurt," Dan blessed himself again and mouthed a silent prayer of thanks, "I'm calling it an ill-conceived prank gone terribly wrong."

Dan nodded and Liz let out a sigh. She felt like she had been holding her breath since she came to the office.

"But," John continued, "she can't stay here. There is way too much bad blood on both sides. It's not safe for either Amy or her schoolmates."

"Her tormentors, you mean." Liz was recovering from the shock and her anger. A sense of terrible loss was building inside her. "I really can't say I blame her." John looked at her sharply and Dan gasped. "They made her life a living Hell."

"Still, she wasn't justified in trying to kill them!" Dan snapped.

"She's eleven, dammit. In her mind, they tried to kill her with a thousand cuts every day."

John stopped the argument with his raised voice. "That's why I'm sending her to another Enclave settlement. Tonight. Karl is making the arrangements now."

Liz looked stricken. "Tonight? I just promised I'd stay with her tonight." She swallowed a sob. "I need to at least say goodbye."

Dan started to speak, but John cut him off with a hard shake of his head. "It's best if we slip her out tonight before the villagers show up with pitchforks and torches." His demeanor told them he wasn't joking.

"I can't just lose her like that." Liz snapped her fingers. "I've...I see so much of myself in her that I've...I've grown very attached to her."

She broke down and the tears came in sobs. Dan stepped toward her to comfort her, but Liz turned and stepped quickly away.

"That's why she has to go tonight, *incognito*. You see, we know of your forays with her in the middle of the night."

Liz turned to John with tears streaking her cheeks. "The little pranks you two have been pulling at night. I've let you have your fun because it seemed harmless—up to now."

"You can't believe that I encouraged her to steal my car!"

"Not directly, of course. But your disregard for the sanctity and rules of this place has been evident since you were Amy's age. The combination of you two is toxic."

Both Liz and Dan shouted at once, but Liz won out.

"Toxic? Our relationship isn't toxic. In fact, Amy is the first person I have…grown attached to in over two hundred years! You want to know why I've been such a cold fish most of my life? Why I keep taking on operations, hoping each time that I won't have the guts to save myself when things go bad? Well, I'll tell you." She turned to Dan. "Get a pen, Father." Turning back to John, she said, "But first, promise you won't send Amy away tonight. Wait until I can hold her…one last time."

PART XIII

Sarah
1779-1780

The quality of the intelligence received through Culper Sr., and of late Culper Jr. has improved dramatically of late. The addition of the help from our friends in the Western forest is the likely cause.

— G. Washington War Journal
New Jersey
1779

Chapter 47

Doubts

Annie helped Sarah get dressed for the victory celebration being thrown by Peggy's parents to honor the heroes returning from the Southern Campaign. She fidgeted and seemed in a particularly bad mood, resulting in Sarah being jabbed with Annie's sewing needle.

"What bee is in your bonnet?" Sarah asked after the second sharp poke.

"I just don't trust that foreign whore." Sarah started at Annie's choice of words, resulting in another stick. "She's always asking questions about your background and Charles's business, like she's spying for that Major. She's neither American nor British. This war has nothing to do with her. She should mind her own business."

The venom in Annie's voice surprised Sarah, but she tried to lighten the mood.

"But your own grandparents were foreigners themselves."

Annie's eyes flashed as Sarah realized her mistake.

"Maybe, but they were brought here in chains in the hold of a ship, not riding on some officer's feather bed!"

"I…I am sorry, Annie. I know your parents escaped and were taken in by The Enclave. That was very insensitive of me."

Sarah's apology did calm Annie somewhat.

"I know, Child. Growing up in The Enclave, you never saw the world my parents and grandparents had to live in. I thank God Almighty every night that I haven't had to, either."

Annie opened her arms and Sarah willingly, thankfully, returned the hug.

"What is your problem with Miira?" Sarah asked sincerely.

"Well, she is living in a nicer house than this, with a staff of four. Just for her."

"Surely Major Andre is covering her expenses."

"No Major can afford that place, and he himself seems to be pretty frugal."

Sarah considered this for a moment. She knew she should trust Annie's experienced instincts more than her own. Her grapevine of servants' gossip was never wrong, either.

"You're right about that. He is the life of whatever party he attends, but never seems to pay for his own drinks at Mr. Rivington's coffeehouse. So, I guess she has her own means of income."

"This far from England? There is only one 'means of income' that she could muster this far from home."

Sarah started to protest, but Annie held up her hand to stop her.

"I'm not saying she is doing that. On the contrary, she is stuck to the Major like nettles on a boot. I've asked around. None of the other house servants have ever seen her invited to their places."

"I have been to her house. It is quite spacious and well decorated, too. So, how can she afford her lavish lifestyle?"

Annie nodded. "Aye, that is the question. She must have brought quite a horde with her, then."

"Perhaps she is widowed, from a rich husband?" Sarah didn't sound very convinced.

"Well, she is certainly wise in the ways of the world. Yet she looks so young. No older than you, Child."

"Are you saying I'm not 'wise in the ways of the world?'"

Annie barked a laugh. "Not like she is. And frankly, your behavior of late with that young Captain is evidence of that."

Sarah saw the deadly serious look in Annie's eye, but couldn't swallow her protest.

"What do you mean? I have him hooked and landed. Just like we planned."

"That was months ago. What have you learned lately?" Sarah's anger rose as Annie continued, "If you give him what he wants whenever he comes around, he won't think there's a price to pay."

"I can't ask him for information straight out. He'll get too suspicious. Besides, he has been away with the Major on this Southern Campaign."

"All I'm saying is, be careful. The way you two flirt and cavort in public, everyone knows you are lovers. The more successful you are in this game, the more dangerous it gets. Remember, it is Major Andre's job to root out the spies in New York. It's true that the last place he would look is right under his own nose, but that is not the case for everyone else. When the end of this charade comes—and it certainly will—you will need to look blameless, at least until we can get the hell out of this town."

Annie's speech had the effect of making Sarah stop and think about how the society gossips saw her relationship with Leslie. What she said made sense, but the thought of someday, probably someday soon, having to leave her Captain Leslie behind made her cringe. And the secret she carried in her belly made her begin to doubt her mission, too.

Daydreams of a simple family life with Leslie somewhere in the backcountry occupied her mind of late. She knew, as anyone growing up in the country did, that it was a nesting instinct caused by the life growing inside her. But daydreams are just that. The reality of her mission as an Enclave operative was the life she had chosen. Still, she knew there would be a reckoning coming, and soon.

Chapter 48

Deception

Although Gen. Howe's victory in Charleston appeased his chain of command back home, Major Andre was still in hot water over the currency debacle and in desperate need of a counter-espionage victory of his own. His increased patrols on the roads around New York netted a lot of smuggling activity, but nothing very substantial until a certain dispatch rider was captured.

Leslie brought the good news to Sarah over dinner.

"The Major's policies of keeping a close eye on the comings and goings of the colonists have finally paid off."

He could barely contain his excitement, and Sarah smiled broadly, though she knew the crackdown Andre ordered had resulted in many innocent citizens being arrested and beaten.

"Well, you have been telling me all along that it was the right thing to do. I would bet that it was you who put that idea in his head."

Leslie's grin grew even wider with her praise. "I was certainly involved in the planning of it," he said, trying and failing to sound humble while he refilled his wineglass. "But that is nothing compared to the big *coup* that is coming."

Sarah picked up her own glass and swirled the contents, but didn't sip from it.

"What is this 'big *coup*' you have engineered?" she asked.

Leslie beamed. "Our men intercepted a dispatch rider carrying some very revealing papers." Sarah tilted her head, encouraging him to continue. "It was a notice from Washington himself!"

Sarah gasped, but covered her shock with an eager smile and nod as if to say, "Go on," which Leslie did. "It was nothing less than the time and location of the arrival of those bastard French!"

Like all British soldiers, Leslie hated England's mortal enemies.

"Why, that is wonderful! Y'all can lay an ambush and sink them before they even make landfall."

Despite her apparent enthusiasm, inside Sarah was terrified for the rebels. Worse, if the English Crown learned of The Enclave's behind-the-scenes involvement in the French crown's decision to support the Americans, there would be devastating consequences for them across the entire British empire.

Leslie sat back in his chair and drank from his refilled glass, all the while watching Sarah as if seeing her in a new light. Finally, he spoke.

"What do you know about 'laying an ambush' and military tactics, My Dear?"

Pretending not to hear the suspicion that had crept into his voice, Sarah just laughed. "I don't know anything about military tactics, Silly," she said. Then her voice got much more serious. "But my Daddy taught me that an ambush is the only way to bring down a wild boar."

Taking his wineglass from him, she straddled his lap. She knew the best way to deflect any of his suspicions. At least for an hour or so.

❧

Sarah sent an urgent coded message the next morning.

British know French landing time and place.

Along with Robert Townsend's and James Rivington's reports of increased provisioning and preparations being made by the British navy, Sarah's enciphered note was carried directly from Benjamin Tallmadge to General Washington's headquarters. It was obvious to Benjamin that the British planned to ambush the French, and Washington concurred. At a hastily arranged meeting of his staff, a brilliant plan to blunt the British plans was born.

Washington wrote out two orders for Benjamin to deliver to commanders in the field. One was legitimate—he ordered one army to move a small force as a feint within sight of the British pickets in New Jersey.

The other command was never intended to reach its destination. Instead, Benjamin asked for a volunteer from his Dragoons to carry a *false order* close enough to the British lines in Harlem to provoke a chase. When he was sure the British, riding their slower war horses, were close enough to see, he was to 'lose' the dispatch bag containing the bogus orders calling for an invasion of New York. Having dropped the bait, he could make his escape.

The operation worked perfectly. The British found their prize, and when Major Andre read the note, signed and sealed by George Washington himself, ordering preparations for an invasion of New York, he reacted as General Washington and Major Tallmadge had hoped.

The planned excursion of the British navy to ambush the French off Rhode Island, which would have left a small garrison force in New York, was canceled and the city's fortifications were built up. Of course, there was never an invasion planned, and the French fleet with their desperately needed six thousand reinforcements safely landed in Rhode Island.

The interception of the *faux* invasion orders was another feather in Andre's cap. Even though the French fleet disembarked its entire complement of soldiers unabated, the British officers, in their arrogance, simply disparaged the capabilities of the French army. They couldn't imagine how a traditional European army, used to operating on open and mostly flat terrain, could be effective in the wilds of America. Of course, they failed to take into account the influence of the native rebel forces whom the French had come to help.

Chapter 49

Treason

Must we throw yet another party? Especially for that blow hard?"

Unlike most of the others in New York society, Charles had never liked Major John Andre, and he was growing quite tired of playing the drunken, clueless husband.

Andre's talents on the harpsichord and dance floor, along with this seemingly spontaneous recitation of doggerel poems of his own composition, made him the darling of New York society. Added to that were the indiscreet whispers detailing his exploits as the British spy master. Most of the rumors, though, were either greatly exaggerated, or orchestrated by Andre himself to enhance his reputation. So, when the gossip spread that he was working on a plan that had the potential to end the war, Sarah's interest was piqued.

"Something is going on, Charles. Rumors of some big plan are swirling around him," Sarah replied. She and Annie relaxed in their parlor chairs while Charles paced, his heels clicking on the parquet floor.

Annie nodded her agreement. "Aye, I've heard the same rumors among the servants."

This information carried more weight with Charles since, in his experience, servants, being invisible to their English masters, were often closer to the source than oft-repeated and embellished rumors and gossip.

"So, what else have you heard?" he asked Annie.

"Nothing more than Sarah has said. The officers meet daily, but stop talking when the wine is brought in. When the meeting is over, they seem 'very full of themselves' according to Sally, the Major's maid."

Charles turned to Sarah. "Has Leslie had anything to say about this?"

Sarah shook her head. "No, but he has been particularly randy of late." Annie snorted a laugh, but Charles just shook his head. Sarah continued, "And as soon as I ask even the most innocent question about his work he changes the subject."

"Maintaining operational security," Annie said.

Charles nodded his concurrence. "Alright. Send out the invitations, but don't schedule the party until the week after next. I have another resupply trip planned for this week."

Charles ventured out every month or so to resupply his stores from local farms in British-held territory.

"Thank-you, Husband," Sarah said with a wink. "I'll visit Mr. Rivington tomorrow. Perhaps he has heard more from his sources."

Sarah discussed the upcoming party with Peggy Arnold and Miira over tea.

"The Major has been a little, ah, detached lately." Miira was her usual cool self—personable, but slightly distant—since their earlier rift. "I think an evening of frivolity would be good for him."

"All of the officers seem preoccupied of late." Sarah turned to Peggy, "What do you think of the idea, My Dear?"

Peggy, who had been lost in thought, was startled by the question. "Well, parties are always fun, aren't they?"

Sarah and Miira looked at each other, then Sarah said, "You, too, have seemed very distracted of late. Can we help?"

Peggy looked from Sarah to Miira with a hopeful look that turned after a second to one of anxiety.

"Ah, no, nothing is bothering me." She could barely get the denial out and hold back the tears.

Sarah sensed that Peggy might actually know something useful for a change. She leaned forward and took her hand.

"Sometimes just listening is the best help. We are here for you whenever you need to unburden yourself. Discreetly, of course."

Miira watched this exchange with hawk-like focus. Though Sarah's probing for more information was taken as sincere by Peggy—she raised her head and the hopeful look was back—Miira's deadpan look, with just a single raised eyebrow, showed that she saw the gambit for what it was.

"Really? You would keep it just between us?" Her eyes flicked from Sarah to Miira, who simply nodded, and back to Sarah.

"Of course, My Dear. We all have our secrets, do we not?" Sarah gave her a wry smile.

Peggy nodded vigorously. "Yes. Yes," her face darkened, "but some are more…secret than others." Sarah waited silently for her to continue. "I'm afraid that…" Peggy took a deep breath and let it out as a sigh. Then the words came tumbling out. "I'm afraid Benedict will bring ruin to us."

Miira sat stoically, and Sarah looked on questioningly. But, when Peggy failed to continue, she spoke to her quietly, "Frankly, I have never understood why your parents let you marry a…a rebel."

As expected, Peggy rushed to defend her husband. "Oh, but he was not a rebel when we wed. My father saw Benedict's ambition as an asset and fully expected him to join my his business, which we would inherit one day."

"So, how did he come to be a General in the rebel army?"

Peggy sighed again and shook her head. "He never expected things to go this far. He thought if he was an officer inside the Colonial Army, he could convince cooler heads to prevail and get them to stop this silly rebellion."

Keeping her face as sympathetic as possible, Sarah thought it wasn't the rebellion that was 'silly.'

But she kept these thoughts to herself and asked, "How did he become so important in the rebel army, then?"

"Well, you know he is so brilliant that he will just naturally rise to the top of whatever he sets his mind to."

"Of course." But Sarah had heard Leslie and his officer comrades laughing behind their hands whenever

Benedict Arnold's name arose in conversation. Mostly he was the topic of derisive discussions about some letter that he had sent the British command. It had been passed on to Major Andre, so Sarah was all ears.

Reacting to the welcoming reception her words were receiving, at least from Sarah since Miira maintained her silence throughout, Peggy said proudly, "He has most recently won a very prestigious commission, actually."

"Oh?"

"Yes, that rebel fort north of here on the Hudson River, ah…"-

"West Point?" Sarah blurted, earning a sharp look from Miira.

Belatedly, Sarah realized that Major Andre would surely be interested to know that she knew about the fort at West Point, which controlled all traffic up and down the Hudson from its strategic location.

"Yes, that's the one. He says if West Point falls, the British will control the entire Hudson Valley up to Canada. That would be bad for the rebels, apparently."

"It would cut the Colonies in two," Sarah mused. "So, you think this commission puts your position here in New York at risk?"

Peggy was confused for a moment. "No, it's not that, exactly. Although I have heard some of the more Tory families here have publicly questioned our family's loyalties."

Sarah had heard the same, and the accusers were getting more vocal.

"Surely they understand the circumstances," Sarah said, although she didn't understand them herself.

"But they fail to," Peggy said. "And if they knew the real circumstances, they would see Benedict for the hero he is."

Peggy was getting more agitated, so Sarah pressed harder. "Just what are the 'real circumstances' that we don't know?"

Peggy gulped back tears. "He has sold this fort, this West Point for ten thousand pounds and a Generalship in His Majesty's army!"

Sarah gasped in surprise, but Miira's expression was much darker, as if she already knew of the treachery and didn't approve of Peggy telling Sarah about it.

"If his plan fails, he will probably be hanged by the rebels as a traitor. And even if he succeeds by breaking his oath to the rebels, no one in Society will see him as a gentleman."

Her tears finally burst forth. Sarah took both of Peggy's hands in hers to console her.

"I am sure that if he is working with Major Andre," Sarah glanced at Miira, but got no sign of acknowledgement. "I am sure their plan will work flawlessly."

It took the better part of an hour to calm Peggy's fears to the point where she could go home. Miira was of little help, and in fact took her leave shortly after the revelation of Benedict Arnold's plan.

When they had both departed, Annie walked into the sitting room with her mouth open in shock.

"You heard?" Sarah asked, although she knew Annie had been in her accustomed hiding place throughout the entire conversation.

Annie didn't bother to answer the question. "You must get word to Major Tallmadge."

Sarah was surprised for a moment that Annie would know the name of her contact. But then again, Sarah had long suspected that there was a lot about Annie and Charles that she didn't know.

"Of course." She was already heading for the spare bedroom upstairs, where she kept her store of invisible ink. "Has Major Andre responded to our party invitation?"

"Yes. He and Miira will be attending tomorrow night."

"Good. Then we have at least a day."

She gathered her skirts and practically flew up the wide stairs.

"What are you doing here, Mrs. Webster?"

James Rivington came from the back of his shop where his apprentices were pulling the long levers of the printing presses and swapping blank pages for freshly printed ones. The rhythmic sounds and motion normally induced a sense of calm in James, but the sudden appearance of Sarah shattered that calm. His agitation was apparent as he stepped up to the counter of the small storefront where Sarah waited. Sarah nodded her head to the door separating the two spaces and waited until James pulled it shut.

"I have a very urgent order that must be completed as soon as possible," she half-whispered as she took a sheet of paper from her coat.

James looked left and right before leaning forward to answer. "That is not possible! You sent me an 'order' two days ago. That one is still…being filled."

"But this one is of the utmost importance. Without it, our whole party will be ruined!"

James could hear the urgency in Sarah's voice, but there was nothing else he could do. The spy ring's courier, Caleb Brewster, would not be back in New York for at least another couple of days, and possibly a full week.

"My Lady, I will be happy to do the work you request," he said as he took the paper from Sarah's hand, "but it will have to wait at least a few days."

Sarah searched James's eyes for some hope, but all she saw was his pained expression.

"Very well. Please do your best. I really *need* this order filled before my party."

Chapter 50

Risking It All

The party was in full swing when Sarah, with a light pressure on Leslie's arm, pulled him to the chairs lining the long wall of the ballroom where they sat, their knees just barely touching.

"I have never seen the Officers in such high spirits. I hope Charles has laid in enough wine."

Leslie couldn't suppress the grin on his face. "Yes, well, we have much to celebrate this evening."

"Oh, and what might that be?"

"Why, just being in your radiant presence, My Dear," he said with an air of gallantry.

Sarah returned his exaggerated compliment with a rueful smile.

"My Lord. You have been taking lessons from your Major, I see."

Leslie chuckled. "I cannot imagine a better teacher."

At that, they both laughed, but then Leslie became thoughtful for a moment.

With a voice lowered so much that Sarah could barely hear, he continued, "I have learned much more than overdone gallantry from the Major. His schemes to defeat these rebels have been brilliant, if not properly executed by others." He looked left and right to be sure they were not being overheard. "And tonight we are celebrating his most brilliant one yet."

The excitement in Leslie's voice was obvious despite it being barely above a whisper. Sarah knew she needed to learn more about this latest scheme, but a direct assault of questions would be too obvious. Instead, she decided to bide her time until they were alone in her bedchamber later.

"Well, I certainly hope you are successful, and you put an end to this interminable war." She dropped her head and continued almost to herself, "Though I cannot bear the thought of you returning to England and leaving me with my old drunkard of a husband."

Sarah reached her hand out almost involuntarily to caress his arm.

The conflict was obvious on Leslie's features. "I must go where my duty calls me," he said apologetically.

Sarah nodded. "Of course. We all have our 'duty'."

Then, raising her head and looking out on the knots of partygoers, her gaze fell on Major Andre and a group of junior officers surrounding him. They all raised their glasses in a toast to the Major.

These toasts had been happening all evening, so Sarah asked, "Who is this 'John Anderson' that you fellows keep toasting? I am quite sure I did not invite a Mr. Anderson tonight."

Leslie's smile faded and his body language immediately became nervous. "Oh, him." He paused a moment to recover his mental balance. "He is just someone the Major will be, ah, working with tomorrow."

The change in Leslie's attitude made it obvious to Sarah that she needed to know more about this John Anderson. "You should have told me. I would have invited him this evening."

Leslie seemed to have regained his control. "Oh, that would not have been possible, I am afraid. In a few days, though, I warrant everyone will know him." After a long look at the increasingly drunken group around Andre, he said abruptly, "Would you excuse me, My Dear? I must have a word with the Major."

Standing, he offered a small, quick bow to Sarah, then turned and strode toward the knot of officers surrounding the Major. With a flick of his wrist, the more junior officers scattered to other parts of the room. Leslie leaned in and whispered something in Andre's ear, then with a nod from the Major, Leslie made a circuit of the room, whispering to each group of officers in turn.

Sarah didn't know who this 'John Anderson' was, but he was definitely involved in General Arnold's treachery. This was another tidbit of information that could tip the balance in the rebels' favor, but she had no way of getting the intelligence to Major Tallmadge.

As Leslie spoke with each of the British officers, they made their way toward the main entrance. Major Andre strode over to where Sarah sat. As he approached, Sarah's eyes fell on Miira, who now stood alone across the room and was watching Sarah intently. But when Sarah nodded a greeting, the mysterious woman simply turned and headed for the door where Annie was handing coats and cloaks to their owners.

Andre approached Sarah, and she offered her hand. The Major took it, bowed deeply at the waist, and lightly kissed it.

"My Lady, may I offer my compliments on a most enjoyable *soiree* this evening? I am afraid I must offer my regrets and those of our officers, however. We have many preparations to complete for tomorrow. I am sure you understand."

"Of course, Major. I hope whatever your endeavors are tomorrow will prove fruitful."

The Major bowed again, spun on his heel, and strode to where Miira stood waiting for him by the ballroom entrance. Together, they departed.

With the attraction of the British officers gone, the remaining partygoers also took their leave over the next few minutes, leaving Sarah, Charles, and Annie to huddle upstairs while the servants hired for the evening cleaned up downstairs.

"You've already broken protocol by going directly to the printer," Annie said. Charles nodded his agreement. "Your position—our position—is very precarious. Sooner or later, someone is going to realize that every time Leslie sleeps with you, some operation goes badly."

Sarah was not swayed. "It is not every time." Then, realizing what she had just revealed, she blushed bright red.

Charles barely hid his smile, but Annie just harrumphed.

"What I mean," she said, recovering her voice, "is I have been extremely careful. None of our successes—not the counterfeiting debacle, not the false invasion that saved the French, nor any of the myriad other pieces of information passed on to General Washington—can be traced back to me."

Annie wasn't appeased. "That is because you followed protocol with multiple cut-outs and indirections. Breaking protocol, as you're suggesting now, is simply madness."

Sarah responded in a calm, controlled voice. "If Andre's plan succeeds, the American colonies will be split in two. England will win this war, and The Enclave—our home—will be at risk. You forget my training. I may playact a foolish young country wife, but my personal history is a little more robust than that."

Annie was abashed, so Charles spoke for the first time, "I agree. If our involvement in this war on the rebels' behalf is discovered, the consequences for The Enclave, not just your village, but throughout the world, will be devastating."

Sarah looked at each in turn with a steely gaze. After a moment, she spoke in a commanding voice. "Make the arrangements for our evacuation plan." She ticked off the agreed upon steps on her fingers. "If I don't return by daybreak, make your escape. In the meantime, I need a fast, dark horse waiting on the far side of the Hudson River. I also need a canoe to paddle across."

Charles nodded quickly, and after a moment's hesitation, Annie did as well. Sarah, was no longer the naïve *ingénue*. She was an Enclave operative and the leader of their operation, and she had made her decision and issued her orders. Annie and Charles were duty-bound to follow them.

"There is a farm north of Wihook where a…friend of the Order lives. He will have a horse you can borrow," Charles said.

"*Borrow?* So, not a great friend, eh?" Charles just shrugged. Frowning at the thought of stealing someone's horse, Sarah continued. "How will I recognize this farm?"

"Cross just north of the town and it is the first farmstead you will come to." Charles chuckled humorlessly. "It is called 'Orderly Farm.'"

Sarah smiled a little and nodded. The smile faded when she saw the look on Charles's face, however. He obviously felt the need to remind her of what she faced if she was caught.

"Use your formidable skills to the utmost. If you are caught, you will likely need to use that cross at your throat." Sarah's hand reached for it where it always hung. "If you survive your capture, which is not at all guaranteed, you will be sent to a prison ship in the harbor. Those ships are like the pits of Hell, by all accounts. Do what you need to do to survive. On each of the next two new moons, look for a cook fire on the northern bank. We'll be waiting there. You know what you need to do?"

Rather than frightening or dissuading Sarah, knowing that Charles had a plan for her 'rescue' strengthened her resolve. She simply nodded in reply and headed for the spare bedroom where her black operative clothes were hidden.

When she had left the room, Annie turned to Charles. "Do you really think she is up to this?" Her voice was full of concern for the young woman she had come to admire.

"I've seen reports of her training. She is not just the socialite you have seen. Even so young, she is already a confirmed killer. With no weapons but her own hands, I might add."

INTERLUDE

Dan and Liz
Present Day

John held up his hand, pausing Liz's recitation.

"Why don't you finish telling your story to Father Dan? I have arrangements to make."

The dismissal was obvious, and Liz didn't have the energy to argue. She and Dan turned to leave the office together, but she paused in the outer office, staring at where she had last seen Amy crying her eyes out. Her own tears came, but silently this time. With a light touch on her arm, Dan guided her to a chair. Together, they sat down.

"John has made his decision and you, of all people, you should know how stubborn he can be," Dan said. Liz just nodded. "The only way to convince him otherwise is to give him a better option."

Gathering her composure, Liz asked, "Like what, Father?"

Dan knew she wasn't ready to accept his suggestion yet, and he had to understand why before making his proposal. Perhaps he could find the root cause of her shuttered heart in the rest of her story.

"We need to think on that. In the meantime, tell me how you got word to Major Tallmadge."

Liz nodded and gathered her thoughts.

PART XIV

Sarah
1780

As life and fortune are risked by serving His Majesty, it is necessary that the latter shall be secured as well as the endowments I give up, and a compensation for services agreed on, and a sum advanced for that purpose...

— Letter from Gen. Bendict Arnold to Major John Andre
West Point, New York
July 12th, 1780

Chapter 51

Operation West Point

The air above the river was brisk, but Sarah's exertions kept her warm. A hastily written note, intended for Major Tallmadge, describing Benedict Arnold's treachery and his contact, a Mr. John Anderson, whom Sarah was certain to be none other than Major John Andre himself, was stuffed in her tight-fitting bodice as she paddled her way across the Hudson.

She had to fight the current to stay above the town of Wihook. The current was not very strong, but her arms ached with the effort by the time she finished her crossing. Being free of the boned corsets and stays of the life of a lady in New York society was invigorating, and she welcomed the discomfort of her little-used muscles.

Reaching the New Jersey shore, she beached the canoe and dragged it into a thicket of bushes. Staying low to the ground, she climbed the steep slope of the bank into the trees lining the river. Quickly getting her bearings, she began creeping through the forest, away from the sound of the flowing water. Within a quarter of a mile, the cover of trees abruptly stopped, and Sarah crouched at the edge of a road running through the forest. Turning to her right, she set off northward at a run on the hard-packed dirt.

The months of high-society life had taken their toll on her conditioning, so Sarah was breathing heavily when the trees along the left side of the road gave way to open fields. Another few hundred yards brought her to the farmhouse. On a trellis above the front walk was an ornately carved plaque. The waxing moon had just risen above the trees to the east, so Sarah could easily read the name inscribed there—"Orderly Farm."

Observing the layout of the farm from the cover of the trees across the road, Sarah could make out the main house, a barn, a stable, and two additional outbuildings. She had no intention of waking the residents, even if they were "friends of The Enclave," as Charles had said. Instead, she planned to borrow a horse and tack and return them well before daybreak.

Being isolated from the town and with no other farms in sight, Sarah knew the Orderly Farm would be well protected from marauding soldiers of either side. Cupping her hands to her mouth, she took a chance and let out a low, warbling whistle. To most people, it would sound like some night bird, but to any dogs trained at The Enclave, it was a friendly greeting. As she had hoped, the two bull mastiffs that came trotting from behind the barn must have been Enclave-trained, since neither emitted even the hint of a growl.

Stepping from the trees to the middle of the road, Sarah whistled again, this time as quietly as she could. When the two massive dogs reached their side of the road, both sat on their haunches and eyed her suspiciously.

With slow, deliberate steps, Sarah approached the sitting dogs with her hands held low to her sides, palms up. When she reached their side of the road, the dogs stood as one and sniffed at Sarah's offered hands while she whistled her own signal, repeating it three times. Satisfied, the dogs turned and trotted back to their coup.

Sarah followed them across the mown grass for a few yards, then veered off toward the stable. With yet another whistle, she calmed the horses inside before opening the stable door. The door opened silently on well-oiled hinges and Sarah switched from whistling to a low, quiet humming that kept the three horses inside calm.

While humming, she lit a candle she drew from a pocket, located the tack room and brought out a bridle and reins. She eyed the two saddles sitting in their cradles, but decided instead to rely on her own horsemanship.

One of the horses was a broad draft horse, which Sarah patted on the cheek as she passed it by. The second horse was a chestnut mare, who lay in the corner of her stall. Seeing her girth and lethargy, Sarah knew with a sense of comradery that the mare would be foaling in a few months.

The third horse, a black stallion, seemed to know he was about to go on an adventure. He stamped his feet when Sarah pulled a piece of carrot from her pocket and offered it to him. He slurped it up, chomped on it a few times, then waited while Sarah slipped the bridle over his head and fitted the bit in his mouth. She then opened the stall door and led the tall, well-muscled steed out of the stable.

The stable door closed as silently as it had opened, and Sarah jumped up and levered herself onto the horse's back. With a flick of the reins and a firm kick, she and the stallion crossed the yard to the road at a trot, then with another kick to the ribs, they were off at a gallop northward up the road.

What the American spymaster, Major Tallmadge, didn't know was that intelligence being gathered by his spy ring in New York had been flowing both ways. The Enclave had been in this game for centuries, and Charles received regular reports from the Order's own network of spies throughout territories occupied by both armies. As a result, Sarah knew that Benjamin was encamped with his Dragoons about twelve miles to the north of Orderly Farm at the top of the palisades overlooking the river.

With an unfailing sense of distance honed over many years of nightly excursions from girlhood through her intense operative training, Sarah rode her mount hard for ten of those miles. Dismounting, she walked the horse into the thickest part of the forest next to the road. She noted with appreciation his owner's care for the animal, since the stallion was just as fresh as when they had started out.

Shrugging out of her backpack, Sarah withdrew a long coat and a hat of the kind favored by the rebels—a three-cornered affair with turned-up brims. Donning the coat and tucking her hair up into the hat that she pulled down low over her eyes, she climbed back aboard her mount and set off at a trot once again.

Judging herself to be about a mile from the encampment, Sarah slowed her horse to a walk. Within a minute, the expected sentries emerged from both sides of the road, muskets held at the ready.

Keeping her head down so the hat shadowed her features, she held up her right hand with her middle, ring, and pinky fingers extended and called out in a husky sotto voce, "A penny saved is a penny earned."

She held her breath, hoping the pass sign and password had not been changed since the last report Charles had received. Apparently, it was still in use and acceptable to the sentries.

"State your business," the one to her left called out.

Trying to keep her voice as masculine as possible, she replied, "I carry an urgent message for one Major Benjamin Tallmadge."

The two sentries exchanged a look and the one who spoke first continued, "What unit is he with?"

Letting a tinge of impatience into her voice, Sarah replied, "The Second Light Dragoons."

With another nod from the sentry in charge, both men stepped to the side of the road.

"He is encamped about a mile up the road a hundred yards or so in the forest to the west."

Sarah nodded and touched the front corner of her hat, further hiding her face as she walked the stallion between the two sentries, then with a kick and flick she set off again at a gallop.

A few minutes later, Sarah stopped and hid her mount when she could see the glow of campfires through the trees to her left. A whispered command known only to The Enclave and their horses told hers to wait silently for her return. She knew her rough disguise, which had fooled the sentries in the dark, wouldn't pass in the light of a campfire, lantern, or even a candle. So, shedding the coat and hat, she patted the horse on his neck and set off silently through the woods.

Surveying the camp's layout, Sarah realized it would take her utmost skill to reach the Major undetected. His tent, obvious because it glowed with the light of candles or lanterns burning inside, was pitched close to the center of the camp on the other side from where she crouched.

A few soldiers sat around dying campfires having a smoke on their clay pipes before turning in. Sarah knew, though, that just outside the light of the fires would be a ring of sentries facing into the darkness. She needed a distraction to draw at least one of them from his post, preferably the one closest to Major Tallmadge's command tent.

The Second Light Dragoons was a cavalry unit. Their horses were their most important possessions, since without them, they were completely powerless. Not surprisingly, Major Tallmadge's tent was pitched close to the makeshift corral where the horses were tied up. A disturbance among the horses would bring quite a reaction, she knew.

Melting back into the forest out of earshot of the ring of sentries, Sarah began gathering what she needed to put her nascent plan into action.

∽

It took quite a bit longer than Sarah expected to gather her materials, which were strapped tightly to her back. The good news was that the camp was almost completely dark by the time she returned to its perimeter. Campfires had been banked to preserve coals for the morning cook fires, and the Major's tent was dark. That made it easier for Sarah to move about undetected, but it also meant the camp's reaction to her diversion would be slower and might not even evoke the response she needed.

Judging by the position of the moon, she knew the delay meant she wouldn't make it back to Charles and Annie before morning. But that was a problem for the morning.

Keeping to the deepest shadows, Sarah crept forward. The sentries' restless shuffling of their feet and a not quite stifled yawn let Sarah identify where the two sentries flanking the corral stood. When she reached a position upwind of the corral and about fifty yards deeper into the woods, she set about preparing her diversion.

With utterly silent movements, she unbundled the dry and wet leaves, twigs, and small sticks and assembled them into the makings of a fire with the dry leaves and twigs at the center, surrounded by the wet leaves, then a layer of the small sticks. The carefully crafted assemblage would issue a pall of smoke for a few minutes before bursting into open flame.

Next came the part that represented the greatest risk of exposure. Lying flat on her belly, Sarah drew a flat piece of flint and her short-bladed knife from their sheaths at her belt. Holding the flint deep in the pile among the kindling, Sarah stuck it sharply with her knife. Her movements were restricted to flicks of the wrist, so it took three of them to spark enough to catch the dry leaves. Blowing gently into the newly born flame, Sarah saw and smelled the wet leaves begin to catch.

Her bait set, she circled the camp to a point directly behind the command tent. Just as she reached that point, the first hint of smoke reached the horses. Being naturally frightened of fire, they first snorted their alarm, then as the smoke became heavier, their snorts became whinnies and stomping of feet. By that time, the sentries, whose sense of smell was much weaker than their horses', also caught the scent and began yelling the alarm, "Fire! Fire by the horses!"

Just as Sarah had expected, the camp came alive, with half-dressed soldiers pulling on their boots as they ran toward the noise. Taking advantage of the distraction and confusion, Sarah crept quickly from shadow to shadow until she lay on the ground at the back of the Major's tent. With her ear pressed to the tent canvas, she heard Benjamin pulling on his britches and boots.

He burst through the tent flaps, demanding to know what the ruckus was about. Without hesitation, Sarah pulled free the pegs holding down the back panel of the tent and wriggled under it. Inside, the tent was darker than the moonlit night outside, but Sarah couldn't afford to wait for her eyes to adjust. She found the camp cot easily with her outstretched left hand and pulled her note from between her breasts, where it had been hidden throughout the evening's adventure.

Unfolding the note, she lay it flat on the thin pillow and scrambled backward beneath the canvas and out again into the night. Replacing the tent pegs, an unnecessary delay and a bit of arrogant bravado, Sarah heard the sentries find her diversionary fire, which had finally broken into open flame.

They would soon realize they had been duped and launch a full-scale search for the perpetrator. So, Sarah made her way with more speed and less stealth than she normally would back to where her stallion waited. She was counting on Benjamin's intelligence and their previous interactions at Valley Forge to cut the search short, however.

Just as she had expected, Benjamin rushed back to his tent to arm himself and lead the search for the intruder. When he lit a candle, however, he spied the note written in a familiar hand, one which he had not encountered in many months. Plucking it from his pillow and reading it by candlelight, he rushed outside and issued new orders to his men.

"Call off the search. We have bigger fish to fry!" Seeing the looks of confusion on his subordinates' faces, he held up the paper. "Our nighttime visitor is a friend. We have nothing to fear from...them." Best not to let his men know they had been hoodwinked by a woman. "In fact, they have brought news of a most dangerous plot that we must do our utmost to stop."

It was a testament to the Major's reputation and the trust his men placed in him that word immediately went out to stand down and call off the search. Instead, Benjamin's officers gathered in his tent to receive their orders.

In the meantime, Sarah donned the coat and hat, remounted and set off back south at a full gallop.

As she rode at full gallop past the sentries, Sarah called out the pass phrase without slowing, hoping they would assume she carried an equally urgent response to her previous passage and not pursue her. When she heard "Godspeed" called in response, she turned her thoughts to her next problem.

The operation, which had started on a very tight timeline, had taken much longer than she had planned. When the road climbed to the top of the palisades along the river, she could see the sky lightening in the east. She was certain now that there was no possibility of returning the horse, making the crossing, and returning to her house in town by morning.

If Charles followed her orders, which she had every confidence he would, he and Annie would evacuate New York at first light. That meant she had several decisions to make. She could abandon any hope of returning to New York and hole up somewhere until the next new moon, a full two weeks hence. Charles would assume her absence meant that she had been captured and would institute his rescue plan.

His plan was to affect a 'rescue' on the nights of the next two new moons. If she could evade capture until then, she would need to preempt those efforts to keep Charles and Annie from risking being captured themselves.

This was the most logical and safest plan, but Sarah had another consideration on her mind and in her body that she couldn't ignore. She knew in her heart that the secret she carried forced her to return to New York.

These thoughts swirled through her mind as she raced south. At every break in the trees to her left, she watched the eastern sky brighten. At last, though, the countryside opened up and she approached Orderly Farm.

Slowing her mount to a trot, then a walk, she approached the farmstead. She dismounted and led the stallion while whistling her greeting signal. On cue, the giant dogs loped from behind the barn to meet her. They walked alongside the road, then at Sarah's side like escorts, as she crossed the yard to the stable.

There was no sign of activity from the house, even though the ambient light was growing by the minute. Sarah expected a confrontation at any moment, but she entered the stable unimpeded. Although the day was brightening quickly, the inside of the stable was still nearly pitch black, forcing Sarah to leave the stable door open to provide at least some light.

Once inside, she removed the bridle and carried it to the tack room. Returning to the stall with a brush and currycomb, she heard the click of a flintlock hammer as a figure in the doorway blocked the meager light.

"I wondered where you might be," Sarah said calmly as she slowly turned to face the silhouetted figure. The man held the flintlock pistol at his side and remained silent. "My compliments on your stallion here," she continued as she turned her back and started brushing him down. "What is his name?"

The man lowered the hammer on his pistol and stepped forward.

"Let me help." Sarah handed him the currycomb and continued with the brush. "His name is Fury."

The man looked Sarah up and down, taking in her unladylike operative clothing. If he was surprised to see a woman operative, he gave no indication.

Sarah nodded. "And yours?"

"Andrew. Andrew…"

Sarah interrupted. "That is all I need to know. You can call me…"

"Nevermind. Best that I not know." Sarah nodded her assent. He continued. "It's getting light. You need a place to spend the day?" Sarah nodded again. "I have a hidey hole under the barn. Not very comfortable, but I imagine you can sleep anywhere."

Sarah shrugged. When they finished their ministrations on the horse, Sarah led him to his stall and Andrew scooped oats from the feed bin into the stall's trough. Sarah leaned in close and stroked Fury's neck.

"Thank you, Fury. You did well tonight." He snorted and tucked into the oats.

INTERLUDE

Dan and Liz
Present Day

Liz slumped in her chair. She had been talking uninterrupted for over an hour.

"I think we both need a break," Dan offered. During Liz's recitation, they had walked from John's office to Dan's apartment above the chapel and settled at his kitchen table. He stood and stretched, looking longingly at the coffee machine on a sideboard.

But Liz shook her head. "No. I've got to finish this. I've never told anyone the rest of this story, and if I stop now, I won't be able to get it out." Her voice choked on the last few words.

Dan nodded and returned to his seat.

Chapter 52

Daydreams Dashed

S arah slept during the day, but fitfully. While awake during the hours hiding in darkness, she listened to the field mice scurrying about, disturbed by her presence. The choices of what to do next kept going around and around in her head.

Should she go back to The Enclave and try to get word to Charles and Annie that she was safe? Surely, they would be in contact with Abraham. The operation was over, whether for good or ill. Either her mission last night was successful and the plot to surrender West Point had been thwarted, or the colonies would be split in two. Either way, she was almost certainly compromised.

There was no logical reason for her to return to New York, and every reason to stay in rebel held territory on her way back to Pennsylvania. Traveling at night, even on foot, she could make it in a week, ten days at most. No, there was no logical reason for her to return to British-held New York, but logic was not the determining factor in her decision. The spark of life that Leslie had struck in her compelled her to return.

Her Leslie was a gentleman, after all. When she gave him the news, she was sure he would do the right thing, protecting her from arrest so they could be together. During that long day in a hole in the ground, her still girlish mind spun innumerable fantasies of their life together after the war, either here or in England. Those fantasies overwhelmed the prospect of an Enclave operative's life, despite her years of training and the admittedly thrilling activities of the previous night. Her snatches of sleep teemed with alternating dreams of an idyllic life with her steadfast Leslie and nightmares of subterfuge and killing as an Enclave spy.

So, when her host opened the trapdoor over her head, her mind was made up. The brisk fresh air that rushed in invigorated her, and the smell of the steaming bowl he held made her realize how famished she was.

"I make a mean rabbit stew," he said as he handed Sarah the pewter bowl and a wooden spoon.

"It smells delicious. Give my thanks to your wife."

But he shook his head in response. "No wife, I'm afraid. Just me, my horses, and two worthless guard dogs."

Sarah spoke around a spoonful of soup. "Not worthless. Very well trained, in fact. You must have spent time at The Enclave?"

The man shrugged. "I've, ah, followed the doings of…Abraham…and his fellows for many years. We have helped each other on more than one occasion."

"Well, I thank you sincerely for your help and kindness, Sir. I will take my leave as soon as it is fully dark."

"Yep, that would be best. Just leave the bowl and spoon down there." He reached for the trapdoor, but paused and met Sarah's eye. "Your order's work is, on balance, for the good, but it is often too easy, or expedient, to stray from that path. You should guard against that as you live a life filled with secrets."

Sarah's breath caught in her throat. "I'm not sure that life is the one for me anymore."

His shoulders slumped and his voice was filled with a sadness Sarah had never heard before. "We have no control over the outcome when someone else casts the die," he whispered, then brightened. "I have no doubt you will do your best to do the right thing."

With that enigmatic proclamation, he lowered the trapdoor, but wedged a rock under it so Sarah had the benefit of the fresh air and fading light.

The return trip was as uneventful as the original crossing. As the half-moon rose, Sarah slipped through the streets and back alleys of New York to the house that had been her home these past months. As she slipped in through an unlatched basement window, she froze for several minutes, listening for any sound or sign of habitation. Satisfied that she was alone in the house, she crept up the stairs to the first floor. Again, she waited, listening. Still hearing nothing, she made her way silently up to the spare bedroom.

Stripping off her now filthy clothing, she lit a candle and studied herself in the full-length mirror. Her 'condition' wasn't showing, but everything about her felt different, even if she didn't look any different yet.

With Charles and Annie gone, it would be difficult to contact Leslie, but she would make an excuse for their absence in the morning. Tonight though, all she wanted was to bathe herself and sleep in a bed.

So exhausted was she that she slept right through the insistent pounding on the front door of the house. It wasn't until the door was smashed in with a resounding crash that she came awake. A moment's disorientation quickly changed to alarm when she heard the heavy boots pounding up the stair. She managed only to climb from her bed before Leslie and two armed soldiers burst into her bedroom.

Seeing Leslie brought momentary relief from the panic Sarah was trying and failing to suppress as she pulled a robe over her nightgown. When her robe was belted, she threw her arms wide and stepped toward him. But instead of accepting her embrace, he backed away and signaled to the soldiers, who grabbed her by the arms and held her firmly between them.

Her panic immediately turned to outrage at being manhandled by two strange men.

"What is the meaning of this invasion of my bedchamber?" Her voice was even, but her eyes burned with fury.

Taken aback by the fire in her eyes, Leslie paused a moment before regaining his composure. Drawing himself up to his full height, he recited, "Mrs. Charles Webster, you are under arrest by authority of His Royal Majesty George the Third."

Sarah stared at him in disbelief, but replied, "That is outrageous. On what charge am I arrested?"

Despite the coolness of the night air, sweat beaded on Leslie's forehead.

"That you did conspire to spy for the filthy rebels." He almost spat the words, "And that information you passed to said rebels resulted in the capture and hanging of a British officer, one Major John Andre!"

Sarah gasped. So fast! Pride mixed with the fear and anger she already felt. "Who accuses me so?"

"Major Andre's own…friend, Miira called at this house several times yesterday, though no one answered her knock. She had previously observed your husband and servant fleeing to his merchantman, which then set sail for parts unknown." Leslie paused, but cut Sarah off before she could reply. "And now here you are alone after sneaking into this house, despite the fact that we had sentries watching it all evening."

"My accuser is the adulteress, *Miira*? You believe a foreign whore over me?"

He shook his head and his voice softened a bit. "If you had fled like your husband, you would have been safe."

This encounter was not going at all as Sarah had planned. Wrenching free with a surprising burst of strength, she rushed at Leslie, but he caught both of her arms and held her with his arms extended.

They locked eyes, hers pleading and his hard.

"Leslie, my Love," she whispered. He jerked his head back but remained silent. "Stop this madness, I beg you. I love you. I love you, and…and I carry your child."

Although his look softened as she professed her love for him, the revelation that she was pregnant had the opposite effect.

"You foolish, foolish child!" His face was crimson, and spittle flew from his mouth as he shoved her violently back into the grasp of the soldiers. "I am a married man! I have a wife and child that I love with all my heart. You…you are nothing to me!"

The two soldiers, clearly enjoying this tete-a-tete, loosened their grip on the young, small woman between them. As they did, realization hit Sarah in a flash that all her fantasies of a life with Leslie were just that, empty daydreams. Anger at her own foolishness ignited her training and, with the back of her head, she broke the nose of the guard to her right, who dropped to his knees. Then, leaning to her right, she kicked sideways into the knee of the one on her left. A satisfying crunch of cartilage resulted. With a wail, he grabbed at his broken knee, freeing her. Leslie reached for the pistol at his waist, but Sarah's next kick sent it flying across the room.

He took two steps backward as Sarah slowly stalked toward him, fury and determination burning in her eyes. She gathered herself for her assault, but her pause had given the guard with the broken nose time to regain his feet.

She had no warning when the rifle butt smashed into the side of her skull.

Chapter 53

Floating Hell

There was no trial, of course. Her punishment was summary, despite a lack of any real evidence. Such was the way of occupied New York. Captain Leslie Alfred strode ahead of two new, uninjured soldiers who carried the still unconscious Sarah, now bound by rough irons at her wrists and ankles. The injured soldiers stumbled along woozily, not yet fully recovered from the blows Sarah had landed.

Once Sarah awoke from her stupor, a brief hearing was held before a fat, middle-aged British colonel. He studiously ignored Sarah, despite her protestations of innocence. Without ever actually looking at her, he signed and stamped a previously prepared warrant sentencing her to "detention aboard the HMS Wildfire for an indefinite period of time".

So it was that by daybreak Sarah was transferred aboard a prison ship anchored in the harbor. A rope was tied to her wrist shackles, and two of the ship's crew hauled her up from the rowboat that had ferried her to the ship. She forced herself to ignore the catcalling from the skiff when the wind blew her dressing gown up around her waist.

She had a feeling that would be the least of the humiliations to come.

The ship's captain sat behind a desk carved with sea serpents, mermaids, and whales. But the first impression Sarah had was the smell. Strong tobacco, months of sweaty body odor, and whiskey-laden breath almost took her breath away when a mate thrust her into the captain's cabin.

"Well, well, well, what have we here?" Despite the early hour, the captain's words slurred a bit.

"A rebel spy, they say."

"Another one? They's breedin' like rabbits!" The captain roared with laughter and the mate chuckled. "This one looks a might young, though," he said as he stood and rounded the desk.

"Young and pretty, she is." The mate leered at Sarah.

The captain stood in front of Sarah and looked her up and down. "What do you call yo'self, Missy?"

Sarah raised her head and met his eyes. "I am Mrs. Charles Webster."

"A 'Missus', eh?" the mate cackled behind her. "Broken in good, then, I'll warrant." He came up behind her and rubbed his crotch against the back of her dress, at which point Sarah spun with her elbow flying. The weight of the manacles made her elbow miss his nose, smashing into his grinning mouth instead.

Sitting down hard on the deck, the mate covered his face with his hands, and seeing the blood dripping from his mouth, he spit out a tooth amid a mouthful of blood. Scrambling back to his feet, he drew back his fist.

Stepping between the two, though, the captain said to him, "Hold on there, Jake. We're dealing with a real lady here, not one of your tavern whores."

He chuckled for a moment, then his face lost all expression. "Throw her in the hold and let the animals down there soften her up."

The captain's cabin was a perfumed boudoir compared to the smells that assaulted her after being unceremoniously dropped into the cramped prison hold. Below decks, the floor of the hold was perhaps forty feet long by twenty wide. The long walls curved away from the floor up to a low, four-foot ceiling of open beams topped with the floorboards of the deck above.

When the mate and another sailor opened the hatch and pushed her into the open hole, Sarah landed nimbly on her feet, surprised by how short the fall was. In fact, she was looking directly at the mate's shoes when she heard his cackle and realized the hatch was swinging down onto her head. She ducked down, but not quickly enough to avoid a good rap on the back of her skull.

Through the pain and nausea brought on by the second blow to her head in as many hours, Sarah heard the latches of the hatch being thrown above her.

Since the hatch closed off the incoming light, she steadied herself by reaching out to the rough-hewn beam just above her head. The mixture of salt crust and pitch covering the massive piece of oak spanning the space stuck to her hand when she drew herself into a crouching defensive posture.

"Look at this one, ready for a fight," came a disembodied voice from the dark to her right.

"At least she ain't cryin' like a babe like you was," came a reply from her left. A few chuckles were mixed with a chorus of low moans.

The voice to Sarah's right fell silent, but the one to her left continued, "Relax, Missy. You're among friends down here…or at least most of us are."

Sarah had the distinct impression that Mr. Left's last comment was directed at Mr. Right.

But Sarah didn't relax. In fact, she shuffled backwards a step, her right foot encountering a soft obstruction on the floor.

"You don't want to go back there." Mr. Left's voice held a sharpness it hadn't had before. In an instant, Sarah understood why. The smell of a decomposing corpse suddenly overwhelmed the horrendous mixture of sweat, shit, piss, and vomit that made up the normal toxic background.

Mr. Left continued as Sarah returned to her original position below the hatch. "The bastards haven't taken Roberts away yet. He's been dead a day or two by now…it's tough to tell down here."

"Why don't you shut yo' mouth, Jones," Mr. Right mumbled. "She won't be around long enough to need the full tour."

"She just might if she knows ahead of time to avoid your sort, Lewis," the one called Jones countered, but with a note of resignation in his voice.

During this exchange, Sarah had maintained her crouching stance and remained silent, letting her eyes adjust to the faint light that leaked between the overhead deck boards. What she saw arrayed before her sent a wave of fear that she tried to calm with deep breaths, but they only drank in more of the toxic air.

The space she crouched in directly below the hatch was clear for a yard or so around. It was bordered by the bodies of unconscious men to the front and sides, and by the dead piled to her rear. Beyond were perhaps forty or fifty men, either flat on their backs or curled into fetal balls of pasty skin and protruding bones. The strongest among them lined the curving walls, either sitting or reclining against the hull planks.

"What's your name, Girl?" Jones asked.

"Mrs. Charles Webster."

"Did they nick your husband, too?" Sarah remained silent. "Probably not, or he'd be here instead."

"Unless the coward turned her in to save his own skin," Lewis said.

He was going to be a problem she'd have to deal with.

"You of all people should know that don't work," Jones countered.

Lewis muttered curses in reply.

Jones elbowed the man half-asleep to his left. "Make a hole, there."

A ripple flowed down the side of the ship as each man shifted in response to the nudging and shoving. Jones patted the newly opened space to the left of where he sat leaning against the hull.

"Sit and save your strength."

Seeing no alternative, Sarah stepped gingerly over the ring of the unconscious and lowered herself into the proffered spot.

"Pleased to meet you, Mrs. Webster. Name's Jones," Jones said over his outstretched hand. Sarah tentatively clasped it, feeling the heavy callouses. She nodded, but offered no greeting in return.

Jones seemed to accept her reticence. "Stick with me. I'll look out for ya," he whispered.

With that, he crossed his thick arms across his chest and closed his eyes. Sarah also lay back against the rough planking, but rather than sleeping, she studied every detail of her prison through half-lidded eyes, and every sound, smell, and motion of the floating circle of Hell.

A motion to her right brought her to full alertness from the half-sleep that had overcome her. Feigning sleep, she lay still as a large, rough hand brushed her right breast.

So much for 'looking out' for her. It was lesson time for all of them.

Sarah let out an inviting, near-silent moan. Encouraged, the hand squeezed roughly. Taking the initiative, Sarah rolled toward Jones and sensuously slid on top of him, straddling his thighs. Sitting back, she saw the surprise and delight in his eyes just before her right hand darted forward with extended fingers, striking and crushing his windpipe.

She locked her legs around his as he started bucking, trying to draw in air. Staring blankly into his panicked eyes, she drove the heel of her left hand upwards into his nose, driving his ethmoid bone deep into his brain.

When his death spasms subsided, she dragged the corpse to the center of the open area beneath the hatch.

That message should be sufficient, she thought as she returned to the now doubly empty space and fell fast asleep.

To say Sarah's life settled into a routine greatly diminishes the torment she suffered over the next two weeks. When she awoke from her dreamless sleep, some indeterminate amount of time after she had dispatched Jones, it was soon apparent to her that everyone in the prison hold—at least those who were capable of coherent thought— was aware of what had happened.

No one, least of all Lewis said anything to her, but when the hatch latches rattled and the blinding sunlight and welcome fresh air poured in, she saw that Jones's body had been dragged next to Roberts and the area below the hatch was once again clear.

A strand of hemp rope was lowered through the hatch, and a rough-hewn wooden bucket was passed by hand from the darkness. Someone across the hold from her tied the empty vessel's handle to the end of the rope. It quickly disappeared up through the hatch along with the stench of Roberts's rotting flesh, eliciting retching sounds from above.

Without a word of command from above, or any discussion below, a canvas shroud was dropped through the hole and two prisoners came forward to wrap the bloated corpse in it before it was hauled up. From her vantage point against the hull, Sarah heard the splash as what was left of Roberts went over the side into the harbor.

Not wanting to miss an opportunity, one of the emaciated prisoners, his remaining hair standing straight out from his head, called up through the hatch, "Another one."

The canvas dropped back down and the two men rolled Jones's more robust corpse onto it. Grunts could be heard above as the body was hauled up.

"'At's a fresh one," a disembodied voice floated down. "You rats makin' room for more, are ya?"

Laughter was mixed with grunts of exertion and the sounds of the body being dragged across the deck above.

"'Is one won' fit through the scupper."

More grunts as Jones was lifted over the rail and another, more resounding splash followed.

The old bucket was lowered down the hatch and was quickly untied. As soon as the rope disappeared upwards again, the hatch slammed shut and was dogged tight. Sarah watched all of this activity and the automatic movements of the men with the realization that this was her life now, for however long it was going to last.

Fighting the despair that threatened to overwhelm her, she fingered the wooden cross at her throat. She knew the plan that Charles had laid out before she had set off to find Major Tallmadge, but now doubts of whether she would survive to the next new moon, let alone how she would know when it was, or how she would get out of this deathtrap filled her thoughts.

The hold seemed suspended in a moment of stasis as everyone's eyes readjusted to the dark. Gradually, Sarah could make out a figure kneeling before her holding the bucket out to her. Realization came with the smell of hardtack biscuits from the offered vessel. Reaching in, she felt perhaps a dozen of the hard, round buns floating in liquid. Pulling a biscuit out, she could see all eyes of those awake staring at her. Feeling like the old priest back at The Enclave, she pulled from the water-softened morsel a meager portion and handed the majority to the starving man kneeling before her. With a cocked head, he followed her lead and pulled off his own mouthful and passed the remainder on.

This strange communion continued when he dipped a ladle into the water and offered it to her. She drank restrainedly and nodded her thanks as he moved to the next prisoner. When he had made the rounds of those who were still able to eat and drink, he returned and held out a final piece of bread to her.

Sarah had the distinct impression that this was the first time in a long time that everyone who could eat had eaten. She shook her head to the offer, at which point, her server grinned a gap-toothed smile and popped it into his own mouth.

There didn't seem to be any schedule to when the prisoners were fed and their dead thrown unceremoniously over the side. It was on the fourth such feeding that a voice called from above after the bucket was untied.

"Yo, Missy. Get yo' bum over here."

"'At's if yain't too sore!"

A chorus of raucous laughter followed. Surprised, but thankful for any excuse to get out of there, Sarah crawled to the hatch. It was a struggle to stand, having been sedentary for so long. Her struggle to make her legs work confirmed the sailors' suspicions, resulting in another round of laughter and ribald comments. When she was able to poke her head through the hatch, she was grabbed under her arms and lifted bodily onto the deck. As she was half-dragged toward the captain's cabin in the stern, she heard the hatch slam shut.

The strange and unexpected smell of perfumed soap greeted her as she stepped inside. To her amazement, she saw a bathtub full of steaming water to her left and a table set for a dinner for two on her right. The captain, himself clean shaven and distinctly less foul smelling, stood in the middle of the cabin. He bowed deeply to her when their eyes met.

"Welcome, My Dear. I expect you'd fancy a bath," he swept his right hand toward the bathtub and, as she now saw, towels and a simple but clean dress draped over a chair behind it. Indicating the table to his left, he said, "And a decent meal."

At a complete loss for words, Sarah nodded quickly, but remained silent.

"Yes, well, I'll let you bathe in private, then. Rap on the door when you're decent again."

With that, he rattled a ring of keys and released her wrists from the manacles. Hanging the heavy restraints on a hook next to the door, he bowed again and left the cabin.

Suspecting that the captain, and maybe his mate, were lurking just outside peering through some spyhole, Sarah decided she didn't care and stripped off the fouled and torn bed clothes she had been wearing since her arrest.

The chill of the autumn air soon cooled the hot bath, so Sarah didn't linger in it longer than it took to scrub off the stink and wash the accumulated sweat and hull planking pitch from her hair. The dress was cut in an old style that included enough stays and ties to accommodate even her much thinner frame. Without any bows or bonnet for her head, she simply combed her hair and let it fall straight down her back.

Her toilet complete, she knocked three times on the door and stepped back to the middle of the room. As expected, the captain must not have been far away, since he opened the door immediately. Deciding to play along, for the time being at least, with whatever fantasy he was creating, she curtsied demurely. After a quick intake of breath, the captain bowed in response.

After their surprisingly tasty dinner, the captain poured them both a dram of sherry. He raised his glass but didn't drink. Instead, he just peered over its rim at Sarah. She returned his gaze levelly for a minute before he finally spoke.

"Am I going to have to tie you to the bed?"

Expecting just such a question, having known exactly where the evening was headed, Sarah just smiled resignedly and said, "That will not be necessary, Captain."

Manacled again after the second of their weekly 'dinners', Sarah paused as she was being led back to the prison hold. Looking out over the harbor as she had done on the previous visit to the Captain's cabin, she saw for the first time the flicker of a campfire on the far bank.

The time of reckoning had arrived at last.

Can I really do this? I don't want to die! Even if this godforsaken plan works, what will I be afterwards?

Her guard, an easy-going older sailor prodded her with a poke in the ribs.

"Move it along, there. Back in the 'ole with ya'."

With a long, lingering look at the flames of freedom and an unknown future, Sarah nerve failed her, and she turned away from the rail.

INTERLUDE

Liz fell silent, exhausted. Dan sat stunned.

He gathered Liz's hands in his. "My Child, I can't imagine the pain you have endured. Please believe that I am here to support you in any way I can."

Liz looked deeply into his eyes. "Thank you, Father." She smiled a little. 'My Child?' Really?"

Dan chuckled in response, but got serious again. "We've come to the crux of it, haven't we?"

Liz knew Dan meant more than just the end of her story. She knew he referred to the core of her inability to feel love for another. Or at least to admit her feelings to herself. She doubted, though, that her tale would be the catharsis Dan was expecting.

Chapter 54

Death, Resurrection, and Sacrifice

Taking her usual deep breath of the fresh sea air, Sarah exhaled clouds of steam. The last week had seen the temperature drop enough to signal the coming of winter, one that promised to be early and hard. A multitude of stars shone in the cold, clear night sky, undimmed by the meager ship's lanterns hung fore and aft.

As she did after each of her weekly ordeals in the company of the Captain, her eyes scanned the banks of the river. Tonight, no moon shone on the water, and it took several seconds for Sarah's eyes to adapt to the darkness.

Please, please be there, her thoughts pleaded to a God she had never really believed in.

Tonight was the new moon and probably her last chance to escape. The Captain had become increasingly violent, the novelty of having a helpless young woman at his disposal having worn off. When she resisted his disgusting demands, he threatened to turn her over to his crew. She knew, though, that they would be raping a corpse, because she would fight them to the death.

The depression she felt, and the self-recrimination for not having had the courage to leap the rail and escape from this living hell last month, ate at her psyche every day. Those feelings were only compounded by the movement she felt inside her womb increasing day-by-day.

Please be there. I need to save my baby, she pleaded again.

Then her eyes saw it. The signal fire burning there on the shore two or three hundred yards away. Her hand trembled as she reached for the cross hanging around her neck. Her guard, himself growing tired of this weekly ritual, poked her in the ribs.

"Get movin'. I want to get to bed."

The manacles she wore jangled as he grabbed her by the arm.

But Sarah didn't turn away from the rail this time. Instead, she pulled the silver cap off the bottom of the cross, exposing a sharp, hardened point. With one quick motion, she jabbed the needle-sharp piece of wood into the side of her neck.

The guard jumped back to avoid the spray of arterial blood that burst forth, which gave Sarah time to jump to the rail. She paused for the space of a single breath, just long enough to see a boat being rowed away from the shore. With another silent prayer, she tumbled over the rail and down into the cold, dark water.

She swam underwater, as best she could with her hands bound, in the direction she hoped was toward the signal fire, passing the point where the ship's lights no longer lit the night. Struggling against the irons dragging her down, her body's need for air finally overtook her. An involuntary spasm filled her lungs, not with life-giving air, but cold, deadly water. Her lifeless, undead body was sinking into the river's depths when Charles found her.

He tied a rope around her waist. When she was secure, Charles blew his breath out of the left side of his mouth, then sucked in air through the flexible reed that connected to a pack on his back. The pack held a sheep's bladder,] which had been pumped full of a few breaths' worth of fresh air. The extra breath or two let him swim silently back to the rowboat where Annie waited. Together, they hauled Sarah up from the deep.

To Sarah, resurrection was like awakening from the deepest possible sleep. When she had stabbed her neck with the simple wooden cross, she had only her faith in Charles and his word that they would be waiting in a boat and ready to recover her drowned body in time. Apparently, they had.

Her last memory was a fight to hold her breath as long as she could. So it was that upon awakening she had to remember to breathe again. When she did, pain exploded in her chest.

After Sarah took a few consciously manual breaths, her body remembered how to do it on its own. Opening her eyes for the first time, she saw that she lay on a cot in a tiny room. Annie rose from her chair and came to Sarah's side when she saw her eyes flicker open.

"Ah, here you are, Child, back from the dead."

Sarah tried to speak, but could only croak in reply.

"Just relax, Dear. Your body needs to remember what it should be doin' for ya."

Sarah smiled weakly and raised a hand to her neck. Her eyes went wide when she felt a bandage wrapped around it.

"You gave yourself a good stick with this." Annie held up Sarah's cross. "It did its job, though."

Relaxing a bit, Sarah's hands next went to her belly, but the expected swelling that she had been hiding the past few weeks was not there.

With rising panic, Sarah tried again to speak. It took her three tries to finally croak, "My baby! Where is my baby?"

Annie's cheerfulness evaporated. "Oh, Child, that cross of yours could only bring you back. I'm sorry, but you lost the baby."

Sarah turned away from Annie, and sobbing, buried her head in the pillow.

PART XV

Liz and Amy
Present Day

"Although the operation was aborted, and the operative was forced to employ to her 'emergency measures,' it was ultimately successful as several interventions were affected, which prevented British advancements in the conflict."

— Operative Sarah Harkin After-Action Report, 1780

Chapter 55

Breakthrough

The clock in Dan's parlor struck eleven. Liz was exhausted, both mentally and emotionally. The striking of the clock seemed to break a spell, and Liz stopped her recitation. By mutual, unspoken consent, the two rose and hugged as they parted.

Dan closed the door and filled a travel mug from the coffeepot before heading off to the Vault below the library. He needed to document Liz's story for the archives and confirm what he could from other records.

Liz headed for her apartment, intending to pack Amy's few things to take with her when she left The Enclave in the morning. But as she folded the girl's meager belongings, a resolve grew within her. Given the late hour, Amy would be asleep, and she knew that she would need Dan's support for the crazy idea that she couldn't shake. So, once the bag was packed, she returned to Dan's apartment above the church's sanctuary. Finding his door locked and getting no response to her insistent knocking, she sat down on the step below the door. It was on the landing in front of his door that Dan found her when he returned from the Vault, curled up fast asleep.

"Liz, wake up." He shook her shoulder gently and her eyes fluttered open. "What are you doing here? Do you know what time it is?"

She rubbed her eyes. "Sometime after midnight, I guess. That's the last time I checked my watch."

"It's 1:10," he said without checking his. "Have you been here since our meeting?"

Liz shakily rose to her feet.

"Dan, please help me."

Her voice quavered, and she appeared ready to break down again, as she had several times while telling the most recent portion of her tale.

"I can't lose Amy. I just can't!"

Finally, the tears came. Dan unlocked his door and helped her through into his modest apartment. "Sit down. Let me put some water on for tea."

Liz nodded, sniffled, and sat. Dan tossed a box of tissues onto the couch next to her. After shaking the kettle to gauge whether to refill it, he just lit the burner and returned to the living room, sitting in his overstuffed reading chair.

"Liz, I can see how much she means to you, but she really can't stay here."

"Then let me take her away with me."

Dan leaned back and failed to keep the smile from his face. "Frankly, if you hadn't suggested it, I was going to. But I have a lot of unanswered questions. If you were finished with your memoir, I would fully support you becoming

Amy's guardian. But let's face it, we both know you won't be coming back here to fill in the details."

Liz looked puzzled and started to object, but Dan continued, "Aside from the natives and their pitchforks," this time the comment did draw a rueful smile from both of them, "you won't have a reason to. You can't take on any operations while caring for Amy."

Liz nodded. "Of course not. But I've taken many-year breaks before, which will give me plenty of time to answer your questions." Seeing the skeptical look on his face, she just shrugged. "Besides, that's how Amy ended up as an orphan in the first place. Her parents should have aborted as soon as they knew she was pregnant."

Dan looked aghast, but Liz shook her head. "Not abort Amy! My, God, no! I meant abort the operation."

Relieved, Dan agreed. "That is standard procedure now, by the way."

"It should have been all along. It should have been back when I…on my first mission."

Liz gazed off into space for a long moment, Dan letting her have her space. Finally, he whispered, "I'm so sorry you lost your baby, *Sarah*." She looked at him sharply, but then sighed resignedly.

"The pain is two centuries old, but it still feels like yesterday. And I didn't know the resurrection process would take away any chance of motherhood with it." Wiping her eyes, she asked, "Will you help me convince John to let me keep Amy?"

Dan frowned a little, then took Liz's hand in both of his. "I will, but first you have to tell me, and yourself, what your real feelings are for Amy."

Taken aback, Liz drew her hand from his grasp. She was about to reiterate what she said before about having grown attached to the little girl. But, before she could say the words, a realization that she had been unconsciously suppressing for weeks forced itself to the surface.

Leaning back against the couch, she said quietly, barely above a whisper, "I love her." Then stronger, as her heart filled with joy, "I love her, Dan. More than I've loved anyone, even myself."

Dan smiled, his mission accomplished, just as the teakettle started to whistle. "I better make some coffee, too."

Chapter 56

Rejection

Over tea and coffee for the next hour, Liz and Dan commiserated on lost dreams. When their mugs were empty, Dan said, "Liz, I am so sorry for what happened to you and your baby."

Liz dabbed her eyes a final time.

"That was long ago, Father. We have a child to save tonight."

With that they walked through the dark night from the apartment to The Enclave's Security Office, where Karl Coolbaugh was keeping Amy until her relocation, but Karl wouldn't let them in to see her.

"It took forever for her to calm down. Besides, John gave explicit orders not to let you in." He jabbed his forefinger at Liz.

"Come on, Karl. Just for a minute. I need to make things right between us," Liz pleaded.

But Karl just shook his head and folded his arms across his chest. "John is just respecting Amy's wishes."

Both Liz and Dan looked stunned as he continued. "Amy was adamant. She doesn't want to see you. In fact, she called you some pretty colorful names. Did she get them from you?"

Liz's eyes flashed, but before she could lash out at Karl, Dan interjected, "So an eleven-year old is running the show now?"

Karl shrugged. "It would seem so. The sooner she's out of my hair, the better."

Again, Dan cut Liz short. "That's what we're here to talk to Amy about. Not keeping her here, but where she could go, and with whom."

The implication was not lost on Karl, who just snorted a laugh.

"She doesn't want to talk to you," he pointed at Liz again, knowing it would infuriate her more. "You actually think she would want to leave with you?"

By now, Liz expected Dan's interruption, and with good sense, she let him handle the negotiation.

"And how many times has your daughter given you the silent treatment?" Dan asked with a raised eyebrow.

Karl chuckled. "You've got a point there." He shrugged again, frowned for a moment, then sighed. "I'm probably going to get in trouble for this." He turned to Liz. "Five minutes. Wait," he stopped Liz's thank-you. "He has to go in with you." He turned to Dan. "Father, I want your word that if she," he nodded toward Liz but didn't poke his finger at her, at least, "upsets the little monster anymore, that you will pull the plug. Your word?"

Dan nodded reluctantly, "My word."

Karl reached under his desk and a doorway to their left buzzed.

"Second room on the left. Five minutes," he called as Dan opened the door and Liz flew through it.

Above the holding room door handle, a green message read UNLOCKED—SINGLE ENTRY. Liz eased the door open. Amy was sitting at the small table drawing with the colored pencils that Karl had left with her. She turned when she heard the door open.

"I have nothing to say to you," Amy said quite calmly.

"I know. But I have something to say to you." Liz sat on the bed next to Amy, who was sitting in the desk chair. "I'm sorry I didn't stick up for you when John told me what happened." Amy just stared at her coldly. "I was upset about the car, and it all happened so quickly."

"You still haven't said you want me to stay." Amy's voice was rising in pitch and volume. "You still want me to leave, don't you?" It was an accusation, not a question.

"Amy, please listen to me. You can't stay here." Amy opened her mouth, but Liz stopped her retort. "But I don't want you to leave *me*."

The emphasis caught Amy by surprise. Her features transitioned from anger to hope.

"So, I can go with you? And live with you forever?"

Liz hesitated, not yet ready to make a promise to this child that John might not let her keep.

"I want you to, but I don't know yet. I have to talk to John."

"More empty promises." Amy turned back to her drawing.

"Amy…" The girl let out a blood-curdling scream.

As Dan rushed forward, a voice came over a hidden intercom speaker, "That's it, Father. Get her out of there."

Chapter 57

Hearts Broken, Changed, and Healed

L iz paced the floor of her apartment like a caged tigress, mumbling a conversation with herself.

"You're such a fucking idiot. Why couldn't you tell her what she means to you? It was the 'forever' thing, wasn't it? She doesn't know what 'forever' means to me. I've been trying to live forever for over two centuries, and what has it gotten me? Life after life of pretending and lies, always ending badly."

She stopped her pacing and stared out the window into the early morning darkness.

"You know why you're doing it. You're storing up whatever it is in that damned cross that heals you. Look how fast the cuts on your hands healed." She looked down at her unbandaged hands. "Each time you stay young longer. Someday you won't need their rejuvenation treatments at all. What, so I can live forever? Alone? Now, with Amy, that sounds horrible. I'd rather live a normal lifespan with Amy than a hundred lifetimes by myself."

Saying it out loud, even just to herself, cemented her resolve.

"Well, OK then. Do something about it!"

❧

Liz checked her watch as she climbed the stairs to John's office—3:20 AM. She didn't care what time it was. She was determined to make John hear her out.

But, to her surprise, as she opened the anteroom door, she saw that the inner office door stood open also, and she heard the familiar voices of John and Dan coming from inside.

As she stepped to the doorway, John said, "Ah, so you did come. The good Father here thought you might. That's why he woke me up at this ungodly hour." Dan ignored the jab, so John continued, "He says you might have a proposition for me."

Liz gave Dan a look. "Are you a mind-reader now?" He just shrugged and Liz turned back to John. "I have an announcement and a proposal," she said. "First, I'm formally resigning as an Operative." Both men jerked back in surprise. "That's my announcement. I want you to know that regardless of how you rule on my proposal, my decision is final."

John didn't hesitate, and his voice carried a hint of relief. "I accept your resignation with the undying gratitude of The Enclave for all the work you have done. You have served far longer than any of your predecessors or successors, and I believe a full lifetime of retirement is certainly owed you."

Liz breathed a sigh of relief and nodded her thanks.

"And your proposal?" John asked.

She looked at Dan, who spread his hands to his sides. "I think you know what it is," she said, holding Dan's eye.

"Perhaps, but I need to hear it from you."

He wants to know if I'm really serious.

Liz turned back to John. "Of course. I propose that Amy be released into my care so I may love her and care for her and adopt her as *my own daughter*."

Dan smiled. He hadn't anticipated the last part.

John remained stoic, though. "And you won't go gallivanting around the world as you so often have done?"

Liz smiled. "Oh, I still intend to 'gallivant' all over. What better way for Amy to learn about the world and all of the people in it?"

Convinced that Liz wasn't making empty promises, he nodded. "I agree to your proposal. You clearly have lifetimes of experiences—and wisdom—to teach the child."

"Wonderful!" Liz hadn't realized she was holding her breath until that moment. She let it out, along with a tear or two. "Thank you. Thank you both." She smiled at Dan, knowing he had prepared the way for her by at least hinting to John what was coming ahead of time. "I can be packed in an hour, then we'll start our life together."

But John shook his head. "Unfortunately, Amy has already left. The transfer was scheduled for three o'clock. It's now half past."

Liz looked from John to Dan in a panic. Then she gathered herself.

"I can catch them before they get to the airport." She turned to go but stopped and sheepishly turned back to Dan. "Uh, can I borrow your car?"

Dan rolled his eyes and fished his keyring from his pocket. As he held them out to Liz, John cleared his throat. They both looked at him, holding up his cellphone. Then he dialed.

"Karl? Change of plans. Please return to The Enclave." He paused while his order was acknowledged. "Thanks."

"One other thing, though," Dan said. "Convincing me and John is one thing. You'll have to convince Amy, too."

Liz pursed her lips and nodded, then turned for the door.

"You're welcome." John called as Liz ran through the anteroom. She just waved her hand over her head as a belated thank-you.

Liz waited with her lone suitcase in hand while the black SUV carrying Amy slowed to a stop in front of her. Karl jumped out of the driver's seat, took Liz's bag from her, and opened the rear passenger door.

Liz leaned down and asked into the darkened car, "May I come in?"

Hearing no response, she climbed into the spacious backseat. Amy sat huddled in the far corner.

"Why do you have a suitcase?" the girl whispered.

"Because I'm going on a trip—a long trip." Amy took a wavering breath, but Liz hurried on. "And I hope you'll come with me."

Amy sat motionless, afraid to break the spell. Afraid that if she moved or said anything, the wish that she desperately hoped for wouldn't come to pass.

"Amy, I realized after we talked that you are the most important thing in the world to me." Liz's voice caught as she continued, "My life would be totally empty without…"

Before she could finish, Amy threw herself into Liz's arms and they both cried the happiest tears of their lives.

EPILOGUE

New Lives, New Challenges

L   iz and Amy strode from the First Class lounge to their gate, impeccably dressed in the designer fashions they had bought while deciding where they would go first. "Somewhere far away" was Amy's choice.

Liz decided Paris would be their first stop.

As they looked out the floor-to-ceiling windows at the huge airliner, Liz whispered, "That will take us as far away from The Enclave as we can get."

She squeezed Amy's hand, who squealed with delight.

Dan held Liz's drawing in his left hand and pointed with his right to the faded light brown marking at the left end of the lance's wrapping.

"See? She must have an amazing memory. She got it pretty much exact."

He laid the drawing next to the symbol on the cloth.

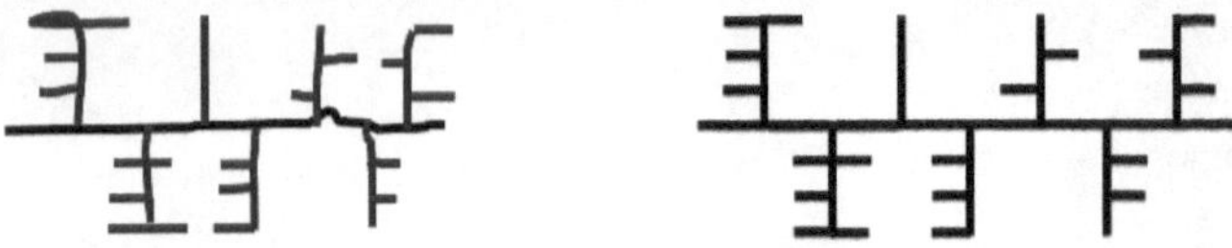

"According to Liz, who heard it from an antagonist almost two hundred fifty years ago, this symbol is pronounced 'Mee-rah'. She said it is the woman's name in her native language."

John shook his head. "I wouldn't be so sure."

He reached into his pocket and held out his open palm. On it sat a rectangle of stiff paper with another similar symbol printed in ink.

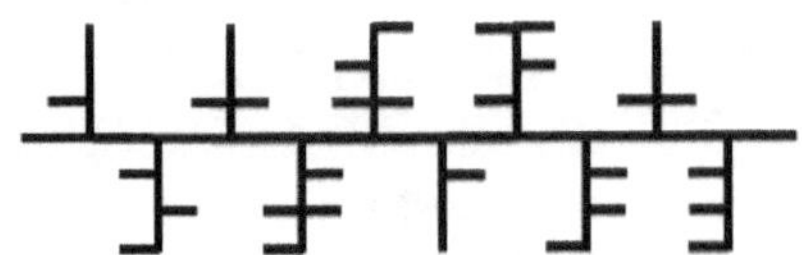

"What is this?" Dan's voice rose in surprise.

"I believe it says 'Alexander'. When I saw what Liz drew, it jogged my memory. I had to dig through some very old papers before I found it."

"What? You knew this Miira?"

"Well, I didn't know her by that name. I knew her as 'Moira' the first time we…met."

Dan was astounded. "The same Moira—"

"Who tried to kill me and steal the Lance over eight centuries ago? Yes, the same woman. When we met again, she used the name 'Mary,' which is why I don't think her pendant spells Miira."

"You met her again? Where? When? How did you get this?"

He brandished the card. John took it gingerly and chuckled.

"That, Father, is a very long story."

UPDATED ENCLAVE TIMELINE

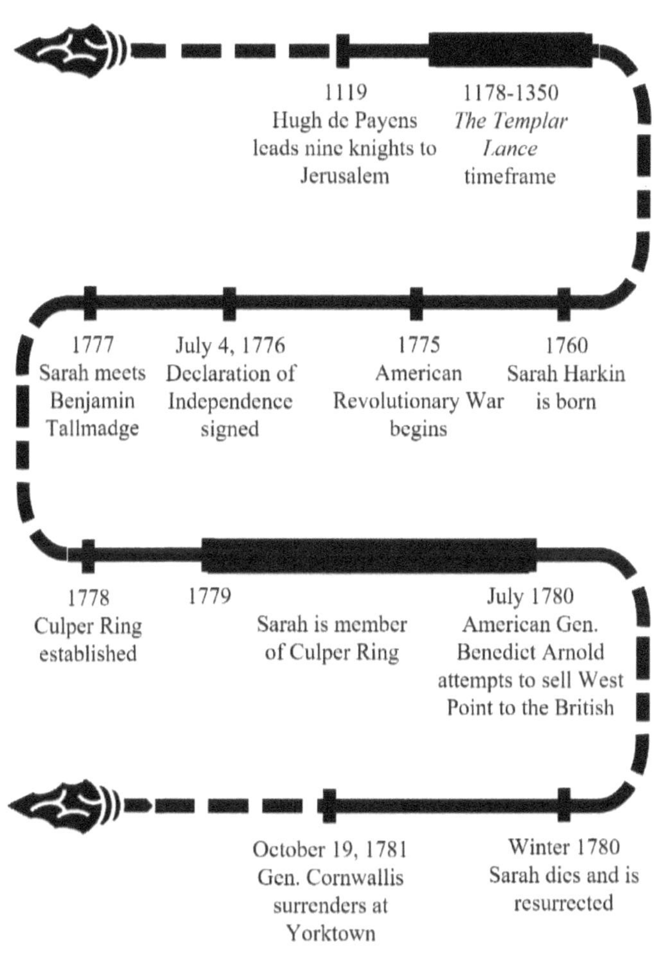

I cannot stress enough the admiration I feel for the patriots, most of whom were simple folk—farmers, tradesmen, and shopkeepers; and their families—who risked everything to ensure that their children's children could live in a land free of tyranny. I tried my best to show their courage in this fanciful tale set amongst them.

First among these common folk, though, were those brave souls known as the Culper Ring. Benjamin Tallmadge, George Washington's real spy master, named this collection of real people after Washington's farmstead in Culpeper, VA.

The core of this spy ring were Abraham Woodhull (known as Culper, Sr.), Caleb Brewster, Robert Townsend (Culper, Jr.), James Rivington, Austin Roe, and the mysterious agent known only by "355", the code number for "lady." To this day, the identity of Lady 355 remains a mystery. That mystery is what attracted me to their story.

Of course, the escapades of my Sarah Harkin as "355" are completely fictitious. What is factual, however, are the key pieces of intelligence that the Culper Ring discovered and exfiltrated to their handler, Major Tallmadge.

First, they learned that the British had, through bribery, obtained printing plates and paper used to make Continental currency. They had planned to flood the colonies with perfect counterfeit money, which would have wrecked the rebel's economy.

Next, they notified General Washington that the British were preparing to leave New York to ambush the French fleet in Rhode Island, resulting in Washington's brilliant use of misinformation, which caused the British High Command to cancel their raid.

The most important of all, however, was the discovery that Benedict Arnold was poised to surrender the fort at West Point to Major John Andre, who was the British equivalent to Benjamin Tallmadge.

All of these intelligence coups are recounted in this book, perhaps with too much emphasis on Lady 355's role, to the detriment of the other Culper Ring members. It was not my intention to slight them or minimize their critical importance to the Revolution. I am a storyteller, after all, and Sarah was my heroine.

It has been speculated that the agent known as 355 was, in fact, captured by the British and sent to a prison ship in New York harbor, where she perished, some say after bearing a child. That bit of speculation inspired the climax to Sarah's story.

I would also like to relate an exploit of the Culper Ring, not covered in the book, which one could argue actually won the Revolutionary War. When the British sailed south to relieve their besieged troops in Yorktown, Virginia, they had naval flag codebooks printed for distribution to all ships in their fleet.

By the time they arrived at the entrance to Chesapeake Bay, however, the waiting French fleet had their own copies of the British codes. Hence, they knew every maneuver the British executed at the same time as the British ships did, and thus managed to completely stymie the British relief effort. As a result, British General Cornwallis was forced to surrender Yorktown and his nine thousand troops, effectively ending the war.

It is quite possible that, while still in New York, the British Command hired printer James Rivington, whom they believed to be fiercely loyal to the Crown, to print the codebooks. How else would the French have their own copies?

I used many different resources while researching the historical facts that fill this book. The key sources I used were: *Major Andre's Journal*, John Andre, originally published in 1903; *George Washington's Secret Six: The Spy Ring That Saved the American Revolution*, Brian Kilmeade and Don Yaeger, 2013; *1776-*, David McCullough, 2005.

I highly recommend that you, Faithful Readers, check them out.

I used a variety of tools to write, edit, format, and publish this book. I write almost exclusively within Microsoft Word, where I also edit with the help of ProWritingAid. Components of the cover art, as well as the Part illustrations were generated under license using MidJourney. Those images were modified using GIMP and Microsoft Powerpoint. The cover design was composited and additional interior illustrations were created using PowerPoint. Interior formatting and layout was also done using Word. Adobe Creative Cloud tools were used for PDF generation, and Calibre was used for EPUB file generation.

Lady 355: Mother of Freedom

As always, you can find me, my flash fiction blog, newsletter sign-up, and anything else I post at RAJohnsonAuthor.com.

Thanks, again, Faithful Reader, for taking some time out of your day to spend with me and this ancient form of mental telepathy called storytelling.

Faithfully,

R.A. (Rob) Johnson
Pennsylvania, U.S.A.
January 2024

ACKNOWLEDGEMENTS

I would like to thank my dear late wife, Ona, for putting up with my mumbling and cursing at the computer when the writing was not going well, and my long evenings spent in my upstairs office when it was.

A special thanks to my beta readers, as well. Judy Maxfield caught all of my typos, misspellings, horrible misuse of commas, apostrophes, and quotes. If any linger in the final version, I put them in after the fact.

Karl Dehmelt gave me very helpful insights as someone who had not read the first book in the series, <u>The Templar Lance</u>. Karl, I'm sorry that draft confused you as much as it did. Hopefully, newcomers who jump into the series with this book will understand things better because of your feedback.

Sarah Inforzato (for whom our heroine is named) gave me excellent feedback from a woman's perspective, helping me make her namesake a much more believable character.

And finally, Elizabeth Devine read the draft in her own unique way. Her take on how the story flowed and how it made her feel let me know what parts of the story *worked* and what parts didn't.

It is virtually impossible to write a book these days without utilizing artificial intelligence to some degree. Accepting any suggestions by the software used for drafting, editing, designing covers, or layouts for the book itself means you have used AI. I am one of those authors who firmly embrace AI as an invaluable resource. I have thus employed AI throughout my process, including its incorporation into the Microsoft Office products, ProWritingAid, ChatGPT, MidJourney, and probably others that I'm not even aware of.

Finally, thank you to all of you Faithful Readers who have stuck with me, Liam/John, Father Dan, Sarah/Liz, Amy, and all the other denizens of this corner of the Fictiverse. Of course, their tales are not fully told, yet. So, stay tuned for the next installment of The Enclave Series, <u>Shroud of Doubt</u>.

To connect with me, check out my website RAJohnsonAuthor.com. There you will find my blog, which contains dozens of flash fiction pieces, and you can join my email list to get monthly newsletters, bonus stories, and special offers.

I am also active in the Fiction Writers Group on Facebook, the APEX Writers Group, Superstars Writing Seminars (yay, Tribe!), the Pottstown Writers Group, The Writers of the Future Contests, and various other challenges and competitions. I'm also a graduate of the Western Colorado University's Creative Writing/Publishing MA program.

You can contact me directly at:
rob@robjohnsonwriting.net

Other Titles by R.A. Johnson

FICTION
The Enclave Series
#1 *The Templar Lance*
#2 *Lady 355: Mother of Freedom*
#3 *Shroud of Doubt (coming soon)*

Ghost Stories
The Ghost of Mackey House

Fantasy
Tales from the Wood: A Modern Fairytale

NON-FICTION
Mental Crudites – Appetizers for the Creative Mind Series
#1 *Helping Science Fiction Writers Get Their Stories Off the Ground*